Wicked Words 8
A Black Lace Short-Story Collection

T0314660

Look out for the nine other *Wicked Words* collections, available in bookshops or from our website www.blacklace-books.co.uk.

Wicked Words 8

A Black Lace Short-Story Collection

Edited by Kerri Sharp

BLACK LACE

Black Lace books contain sexual fantasies.
In real life, always practise safe sex.

This edition published in 2004 by
Black Lace
Thames Wharf Studios
Rainville Road
London W6 9HA

Originally published 2003
Reprinted 2009

Opening Ceremony was first published in the US in *Desires*, Amar Mira
Press, 2000, and *Cycles* was first published in the US in *Best Women's
Erotica*, Cleis Press, 2000

Design by Smith & Gilmour, London
Printed and bound by CPI Antony Rowe, Chippenham, Wiltshire
ISBN 978 0 352 33787 0

Penguin Random House is committed to a sustainable future for
our business, our readers and our planet. This book is made from
Forest Stewardship Council® certified paper.

Printed and bound in Great Britain by Clays Ltd, St Ives plc

Contents

Introduction

I am delighted these wonderful Black Lace erotic short story collections are getting a new lease of life, and in such fabulous eye-catching new covers, too. The series has been hugely successful, and sales of *Wicked Words* anthologies have proven how popular the short story format is in this genre.

The majority of the stories in this collection feature sex with a stranger – a very popular fantasy, as the instinct of natural desire is unencumbered by the emotional investment of real-life relationships. The thought of sex with a stranger frees us up to live for the moment, something us security-conscious modern humans are loath to do. Black Lace books have always revelled in such escapism. Those characters not actually having sex with a stranger are still witnessing or indulging in new sexual experiences, and not always in the bedroom. In this anthology we have people doing the wild thing hiding in a cupboard, over the bonnet of a car in a supermarket carpark and rolling about in the hay in the stables of the Queen's cavalry. Not to mention some very earthy behaviour under the table at a wedding reception – where I'm sure many real life 'sex with a stranger' incidents have taken place. There are some powerful and unusual explorations of erotic subjugation in *First Night* and *The Stranger*. In the former, clothes are all-important; it's good to read a little fetishism from the female perspective. In the latter, clothes don't matter a jot, but the sex is just as concentrated and thrilling for its inappropriateness.

The fun doesn't stop with these reprints. There is much more to come from the series next year. As from February 2005, we will be publishing themed collections – which will be a fun way of diversifying the list. The first books will be *Sex in the Office* and *Sex on Holiday*, and after that we will be having *Sex on the Sportsfield* and *Sex in Uniform*. I can't wait! In the meantime, the first eight *Wicked Words* volumes are available now as of this month – November 2004. If you never got the chance to buy all the books when they were first published, you can now complete your collection and be the envy of your friends! Look out for the colourful covers – guaranteed to stand out from everything else on the erotica shelves in bookshops.

Do you want to submit a short story to Wicked Words?

By the time these reprints hit the shelves, it will be too late to contribute stories to the first two themed collections, but the guidelines for future anthologies will be available on our website at www.blacklace-books.co.uk. Keep checking for news. Please note we can only accept stories that are of publishable standard in terms of grammar, punctuation, narrative structure and presentation. We do not want to receive stories that are about 'some people having sex' and little else. The buzzwords are surprises, great characterisation and an awareness of the erotic literary canon. We cannot reply to all short story submissions as we receive too many to make this possible. Competition-style rules apply: you will hear back from us only if your story has been successful. And please remember to read the guidelines. If you cannot find them online, send a large SAE to:

Black Lace Guidelines
Virgin Books
Thames Wharf Studios
Rainville Road
London W6 9HA

One first-class stamp is sufficient. If you are sending a request from the US, please note that only UK postage stamps 'work' when mailing from the UK.

Always the Bridesmaid
Primula Bond

My fingers were mauve and so were Janie's bare shoulders. Her dream of getting married in spring had been hatched on account of the balmy weather – the cherry blossom, fluffy white clouds and twittering birds – all of which would surely be preferable to the parched grass and blinding glare of a scorching day in June, when everyone would sweat buckets into their raw silk suits. Janie had been certain that the cold weather would be over by April; the sun would be in full swing, and she had planned every detail of her wedding accordingly. Since their engagement, right up until this morning, she had kept one ear glued to the weather reports, nodding or wincing depending on the forecast.

But when she emerged from the pretty church to be greeted by a sharp wind weighted with rain, the bride's mouth dropped in horror. Her new husband tightened his grip round her ivory waist, sensing her tension, but she looked wretched, hunching her shoulders under her veil as if the stiff white netting could warm her. She scowled at the treacherous sky while the photographer manhandled her and Jerry directly into the icy draught whipping round the corner of the church, as we all grouped ourselves around them.

My peach satin dress was also strapless, but at least I wasn't in the spotlight, and I could shiver if I wanted to. The garment clung for dear life round my torso, squeezing my breasts brutally into a deep cleavage and threatening to evict them altogether as they strained against the tight bodice. I feared for the tiny buttons scattered up my spine that had taken the other bridesmaid hours of cursing to fasten, and which were now wrestling with the delicate threads keeping them in place. I had missed the last few dress fittings, much to Janie's fury, and must have put on weight since I agreed to let her truss me up like a toilet-roll cover.

The cold air brought my skin up in goosebumps as I shuffled into the line-up for the photo. I raised my posy of wild flowers to hide the brazen outlines of my stiffening nipples as they poked through the thin material in an effort to get out into the brisk air. The dress was self-supporting. I hadn't known what that meant until I had put it on. Then I realised that the complicated scaffolding of under-wiring and corseting enabled me to throw aside the confines of my bra for the first time since I'd burst like a chrysalis into top-heavy womanhood all those years ago, watched by an envious, pancake-chested Janie. Although it kept my breasts reasonably well contained, the bodice of the dress couldn't possibly hide the determination of my nipples, which always reacted to any change of temperature, whether actual or emotional, and which were my reliable thermometer for testing any promising situation.

A knot of secret pleasure twisted behind my navel at the way they shrank into hard points, pinched into rebellion against the bitter weather. I may as well enjoy this part of it, I thought, lips twitching into a smile, and pulled my shoulders back so that they would press harder against the satin bodice.

'Flowers down,' ordered the photographer, barging up to fuss about with my wrists. I toppled awkwardly on my delicate kitten heels, and the photographer managed to brush his knuckles across my wobbling expanse of bosom under the pretext of catching me. Then he shoved me brusquely between Jerry and another man waiting in the line-up.

'A sight to warm the cockles,' my neighbour murmured into my ear as I obediently lowered the flowers, exposing the double swell of my plump breasts against the shoreline of shiny satin. The tortured follicles of brutally pinned hair prickled against my scalp. 'I suppose everyone else has been on a diet for weeks. But what a difference a real woman makes. You weren't hired as the token fertility goddess, were you?'

I opened my mouth, ready to take offence, and unwound my neck to trace the tall body of the man who had spoken. He was leaning slightly over me, blocking out the watery daylight, and my words were silenced by a pair of eyes the colour of ready-to-eat Bourneville. I gulped and swallowed, and the tip of my tongue slid across my teeth as he stared at me. One of the chocolate eyes winked, and my teeth clamped over the red sliver of my tongue to keep it from flicking out and licking him.

'Facing forwards, please!' called the photographer.

It wasn't until the room hushed for his speech that I saw him again. Thank God Janie hadn't insisted on a marquee, but had reluctantly agreed to hold the reception in the comfort of a posh hotel. Outside it was raining now in earnest. The meal was finished and at last I could give up the good fight to keep a conversation going with some of Jerry's work colleagues. I was also struggling to breathe. My dress was constricting my ribcage after that second helping of lemon mousse. The warmth in the room, combined with the earnestness of my companions on the topic of corporate options, was making me sleepy, but my yawn froze halfway through. The man who'd called me a fertility goddess was rising from the top table. I hadn't noticed him sitting up there. He was preparing to speak. His voice matched his eyes. Deep and liquid, the inside of a liqueur chocolate, gravel shifting under velvet. I didn't hear anything he said. I didn't even gather who he was, or why he had the dubious privilege of sitting with the bridal party. I just let his voice caress the air around my ears.

'Finally, although I know it's really the job of the bridegroom, I'd like to toast the most luscious bridesmaid I've ever seen.'

As he waved his glass towards me over the heads of the crowd, he winked again. He looked like a pirate, tamed for the day into a morning suit, and his out-stretched arm looked as if it should be brandishing a cutlass. Though his dark hair, with streaks of grey that I hadn't noticed before, was as glossy as oil and obviously freshly cut, his chin was shadowed as if a beard would spring forth the moment his back was turned.

My eyes moved from his face. His crisp white shirt covered, I was sure, a broad chest curling with thick hair and the firm, warm stomach of a mature man confident in his prowess. There was no obvious bulge beneath the sober grey trousers, but I could imagine the quiet beast lurking there, resting against his strong thigh, waiting to lift and unfurl into throbbing life . . .

Someone dug me in the ribs and, as I realised that the man was talking about me, a ferocious blush seared my face. Sweat dripped between my asphyxiated boobs as everyone clapped and cheered their agreement and the guests at my table hoisted me up to give a mock curtsey. From behind her bouquet the bride glared, and I heard a squeak of fury from the other bridesmaid at the table behind me.

The applause faded and I was left to bite my lip enviously as the speaker bent to kiss Janie's cheek, obviously charming her back into smiles. I noticed that Janie, too, couldn't resist glancing south of his cummerbund as he murmured a few words into her headdress, and her hand flew up to her throat as he hitched up his trousers to sit down. Then Jerry was upstanding, and the pirate relaxed as if he was on a deck chair. He stretched his legs out under the white cloth of the high table and tilted his head deliberately to stare at me. Everything blurred except his smiling mouth, and I gripped the velveteen seat to stop myself ejecting from my chair and flying across the room.

At last the jokes ended and the music started. The bride and groom started dancing to their tune: Marvin Gaye's 'Sexual Healing'. I bent down to unhook my petticoats from the table leg, ready for my pirate to come and claim me, but when I straightened I saw him give a gallant bow and start waltzing with Janie's mother, his brown fingers fanned out in the centre of her blancmange-pink spine. She batted her eyelashes at him and puckered her lips in a cartoon kiss. Obviously he could ignite any woman just by fixing her with those ocean-deep eyes.

My stomach plunged with disappointment. I started to bully myself out of my trance. Of course he wasn't available. What had I been thinking? He would be married to one of these florid matrons and be dull as ditch-water. He was a no-go area, with duties to perform. Obviously one of the older generation, perhaps a godfather or uncle, chosen for his knack of flattering the females.

I remained in my seat, yanking at the peach satin, tears pricking my eyes.

'Hey, you can't be a wallflower!' The best man was

hovering in front of me, helping me to my feet. He was good looking enough, in a boyish kind of way, and Janie had often tried to pair me off with him. Any other time I would have responded enthusiastically to being folded against his muscular chest, but at that moment I just flopped into his arms like a rag doll. But it was useless to resist his request. He was an extremely strong, extremely virile rugby player. As he manhandled me into an upright posture and fitted our groins together, I could feel the hard, rude tip of his ever-ready stiffy burrowing into the folds of peach silk, which were clinging damply to my sweaty thighs.

'He was right, that guy, whoever he is,' my admirer went on, lacing his fingers firmly just above the rise of my buttocks to keep me in place. We started turning, and I could see 'that guy' on the other side of the room, this time taking the other bridesmaid by the hand.

'What did you say?'

'I said, he's right. You really *do* look sensational today. Outshine everyone. Don't tell Janie I said that. This dress, the way it sticks to you like clingfilm, it looks like you've been poured into it. Is it easy to get all these stupid buttons and laces undone?'

I shrugged, too upset to answer him, but this had the effect of loosening the tenure of the corset around my torso so that when my shoulders settled down again, the bodice had slipped another inch and I could feel one nipple grazing against the tight seam, trying to flick out over the top.

'Let's try it. Let's get out of here! I'll burst if I don't have you!' he said.

My dancing partner clasped me more furiously, and backed me into a less illuminated part of the hall. His eager cock had already doubled its size and had eased itself confidently up into the warm crack between my legs. My head felt heavy and my eyes were still glued to the other man, but my pussy was having none of my casual attitude and was clamouring for instant gratification. I couldn't stop the twitches. They started to taunt me, fidgeting in the tiny hidden places every time his cock blindly poked about and made contact. Despite myself, I parted my legs slightly in response.

'I've always fancied you rotten,' he went on, as if he'd rehearsed it. 'I annoy the hell out of Janie, going on about your voluptuous body, and how much I'd like to get up close to you, just like this; feast my eyes on your tits, just like this. They're usually hidden, aren't they, under shapeless jumpers, but I always knew they'd be this: gorgeous –'.

'I'm not very good at dancing,' I muttered, stifling a yelp as he stood on my toe.

'– if only you'd show your boobs off more often. I've dreamed about shoving my cock into your cute fanny, just like this –'

Across the room the other bridesmaid was giggling, her paw held up over her pink face as the pirate twirled her in a kind of French rock and roll.

'Later, perhaps, John,' I mumbled, wriggling as politely as I could to get his hands off me. But he misread the signal, and his hands lost all pretence of manners and slid down to grab my bum and grind it against his straining groin.

'You mean it? When?'

'When I've had some air. Let me go, John. Please.'

'Don't forget. Best man and bridesmaid. Meant to be together.'

My pussy twitched again in protest as John released me, but the dents in my skin where his fingers and toes and erection had pressed me slowly plumped out again. What was the matter with me, rejecting the offer of guaranteed rampant sex from the second dishiest man in the room? John knocked spots off the groom, but he was a boy. He wasn't what I wanted. A gaggle of girls swarmed round him as I pushed my way through the crowd towards the garden door. Although it was still spitting with rain I edged out along the terrace where the breeze snatched at my breath. I shut my eyes as the cold brushed down my throat and across my half-naked breasts. The music and chatter faded slightly behind me. I realised I was shaking, and there was a patch of warmth deep between my legs. But now I was imagining those other hands pressed against my back, that other mouth nuzzling against my ear, those chocolate eyes undressing me at last.

'It's much warmer inside,' a deep voice murmured into my neck. 'But no fun without you to look at.'

'You sneak about like a panther,' I answered, stopping dead so that he bumped right into my back. 'I didn't hear you.'

'And you sail along like a ship. There's no stopping you.' His hands ran over my hips and up my sides, pausing at the point where my tits spilled over the whalebone bodice. 'They always say it's the bride who should be the belle of the ball, but there's nothing to her. She's not abundant and fruity, like you.'

His palms flattened against my sides so that my breasts rose higher, ready to escape. Those long tanned fingers, which had guided the bride's mother so politely, and twiddled the champagne flutes so elegantly, were now spread confidently over my bosom as if I'd invited them, hovering over each breast as if measuring it. The pounding of my heart made them both quiver like moulds of pale jelly.

I reached behind me and grabbed his tailcoat, pulling him hard against my back. He hooked one finger into the deep cleavage, running it forwards until the dress blocked its progress. Then he pressed each large globe together, drowning the finger between banks of soft flesh.

'Just as I thought,' he gloated. 'You feel even more delicious than you look.'

His voice was intoxicating; and, in any case, flattery always floored me. I was proud of my breasts, but people seemed wary of them, as if they were bouncers blocking the way to the rest of me. Not even John had actually touched them just now. Then again, we had been in full view . . .

But this man knew what he liked, and he was probing for it now, reaching into my dress, sure of my permission, until he had completely encircled my breasts in his grasp. He squeezed them like sponges, increasing the pressure, until the pain started and instantly shifted into pleasure.

My head rested back against his shoulder, my hands sliding round his muscled buttocks. My fingers closed around the thickness of his erection, the smooth shaft concealed beneath expensive cloth. It pulsated briefly under my touch, growing longer and wider and nudging firmly into the cleft of my butt.

'– the bridesmaids? Where's the sexy one, the one who's good enough to eat?' John, or someone, called from just inside the open door. We were only a few yards down the terrace.

Still trapping me against his chest, the man knocked another French window open with his elbow and waltzed me into a cold, unlit sitting room. From there we could hear the reception party raging, and voices asking where we were. We stumbled against some furniture and he steadied me against the wall, releasing my breasts to undo the little buttons of my dress, some of which simply tore off and rolled away under the chairs. He came round in front of me as the dress slithered to the floor, in time to catch my freed breasts, which thumped gratefully into his waiting palms.

We stared at each other, panting greedily in the dusk, and his eyes glittered briefly before his mouth ground onto mine, his tongue parting my lips to explore inside, running along my teeth, finally curling round my own tongue and sucking hard. I felt my knees give but he kept me upright, propping me up with the length of his body. I scrabbled between our stomachs to get at his burgeoning penis and take it out from its respectable hiding place, but he only pressed his groin harder against me so that I could feel it, rigid, even through the layers of skirt.

My breath rushed in my ears. His stubble scraped over my chin and the wall was cold against my back, but his hands were warm as they kneaded my breasts. He found the nipples standing out like acorns and pinched them hard so that I squealed out loud with excitement. He chuckled, pulling away, leaving my mouth open and wet. He let one nipple go, still elongated and tingling on my breast, and started bunching up the layers of rustling petticoat still fastened round my waist.

I couldn't reach his trousers. I was trapped against the wall, and now he let go of my other breast and sank to his knees. I took my aching breasts in my own hands, kneading them furiously. Instead of removing the petticoat, his head disappeared under it. His tongue started slicking like a cat's up the virginal white stockings I was wearing.

'No knickers. I should have guessed!' His laughter was muffled against my thigh. I wanted to tear everything off, especially as he was still fully dressed, but as I twisted to struggle with the hooks at my waistband, a tall shape loomed in the doorway leading from the terrace.

Everything stopped. My breath, the music, my hands; everything except the wet tongue inching over the lace stocking tops into the fragrant shadows at the top of my thighs.

'Jerry!' I croaked, loud enough for the lover hidden under my skirt to hear. The tongue paused briefly, the tip just arrowed into the hairs curling over my pussy. Then it shot inside, parting the damp labia hidden there and burrowing into the dark slit between. My ability to think or speak scattered like so much confetti.

'So this is where you're hiding,' the bridegroom remarked softly. 'Luscious bridesmaid of the year. They're all asking for you, especially young John. And you've put Janie's nose out of joint something rotten.'

'Why don't you get back to her, then!' I gasped again. Jerry folded his arms and shook his head at me, teeth glinting as he stared at my breasts, glowing large and white in the dark room.

'I don't think I can tear myself away. I should have grabbed you while I had the chance. I've often dreamed of seeing you topless,' he chuckled, eyes roving slowly over me. 'And what a sight you are, out of that hideous shiny dress. But why are you all alone in the dark?'

I slapped one hand back to cover my bare tits, supporting my quivering weight with the other, and sighed out as the stranger's tongue circled the frills of sensitive skin surrounding my clit, tantalising in its blind search. Suddenly his tongue tapped the tender bud and flames spread through my pussy. My hips tilted, jerking into his face, and I crashed back against the wall. The tongue started to lick feverishly back and forth across the burning burning flesh. Instinctively I parted my legs wider, both to increase the sensation and to give my pirate more room in which to hide.

'Too hot.' I exhaled the words rather than spoke them. 'So lovely, but too hot in there.'

'And it's freezing in here. We missed you. Come back.' Jerry unfolded his arms and stepped closer.

There was a tiny slurping sound. The invisible tongue had hit its mark; the excitement gathering in my belly descended through my groin to that little point, accumulating at the electric centre of my clitoris. Waves of growing pleasure rippled outwards, blood pumping through me as the pleasure swelled.

'In a minute, in a min–'

The tongue flicked mercilessly between my legs while a couple of fingers combed through the damp bush where his nose was buried, his rough chin adding friction to the soft flesh. His other fingers were crawling between my buttocks, tickling and pushing into every crevice when, suddenly, at least one slid into my pussy, just beside his tongue, thrusting in hard like a penis.

Jerry was beside me now, the rose petals in his buttonhole grazing my shoulder. My skin tensed as his fingertips trailed over the hand that was trying to cover my breasts, and he started to pull at my fingers to release my grip.

'Let me see, let me see,' he whispered, yanking my hand away so that my breasts fell forwards again. He reached out and cupped one of them roughly, breathing heavily. I was startled and excited by his illicit interest but now all my attention was drawn like a magnet to what was happening under my dress, and I closed my eyes. I couldn't wait; I couldn't focus just then on Jerry and the fact that he was ogling his wife's bridesmaid, but my senses were sizzling with the wickedness of it.

I flung my head from side to side as the first wave broke over me, coaxing a groan from my throat as my body shuddered. The long, hot tongue lapped furiously, the fingers screwed into me, and I came, juice dripping down over my stockings and into my lover's mouth, which sucked hard at the honey oozing through his lips.

Shaking with the powerful pleasure, mixed with shivers of reality to see Jerry still rooted there, my legs gave way and I fell to the ground in a puddle of taffeta, panting like a puppy.

'How do you do that?' breathed Jerry, licking spittle from his lips. His hand was shoved down the front of his trousers and I could see the shape of his stiff cock jutting behind the grey material. He glanced back over his shoulder as more voices called out, advancing along the terrace. He ran a finger down my neck. 'Come on. Admit it. It was me standing here that turned you on, wasn't it? So let's get down to it. After all, it's my party.'

My petticoats erupted then, and my pirate with the cunning tongue backed out from between my legs. He squatted down to settle the rustling layers carefully across my knees and then stood up, wiping his hand across his wet mouth and over his hair.

Jerry's jaw dropped, and he whisked his hand out of his bulging pants.

'Not in here it isn't. This is a private party, and I'm just toasting the bridesmaid,' answered the stranger, taking the gaping bridegroom by the elbow and escorting him to the door. 'Something you most certainly are not allowed to do. You have a wedding, and a new bride, to get back to. And just this once I won't let on to the poor girl that your eyes are already roving over the nearest piece of crumpet, not married for five minutes.'

'Like father, like son, eh Dad?'

'It looks that way, son. But as father of the bridegroom

I have the pick of the crop, and I'm free to fuck whom-
ever I choose, whereas you are not. Now get lost.'

Jerry stumbled back onto the terrace, cursing, and was
gone.

Then his father turned back to where I sat on the
floor. He started to undo the buttons of his grey tailored
fly.

'Don't look so surprised,' he laughed, pushing my legs
apart with his knee and holding his thick penis out like
a trophy. I lay back, and weighed its muscled length in
my hand. 'My son's welcome to his skinny bride. I know
which woman I prefer. Now, where were we?'

The Offering Fiona Locke

She was a strange girl. The kind who seemed to know things the rest of us don't. You know the type – imperfect but intriguing looks, art student clothes, long hair and dark eyes that took in her surroundings with an eerie accuracy, seeing everything. Everything you knew and didn't know. Everything you were trying to hide. And everything you lacked the courage to confront.

She was still staring at the board, still watching the races. She had been here for hours, but had not made a single wager. There were far better places to kill time than the race book of the Mirage. Maybe she was waiting for someone. There was a shopping bag beside her on the floor and, from time to time, she peeked inside, as though reassuring herself that whatever she had bought was really there. There was no shop name on the bag, which I found almost maddening.

I was trying to figure her out. At first I had just assumed she was bored; that her husband was off at the craps tables or in the poker room, winning and losing by turns and high on the rush of both. But there was too much power in her eyes; too much of that elusive quality that Hollywood calls 'presence'. She couldn't possibly be some ordinary guy's trophy wife. Perhaps she was just waiting for the right horse to pique her interest. She had refused several offers of cocktails, but my curiosity wouldn't let me stop offering.

'Are you sure I can't get you anything, miss?' I asked politely.

This time she turned to look at me. She had waved me off before, though not rudely. There was an air of sophistication about her that came from something other than old money or a fancy education. She was no older than thirty, and somehow I knew she had experience beyond her years.

Waitresses and bartenders develop a sixth sense about people they serve drinks to. And I never doubted mine. You can tell a lot about a person's basic nature by the drinks they order, the way they pay, the way they tip or don't tip, and what they do while they drink. I sensed in this girl a kind of focused intensity that told me she knew exactly who she was and what she wanted. But it was as though she had just made a painful decision and was gathering the courage to face it. Why did she seem so lost?

She fixed her gaze directly on me and stared for three heartbeats. I wasn't used to being scrutinised so closely. I felt exposed. Then she sighed and said, 'Sure. Can I just have a glass of Merlot?'

'I'll be right back,' I told her, relieved for the moment to escape her penetrating gaze. It surprised me that she asked, rather than stated what she wanted. She was so oddly compelling and I couldn't put my finger on exactly what it was about her. Something in her pensive demeanor; something almost otherwordly. Hypnotic.

I returned with her wine and she tipped me a dollar. I couldn't think of anything to say, so I left again, afraid she might think I was coming on to her if I stayed to chat about the weather. My shift was over, but I couldn't leave. I hung back, watching her from a distance, wondering what she was doing here if not gambling. Was she waiting for someone? If so, I had to see who.

At last she got up and headed for the pari-mutuel

window. So she *was* here to gamble after all. I had to know which horse she was betting on. I had the weirdest sense that she had the answers to questions I didn't even know how to ask, and that her horse would be one piece of that puzzle.

I moved to a better vantage point to spy on her as she watched the race. Her eyes were fixed on the screen, wide and hopeful, as the horses pounded their way down the track, the jockeys spurring them on with their whips.

The horses were exquisite. Their powerful, rippling muscles made me think of all the starry-eyed girls who flocked to Las Vegas to find the American Dream. Or at least something like it. And it's a lurid little underworld they find themselves in, wannabe artists who torture their bodies to perform for audiences that are really only there for a glorified peepshow. They want to be show-girls, but most of them wind up as strippers or cocktail waitresses, waiting forever for their big break. I certainly did.

But the horses were different. They didn't know they were being exploited; they only knew that they were running. As they rounded the final turn into the home stretch, she winced, and I looked up at the screen to see a horse in blue being passed by one in gold. Hers? It couldn't regain its position and it gradually fell in behind the gold horse, falling further and further behind as it tried to muster one last burst of speed. But the poor beast was spent. I turned back to see the girl staring at her hands on the table in front of her as the race ended and the unofficial winners were announced. She sat still for a few moments, and then slowly got up to leave. She hadn't even touched her wine.

I hurried to the table and grabbed her ticket. Number

7, Race 5 at Golden Gate. I glanced at the board. 'Anything For You' was the name of the losing horse. Her wager: five hundred dollars. Ouch.

Gambling means a lot of different things to a lot of different people: fun, cheap thrills, danger, entertainment, junk. And some use it as a sort of divination tool. I'd been guilty of it myself, though no one knows better than the locals what a calculated con game it all is. Casinos are not in the business to lose money. Still, it's hard to resist betting on a horse whose name has special meaning for you. Same with lucky numbers. One of the keys to this riddle was the horse's name: I was certain of it. I tucked the slip of paper in my pocket, though I didn't really know why.

As the girl walked away through the casino, she wiped her eyes with the back of her sleeve, a childish gesture that seemed inconsistent with the enigma she presented. I followed. I was practically stalking her, but she was a mystery I couldn't resist.

It looked like she was heading for the elevators. I obviously couldn't follow her to her room, but she stopped just beyond the last row of noisy slot machines. A man stood there. I was just within earshot.

'I was coming to look for you,' she said, and there was a hint of anxiety in her voice.

'I know. I'm sorry I'm so late. Have you been waiting long?'

The man was both taller and older. Her father? There was some similarity of features, but their body language suggested a different and deeper level of intimacy.

She shook her head and lied. 'No, not long.'

They regarded each other silently for a few awkward moments and then he motioned her over to an alcove near a bank of payphones.

I couldn't hear what she was saying now, but I was

sure she was confessing her wager. As she talked she looked down at the floor. Her hair fell over her eyes like a veil and she smoothed it back from her face. She fussed with the handles of her shopping bag, shifting it from one hand to the other until he took it from her gently and set it down between them.

When she was finished, she looked up at him and her eyes filled with tears as he began to speak. I couldn't hear either of them, but I didn't dare move any closer. The girl was struggling not to cry and she scrubbed away each silent tear with her hand. When she regained her composure, he lifted her chin so that she was looking directly at him. He asked her something and she nodded. She bent to pick up the shopping bag, which she presented to him.

He looked inside and whatever was in it told him the full story. He closed his eyes for a few seconds. This time I could read his lips. 'All right,' he said at last. 'All right.'

He took her arm and led her to one of the back exits and out of the hotel. A split second of indecision and then I was behind them, hurrying towards the exit as well. I had to see the rest of this strange little drama.

I followed them outside and around the building, keeping a safe distance so as not to be noticed. I assumed they would probably just get in a car and leave; that I would never know what it was all about. Not that it was any of my business anyway, but it's human nature to be curious. Nosy. Obsessed.

To my delight, they passed the entrance to the parking garage and kept walking. There was a huge construction site behind the hotel. The workers had left for the day and the couple had relative privacy in the skeletal structure of the promised future casino.

They stopped by a grey stone wall and I ducked behind a forklift a few feet away. My obsession far outweighed any guilt I should have felt over spying on them. Something profound was at work here. It was as though some part of me knew that whatever I was about to see would change me forever.

'Is this really what you want?' There was sorrow and resignation in his voice.

'Yes, sir,' she murmured in response, her head lowered. Sir? Who was this guy? There was no way she was a hooker, and he didn't look like any pimp I could imagine, either. Where had her eloquence gone? She seemed like a frightened little girl now. Her hair was hiding her face again and this time he was the one to smooth it away.

He reached into the bag and, to my astonishment, took out a riding crop. She lowered her head again and he lifted her chin. Then she slowly turned around and bent over, placing her hands on a pile of bricks for support. The man raised her skirt over her hips. She wasn't wearing anything underneath. I couldn't believe what I was seeing.

Without ceremony, he raised the crop and brought it down on her bare bottom with a loud, leathery smack. She didn't make a sound, and I had to cover my mouth to keep them from hearing my gasp. He delivered another stroke. Harder than the first. And another. Even harder.

Then he stopped and placed his hand on her lower back, bending down to look at her face. She said something to him and he resumed his position, took a deep breath and began to use the crop again.

The girl kept silent for a few more strokes, and then she started to whimper. He raised the crop to strike again, but he hesitated at the sounds of her distress. Immediately, she shook her head and I thought I heard her say 'Don't stop.' I had to be imagining that.

I watched as he took a deep breath, steeling himself. Then the real whipping began. He wielded the riding crop with force this time and her soft whimpering turned to yelps of pain. The leather made a loud slapping noise each time it landed and I was horrified. I looked around for other witnesses. There were none.

This time he ignored her cries. He was merciless, raining heavy blows on her unprotected backside, thrashing her like a horse nearing the finish line. Long red weals began to appear, like red paint on an artist's canvas. But this was not art. Not even performance art. This was abuse.

Through it all she remained still, never resisting, never struggling, never pleading for him to stop. Like the horses, it seemed as though she accepted it as part of her due. And as she endured the pain, tears began to stream down her face.

I fought the urge to run to them and tear her away from this man. Maybe he was her pimp, after all. A monster at any rate. How could he beat her and humiliate her this way? I didn't have a cell phone or I would have called 911. Why didn't she run? Why didn't she scream for help? Hell, why didn't she just knee him in the groin and tell him to fuck off?

This was not the same girl who had captivated me all day. What hold did this guy have over her? I didn't know her at all, of course, but that didn't matter; no one deserved to be treated like this. What was *wrong* with her? But then, she was the one who presented him with the riding crop. And she was the one who insisted he use it. His reluctance ... her insistence ... I didn't understand and I didn't know what to do.

The one thing that became clear to me was that I couldn't interfere. I balled my hands into fists at my sides and watched, seething, wondering if I could get the guy's hotel room number and poison him the next time he ordered room service.

Again her hair concealed her face and again he uncovered it. A tender gesture – one which made her squirm and close her eyes. He drew her hair away to one side like a curtain. He gathered it all in his left hand and wound it around his fist, pulling her head back so he could see her face.

Her yelps and cries had turned into sobs. It was torture to see her made a victim like this. I had been so fascinated by the inner power she seemed to possess. How could I have misread her so much? And yet there was still something in her demeanor, even broken and crying as she was now, that exuded that strange confidence and inner peace. The flame that drew me to her like a moth.

He was finished. He tossed the riding crop aside and watched her for a moment while she cried, her hands still clutching the edge of the pile of bricks. He let go of her hair and it cascaded down around her head like a soft waterfall. Her whole body was trembling. Placing both hands on her arms, he turned her to face him. He whispered something to her and she nodded. Then she clung to him, burying her face in his chest and sobbing. I felt a pang of empathy, like a splinter in my heart. He had reduced her to such a helpless, childlike state. But before I could process the thought that he was a heartless sadist, he gathered her in his arms and held her close, rocking her and stroking her hair with an almost fatherly tenderness. Then he raised his head and I saw that he had tears in *his* eyes, too.

Shaking with sobs, she looked as though she would never let go. She clutched him tighter and tighter, as though she could somehow climb inside and merge with him.

'I love you,' he said. 'Please don't make me do this again. Please.' There was a kind of muted desperation in his voice, as though, like the old adage, it had truly been more painful for him than for her.

When her tears began to subside, she grew calmer. She sighed, a long deep sigh of emotional exhaustion. 'I'm sorry. I've just been so bottled up. I need this. I need the trust and the safety to be vulnerable. I can't release it any other way.'

'Yes, but –'

'Shhh.' She put a finger to his lips. 'It's a part of me, a part of who I am.'

'I don't think I can do this.' He was shaking his head.

'You have to.'

He seemed afraid to believe what she was saying; afraid of a strange, secret truth. But her serenity had returned and I was again seeing the lovely ethereal creature I had watched all day.

'I can't ... hurt you,' he said, shaking his head and glancing over at the riding crop on the ground.

She smiled at him with tenderness and touched his face. 'I need you to accept this part of me,' she said. 'And in time you'll grow to love her as much as you love me.'

He kissed her and she weakened, her legs no longer capable of supporting her. But he held her and I could see the bulge in his pants as she pressed her body against his.

At last she unwound her arms from him. Her hands drifted to his pants, unbuckling his belt with the skill of an experienced lover. Their mouths still one, she released his cock and he moaned. The noise was muffled in her mouth and sounded like some beautiful new language.

He took a few steps backwards until he felt the stability of the wall behind him. With eager desire, she raised her skirt and tucked it out of the way as he held her raw and reddened backside. She was very sore and his touch made her jump. She squirmed and twisted as though trying to escape the pain, but he was insistent. His fingers gripped the tender flesh he had punished and guided her to him.

My face burned as I watched their intimate dance. I knew I shouldn't be here. This was their moment, their special union. I had no right to be spying. But my own body was as greedy as hers and I squeezed my legs together, delirious over what I was seeing.

The girl parted her legs to receive him and her breathless cries were indistinguishable from the sounds of pain she had uttered only minutes before. Still cradling her bottom, he turned so that now her back was against the wall. He released her burning flesh and she gasped as he entered her, first with deliberate, sensual strokes, then with hungry urgency.

I watched her face as they became one. Her eyes seemed fixed on some faraway dream, made possible only with the right offering. She had made an offering of herself. One single desperate gesture was all she needed to open the door to a higher realm of intimacy, but she could not enter it alone.

He pushed his hands up underneath her shirt. She was wearing a white lace bra that fastened in the front and he unhooked it to release her. He cupped her small breasts, kneading them gently and then firmly. She moaned and arched back. He caressed her swollen nipples with his thumbs, pinching and squeezing them at irregular intervals, making her gasp.

He kissed her and allowed his mouth to travel the length of her long neck. His tongue made its way to her breasts and he licked the hard little nipples, flicking them and then closing his lips around them – first one, then the other. She rose on tiptoe to offer herself to him even more and he squeezed her breasts harder – kissing, licking, devouring.

She wrapped one leg around him to drive him deeper inside her and he lifted his mouth from her breasts to kiss her, using his tongue as he was using his cock. She uttered short little gasps and sighs, grinding her hips into him hungrily.

Their movements synchronised, she took his hand and directed it to her own pleasure. He filled her with tongue, cock and fingers as the taut muscles of her thighs rippled with the exertion. Just like a horse.

Then she took his face in her hands, telling him that she loved him, needed him, would die without him, and that she needed this strange blend of passion, pleasure and pain. Oblivious to the world around her, she made no attempt to silence her ecstasy; all he could do was release it for her.

I was oblivious as well, hiding like a child behind the forklift as the sun threw lean, spidery shadows over the darkening lot. My own sex yearned for expression and my face was flushed and warm: warm like the desperate wetness beneath my skirt, and I longed to touch myself and bring my body joy.

Spent, the girl was crying again. I sometimes did that too. Sexual euphoria could be so overwhelming that there was nothing to express it but tears. I closed my eyes and listened as she wept.

When she had no tears left to cry, he kissed her; kissed her mouth and kissed away the tears on her matted eyelashes. He hugged her tightly. 'I don't entirely understand. But I want to. I want to be what you need.'

'Promise?'

'Yes. But I don't want you to have to go to such lengths again. Promise *me*.'

'I promise.'

'I love you,' he said. He held her, wiping away tears of his own. He looked as though he truly had felt as much pain as she had. Possibly even more. Her uncanny poise was back, and she seemed utterly at peace. They clung together so tightly that they seemed to melt into each other's bodies, wrapping themselves in one another's pain.

I felt like I had lived a small lifetime with them in this one brief moment in time – sin, confession, penance and redemption. All within the blink of an eye. All through absolute trust and vulnerability. And all for love. So unlike the stifling formality of my harsh Catholic school upbringing. The impersonal priests behind the grille had never comforted me after I bared *my* soul. They never kissed away *my* tears. And they never had the kind of love for me that would go to such extremes as these two had.

I was haunted by what I'd seen. For me it was a privileged glimpse into the power of vulnerability; the power of another kind of love. I pulled the girl's ticket out of my pocket and smoothed it out. Anything For You. I felt very alone.

My husband was probably working late. I wouldn't see him until after I'd eaten dinner alone, no doubt watching a movie I'd already seen before. I wrapped my arms around myself, suddenly feeling the chill of the desert evening. I couldn't remember the last time he had brought me flowers, let alone shed tears over me. I had the crazy image of presenting him with a riding crop to use on me, and I laughed out loud. No, that would never happen. Some of us win, some of us lose, and some of us never even leave the gate.

Now I understood the look I had seen in her eyes, and why she had captivated me so. I had seen myself in her – an ideal and sublime vision of what I could have been.

I took the ticket out of my pocket and turned it over in my hand. Anything For You. The tiny scrap of paper seemed to me like a talisman and I could envision myself carrying it with me everywhere, hoping it would bring me some of the magic it had brought her. Then there was a loud, whistling rush of wind, and it stripped the ticket away from me before I could close my hand. I jumped up to try and catch it, but it swirled up and away, out of sight. I thought I saw it buoying back down at one point, but I couldn't get to it. The symbolism was not lost on me.

And I began to cry as I made my way home and back to my own simple life. My lukewarm, dull, predictable life.

First Night Melissa Harrison

Lauren flicked the lights on and surveyed the room from behind the bar. It was the club's opening night, and the punters would begin arriving in less than an hour. Advance ticket sales were higher than she had dared expect, and many of the city's listings guides and under-ground papers had run articles and interviews in the run-up to tonight's party; in no time at all the place would be heaving. For now, though, it was a dark, empty space. The dancefloor was a huge cavity surrounded by railings and presided over by the DJ box. The two bars – one where she stood and one on the opposite side of the room – were stocked with beer, spirits, mixers, lemons and limes, ready for the clubbers who were, no doubt, already beginning to make their way to the club from houses and flats all over the city and beyond.

Feeling a surge of excitement at the imminent achievement of a long-held dream, Lauren crossed the dancefloor and turned to the right, tying her curly hair at the nape of her long neck with a rubber band as she passed through a dark archway to the room beyond. Here she made her final checks: that the pair of X-frames were securely bolted to the floor; that a black rubber sheet had been correctly fastened to the mattress fitted inside a hanging, steel cage; that there were enough skeins of Japanese rope hanging from the wall-hooks, and that the straps and restraints of the leather horse, her favourite piece of dungeon furniture, were properly attached. Giving the chainmail swing a little push as she passed back through the arch, Lauren headed to the flat upstairs to begin her own preparations. Tall, slim-hipped and high-breasted, she would be wearing scarlet rubber tonight.

A couple of miles away as the crow flies, but a good hour's slog on the city's creaking public transport system, other preparations were beginning. Sarah lived by herself in the flat she'd shared with her boyfriend until a year ago, when it had become clear, to her at least, that they wanted very different things. She wanted a relationship; he wanted an easy life. After an initial period of adjustment, she realised she didn't miss him half as much as she'd feared. This was coupled with the fact that her burgeoning job as an assistant in one of the city's larger investment banks meant she could afford the flat by herself. It was a liberating realisation to know that, at 29, she was more than happy being single.

Now she was awaiting the arrival of one of her closest friends, Mark, who had promised to take her somewhere special tonight. Mark and Sarah had met not long after she became single when, kicking over the traces, she'd spent a month or two picking up guys in bars and sleeping with them – experimenting with all the things she'd never done, pushing her boundaries, learning afresh exactly what she wanted.

Mark was a good head taller than her and had a quiet confidence that set him apart from other guys, who mostly struck her as boys in comparison. Mark had been the best shag she'd had in a long time, but there had never been a repeat performance. They had fallen into an easy friendship that, though it had plenty of room for the spice of drunken flirtation from time to time, had never gone any further. Besides, Sarah suspected that Mark's sexuality had a dark side; there were things he got up to that he wouldn't always talk about, despite her teasing and her morning-after questions on the phone.

Sarah thought that tonight she might get some answers. Standing naked in front of the mirror, she wondered how the evening would end, and whether she would be changed in any way. Her reflection looked back, pale and wide-eyed.

She had dark, nearly black hair cut in a sharp chin-length bob, with a high fringe, dark eyes with long lashes and full lips. Petite and small-waisted, she looked far younger than her 29 years, though her full breasts and round ass-cheeks ensured she was far more woman than girl. She hooked her hair behind her ears then, hands on hips, she contemplated her reflection. She'd already finished her make-up; it was time to get dressed.

Earlier in the day, Mark had dropped a bag off, saying he'd picked up something for her to wear. He'd made her swear not to look at it until it was time to get ready, and said he'd be there at about eleven to pick her up. Opening the bag now, Sarah began to wonder what she'd let herself in for, and whether she was up to the challenge.

First out of the bag was a tartan mini-skirt so tiny she could tell just by looking at it that it would barely cover her buttocks. A typical man-purchase, and not her usual style at all. She laid it out on the bed, already wondering what would happen if she refused to wear it, and what knickers she could possibly put underneath. Next came a pair of black hold-ups with plain tops; she drew in her breath at the brand. Checking the tag, she found they were even more extortionately priced than she had thought. A pair of shoes came next: black patent leather with six–inch stiletto heels, buckles and a platform sole, the kind she knew strippers wore. Sarah began to laugh incredulously; surely Mark didn't expect her to *wear* these? She'd barely be able to stand.

She placed them on the floor and reached again into the bag, touching something smooth yet ridged. She pulled it out and unwound the laces wrapped around it, unrolling it to reveal a beautiful black corset, shot through with steel boning and bound by vicious-looking hooks. Laying it out on the bed with the rest of the outfit, Sarah had to admit that her pulse was quickening, despite a growing feeling that, wherever he was planning to take her, Mark had got her wrong; she couldn't wear these clothes, it was impossible.

The urge just to try them on, however, was irresistible. Sarah drew the hold-ups on, sliding them carefully over her freshly depilated legs and adjusting the tops so that they were even. She fastened the shoes and, gingerly standing up, she discovered that they were much more comfortable than she had expected, though her movement was a little restricted by the slightly intoxicating feeling of imbalance. Once the skirt was on, she could see that there were a good few inches of bare thigh between the tops of the hold-ups and the hem of the skirt. She twisted around to see her ass in the mirror; the crease at the bottom of each cheek was very nearly visible. Crouching by her underwear drawer, Sarah touched herself absent-mindedly with her left hand as her right rummaged through the mess of knickers and bras for something small and lacy. She was surprised to discover how wet she was.

Looking at the corset, she realised she had no idea how to put it on. It wasn't anything like the soft, frilly concoctions the shops had been full of not so long ago; this thing meant business, and was both beautiful and deadly-looking. A 'v' shape in the boning at each side told her which way up it went. Loosening the laces at the back, she opened the hooks and wrapped the corset around her, a 'v' over each hip. Clipping the front together over her breasts, she found her nipples responding instantly to the silk and steel, hardening and threatening to peek over the top of the corset. She wondered how to lace it and began pulling experimentally at the loose ends of the lacing, barely able to take her eyes off her reflection as she did so. There was something about the outfit that made it more than the sum of its parts; something that spoke to her in a way she was both scared and too intoxicated to respond to. And as she looked, the buzzer rang.

She answered the security phone and asked Mark to wait a moment.

'I'm coming in now,' he said. 'Let me in.' Walking carefully to the door, holding the corset's loose lacing in one hand, she did.

Mark stood in the doorway, arms folded over his long coat, looking at her for what seemed like a long time. Unable to endure his gaze, Sarah found herself looking down, a gesture that she noted, with surprise, as uncharacteristic. Walking in, Mark didn't take his eyes off her as he swung the door shut behind him. Sarah took a few steps back into the bedroom, heart suddenly hammering, but he reached out and caught her around the waist, turning her around so that she faced away from him. He placed both hands around her waist, moving them experimentally. Sarah stood motionless, unsure of what was happening, wondering why her will seemed to have deserted her, and which cat had got her tongue. Suddenly Mark walked her roughly forward until she had reached the bedroom wall, in front of the mirror. Holding the corset laces in his left hand, he used his right to raise each of her arms and place her hands on the mirror, as if she were surrendering. Raising her eyes, she stood like this and looked at herself in the mirror, and at Mark, behind her. Though he had let her go, she remained like this, aware of a growing heat and swelling sensation in her pussy.

Finally Mark stepped back and removed his coat. Underneath he wore a black rubber top that was tight over his chest and biceps and which had a zip down the front and a high collar. He also wore a black kilt. With his close-cropped dark hair there was something faintly menacing about the outfit, and it was a moment before Sarah saw the vicious-looking boots, strapped with buckles, and the riding crop and handcuffs that dangled at his waist. Wherever Mark was taking her tonight, he meant business.

'Looks like you're going to need some help with that,' he said, indicating the corset.

'Yeah, sorry, I couldn't manage...' Sarah said, wondering why she was apologising, her words tailing off as he approached.

'Keep your hands where they are,' Mark said, 'and stand with your legs apart.' She did so, and felt him begin to tighten the laces, his efficient manner betraying the fact that he had done this many times before. Bit by bit the boning began to bite but, far from being uncomfortable, the restriction began to feel like the most natural thing in the world. She closed her eyes as her breathing became shallower, jumping slightly as he leaned forward and breathed in her ear, his hand on her neck. 'How's that feeling?'

'Fine,' Sarah whispered, responding unthinkingly to the pressure of his body behind her by arching her back ever so slightly and cocking her ass backwards towards him. Something was overtaking her and it had nothing to do with their friendship. She kept her eyes closed as he finished the lacing and tied off the ends, finally placing his hands around her, where they nearly met around her new, wasp-waist. As she savoured the sensation, light-headed from the restriction of the corset and the imbalance of the stilettos, he turned her around to face him and ran his hands down to her thighs, relishing the contrast between the tops of the hold-ups and the silk of her skin. Then he moved them up, beneath the skirt, until his thumb grazed the warm, damp lace that covered her newly denuded pussy.

'Tut tut,' he whispered in her ear, his thumb stroking her pulsing clitoris through the knickers. 'That won't do.'

Sarah opened her eyes as he removed his hand and stepped back, looking at him quizzically and amazed to find herself blushing.

'Off,' Mark said, gesturing towards her underwear, and strode away to sit on the bed, where he became absorbed in a flyer he'd taken from his coat pocket.

Sarah regarded him for a moment. The compulsion to simply do as she was told was entirely new, and very bizarre. As if aware of her confusion, Mark remained resolutely turned away from her, as if waiting for her to cross her own, personal Rubicon. Wordlessly obeying men was not, after all, something Sarah had grown up wanting to do.

Yet here she was, slipping the knickers down to her feet and kicking them away, unwilling to incur the displeasure of someone she had previously regarded simply as a friend – and equal. She remained there, looking at him, whilst he continued to ignore her, turning from the flyer to check the plastic bag that had held the corset, tartan skirt and shoes. To her surprise, it had one last secret to reveal. As he shook it over the bed, a heavy leather collar fell out, three inches wide and with a single steel 'D'-ring at the front. 'Come here,' he said.

Sarah walked forward carefully until she stood between Mark's knees. He still hadn't looked at her. 'Kneel down,' he said, and she did so, dropping her eyes, looking warily at the implements that hung from the side buckles of the black kilt.

He raised her chin with his knuckle; reluctantly, she met his eyes. Without breaking their gaze, he placed the collar around her neck, fastening the buckle at the front before turning it gently so that the D-ring was under her chin. Placing his hands on her waist, he raised her up so that they were both standing. Then, his right hand grasping the back of her neck, he kissed her, once, gently, exploratively, her body straining up to meet his. When he drew away she realised that he had fastened the hook of a metal chain to the collar she wore, and that he held the other end of the lead. Only then did Mark allow a smile to cross his lips. 'Come on,' he said, 'time to go.' Vaguely Sarah protested that she had no purse or handbag. 'You don't need them,' he said. 'I'm looking after you tonight.'

Draping her coat around her shoulders, Mark led her out of the flat door and swung it shut behind him, pocketing her keys and leading her towards the night beyond the building's main doors.

At the club, the first punters had arrived, and were spreading out through the main rooms. Crowds were forming at both bars, where girls in skilfully cut rubber maid's outfits served the customers. The DJ was playing tech-house in the main room, whilst in the dungeon area bizarre images were projected onto giant screens at both ends of the room: Japanese girls in plaster casts; a man in an inflatable rubber suit; Betty Page in wartime stockings; coy Victorian pornography; surgical implements; a woman mummified in a cocoon of rope and suspended upside-down.

Hardly less eclectic were the crowd who were rapidly spilling into the dungeon, examining its layout and equipment with varying degrees of professionalism: the dominatrices, resplendent in head-to-toe rubber and carrying whips and floggers; male submissives, often naked, sometimes on all fours; a woman wearing an immaculate 1940s-style suit, complete with seamed nylon stockings and a hat with veil; cyberpunks in silver and UV accessories; men in army uniforms; groups of young girls in nurses' outfits; ageing swingers in cheap PVC.

From a raised dais at one end of the dungeon, Lauren surveyed the scene, watching it all come together, buzzing with pride, nodding to the scene regulars she knew, smiling at newcomers and keeping an eye on the dungeon monitors as they discreetly policed any unfolding scenes. She wore a beautiful red rubber dress with long, pointed bell sleeves and a stand-up collar. Falling into a train at the back, it was cut crotch-high at the front to reveal matching red rubber knickers and, below, her thigh-high red boots. Her high breasts were all but revealed by the cutaway neckline. She was hoping she would be able to play tonight, despite her responsibilities as hostess; one of her regulars owed her a new plaything, and she had a feeling tonight could be payback time. Lauren was a 'switch', able to either give or receive discipline, but the lengthy preparations for the opening of her own fetish club had meant it had been a while since she had seen any action. Now, inside her smooth rubber pants, her pussy sweated and swelled like a flower at the thought of exhibiting herself here, in front of this crowd, at her own club. Fingers crossed, she thought. After all, who knew what – or who – the night would bring.

In the main room, Mark and Sarah stood by one of the bars. The leather grip of the lead was wrapped around Mark's wrist; Sarah stood demurely beside him, sipping her drink and looking around, wide-eyed, at the outlandish crowd that surrounded her. Mark had barely said a word to her since they'd arrived but, lost in amazement at this new world he was introducing her to, she didn't mind. She realised that he knew many people there, though none approached. Seeing her, they cast her curious glances, merely nodding gravely to Mark as they passed by. Sarah's initial discomfort with the amount of skin she was showing in her tartan skirt and corset had diminished with the realisation that, compared to many of the other women there, she was positively covered up. Some were bare-breasted; two wore nothing more than tiny chain-mail bikinis; all seemed entirely at ease with their bodies. Sarah began to relax. There was a difference, she understood, between looking and staring; slowly she became comfortable with the appraising glances she was attracting, realising that she was safer here than passing a building site in tight jeans.

As if knowing exactly when she began to feel more comfortable, Mark finished his drink and tugged gently on her lead. Responding from deep within her new obedience, Sarah followed him through the arch to the room beyond, where Lauren watched their entrance from her dais. Seeing Sarah walking behind Mark, Lauren raised a questioning eyebrow. Mark nodded up to her and grinned. She made a half-mocking gesture of applause towards them. Catching the exchange, Sarah followed Mark's glance, but Lauren had already turned away.

The girl tied to the X-frame arched her back, inviting the crop being wielded by the attendant male dom, whose expert discipline had drawn a large crowd around their scene. Her grey skirt and pink G-string had been removed but still remained puddled around one stiletto-clad foot where her ankle – slim and brown in a lace-trimmed ankle sock – strained against the leather straps that bound it to the wooden structure. She wore a white shirt which, from the way it strained high across her back, looked to be tied in front between her breasts; her long, blonde hair was tied in pigtails, secured with pink ribbons. The schoolgirl ensemble was belied, however, by the delicate silver ring hanging from her clitoris; even from behind, where most of the spectators stood, her open legs and arched back displayed nearly the whole length of her bald, wet cunt, her pink lips peeling back to reveal the moisture within.

As Mark and Sarah reached the front of the crowd, Sarah found herself noting the vague sense of envy the girl's position centre-stage provoked in her. She watched the dom caress the girl's buttocks with a gentle, open palm, before stepping back and landing a crack across her round ass-cheeks with his crop, leaving a vivid pink weal. Even as the girl flinched, she continued to arch and invite the next stroke. The dom, tall and imposing in army uniform, reached forward and gently ran a finger down her spine where it was beaded with sweat, slowing as it dipped towards the puckered secrecy of her anus. It lingered there a moment as she froze, then he plunged the finger hard and deep into her open pussy; it emerged glistening with juices. Before resuming his pun-ishment, he reached forward and gave her the finger to suck, all the while surveying the watching crowd, tap-ping his crop ruminatively at his jackbooted calf. Appalled at the simple Pavlovian nature of her response,

Sarah felt a slick pearl of cunt-juice slide from between the swollen lips of her own pussy as his eyes met hers. She looked down, her face on fire, but her confusion did not go unnoticed by Mark. Hands on her waist, he moved her to stand in front of him. She could feel the nudge of his erection at her buttocks through the material of his kilt. With a finger hooked through the back of her collar he tugged her head sharply back and, at the same time, lifted her tiny skirt to caress her smooth buttocks. Parting her legs slightly, she gasped as he slid his middle finger up her crease, drawing her moisture up towards her asshole where his finger remained, beckoning slightly. Finally he released the collar, allowing her gaze to return to the scene fast developing in front of them.

The dom had beckoned a red-headed girl out of the crowd; giggling, she still looked back towards her posse of friends where they stood beside Lauren. Taller by a head than the other girls, and marked out by her scarlet rubber gown, Lauren stood with arms folded, in the midst of the crowd yet not part of it, appreciatively watching the dom's control of the scene. Now, with his crop he gestured towards the trussed-up schoolgirl's cunt where she continued to present it towards the crowd. The red-head, in cheap PVC, knelt down and grasped the sub's butt-cheeks, pulling them apart to reveal the stretched, splayed lips where they glistened in the dungeon's dim light. Still giggling, she leaned forward and drew a pink tongue under the pendulant clit-ring, nibbling it as the sub shuddered under her lip-glossed mouth. Looking up at the uniformed dom for further instruction, he passed her the crop but, instead of wielding it, she turned it around theatrically, enjoying the attention now, and slowly pushed the cold, thin metal handle far up into the blonde sub's pussy. Drawing it out, a delicate string of moisture attended it. Gently she popped the rounded tip into the girl's ass and moved it smoothly in and out.

After a moment, the dom took the crop back and spoke briefly to the red-headed girl. She nodded, and, standing and bending at the waist, began to eat out the helpless sub's pussy, burying her mouth and nose in the glistening flesh. The dom strode behind her and lifted her dress with the very tip of his crop; then, unbuckling his belt, he revealed a cock already straining and engorged. Pulling the damp crotch of her G-string roughly aside, he began fucking her hard and unceremoniously as the crowd watched, finally withdrawing in just enough time to shoot a thick spurt of come over her pussy and ass, where it looped in sticky trails down to the crotch of her knickers. He rubbed it over the smooth skin of her ass, making it shine in the dim light, as, with her tongue, the red-head brought his tied-up sub to a whimpering, twitching orgasm on the wooden frame.

Removing his inquisitive finger from her butt and tugging gently on her lead once more, Mark began to lead Sarah to the ugly-looking leather horse a little further away. Many in the crowd watched their progress, a few strolling speculatively behind them. It seemed that the scene that had just ended had given him ideas.

'What are you going to do to me?' Sarah asked urgently above the noise of the club, as Mark roughly pushed her face-down onto the leather.

'Nothing I shouldn't have done a long time ago,' he replied, parting her legs with his knee. 'And nothing you're not gagging for, you dirty little slut. Don't think for a second that I don't know how to deal with you. Now shut up and behave – we've quite an audience.'

The tough straps were beginning to bite into Sarah's

forearms and calves as she surrendered to the gaze of the crowd that was rapidly gathering around the wood and leather horse. The angle of the padded cushion, which took her weight, ensured her ass was raised high in the air; her legs were straight where she stood nearly on tip-toe, fixed securely to the contraption's legs. She struggled futilely for a moment, knowing even as she did so that there was no point. At least her head was free. Seeing the encircling shoes and boots of the watching crowd, she raised it as far as she could, looking for Mark. He must be behind her, she thought. There was nothing to do but let it happen.

Gently Mark lifted her little kilt, draping it carefully over her lower back and revealing her ass. Sarah's heart began to hammer at the thought of the dozens of strangers all looking at one thing – her pussy. Despite her fear, she realised it was a delicious thought, made all the more enjoyable by the fact that she could do nothing about it. Mark was exhibiting her to the crowd – to people he knew – like a particularly rare and desirable object, and Sarah was intoxicated by the sensation. She could feel her cunt pulse and shift, swelling and inviting the thrust of something, anything, deep into her. Mark began to caress her buttocks, his hands moving nearer and nearer to her lips. Sarah felt her secretions start to flow from somewhere deep inside. Was it her imagination or was the crowd moving closer? She could see a pair of red thigh-high boots and the train of a red rubber gown sweep the floor directly in front of her; evidently someone who preferred to watch her reactions from this side, rather than Mark's expert teasing at her ass. Finally his thumb grazed her delicate inner flesh. She jumped as if electricity had been applied, and the crowd sighed audibly at her reaction. Slowly Mark sunk a finger deep inside her, then two; the sucking noises his movements made were audible even to Sarah. She closed her eyes, shuddering, surrendering. What would be next?

Sarah started as she heard her name. Despite her position, she could see that the woman in the red boots was having a conversation across her back with Mark, who was still engaged with her pussy; it felt to be gaping and sodden at this stage. They were evidently discussing what to do with her. Did they know each other? Despite herself, Sarah couldn't help hoping that she was making a good impression. Suddenly the woman bent down slightly so that Sarah could look up at her face. 'I'm Lauren,' she said, kneeling down in front of Sarah and smiling. 'I own the club. I hear you're here for me.' She began to kiss Sarah on the mouth.

This new element was all but causing Sarah to reach her climax on the spot. Lauren's gentle, lingering kisses were nothing like those of a man; her lips were incredibly soft and her tongue was exploratory, slow, sensuous. Moreover, Sarah could feel the small smooth ball of a tongue stud as their kisses became deeper. The thought that she had been given to this complete stranger somehow increased her value, she instinctively knew, rather than demeaned her. She was in someone else's charge now – someone important – and there was nothing for it but to give in.

Behind her, Mark had paused in his manual invasion; but no sooner did Sarah have time to wonder what he was doing than there came a signal from Lauren and she felt the smooth head of his cock part her pussy lips, sliding teasingly up and down. She strained backwards against the restraints to meet it, her body a deep, open channel, begging with her spine, her hips, her tautened legs, her whole body, for the first thrust of Mark's penis. He rested one hand on the arched small of her back, holding her there like a rodeo rider for the crowd to admire, before plunging his thick cock into her, making her throw her head back with joy at the deep, bruising thud that she so loved, that told her she was full. It didn't take many slow thrusts before she felt Mark's come blossom hotly inside her, making her climax in turn, wave after muscular wave squeezing every drop out of Mark's cock and into her, her body jerking convulsively on the horse.

It was not over yet. As her muscles quietened, Sarah opened her eyes. The floor below her head was already decorated with several spurts of come; she wondered whose, and felt her nipples stiffen at the thought of tasting it. Raising her head slightly, looking through her now-bedraggled bob for Lauren, she could see men around her, cocks in hand, openly wanking over her. One smoothed his foreskin over the huge purple head of his cock and pulled it back again, over and over; one, circumcised, was stroking glistening pre-come over his entire shaft, his hands sticky with it. As she watched, Sarah felt Mark's hot semen begin to slide from between her pussy-lips onto her thigh.

But no sooner than she had regretted its loss than its progress was halted. Sarah felt a hot breath on her cunt, and a tongue with tell-tale ball-piercing moved towards her slit, taking the come with it. Now she understood where Lauren was. Hands pulled her ass-cheeks apart and suddenly Lauren's face was buried in her, sucking Mark's semen from inside her and bringing her immediately to a state of engorged excitement again. Now Lauren was lapping at her in long, smooth strokes, the piercing causing her clitoris to twitch uncontrollably every time it passed over it.

As she sank into the sensation, another orgasm beginning to build, her hair was roughly pulled back, raising her head. She fought the gag reflex as a cock was thrust into her mouth, and wondered at how Mark had got hard again so fast. Unable to move her head, she closed her lips around its girth and let him fuck her mouth, giving in, allowing herself to be used. Then, as that expert tongue teased another bucking climax from her gaping pussy, Lauren's mouth moving with her to drink the last of Mark's come from her cunt as the contractions forced it out, Sarah began to feel the splatters of other ejaculations land on her ass and face. And as hot semen suddenly filled the back of her throat, those strong hands tightening in her hair, Sarah opened her eyes to see Mark disappearing into the crowd. Now the circle of strangers closed in on her relentlessly, dozens of hands grasping hungrily at her slick, trussed-up body, pressing for her final, total submission.

On Show Madelynne Ellis

The last of my breadcrumbs drift over the black oily water of the duck pond as I crumple the empty packaging and dispose of it in the gaudy waste-bin. In the middle distance, the street lamps burn with an early evening orange haze; autumn has arrived and fallen leaves already litter the footpaths. Most people avoid the park at this time of day, afraid for their wallets, and wary of the prowlers in the shrubbery. Not me. I know that the shadowy figures have other things on their minds, for this is the local gay cruising ground.

I stand out in this male paradise. The only woman to brave the walkways after dark. Every few yards, I catch a glimpse of a solitary figure leaning against a tree, or a man strides past with the familiar swagger of a beast on the prowl. I love to watch these men when they meet: whole paragraphs of conversation are condensed into a simple sweeping gesture of the eyes, down to the crotch and back, followed by a nod or a resigned frown.

When their eyes lock with mine, the reaction is one of surprise. The casual glimmer of hope vanishes; some ask me the time, while others hurry away. Occasionally, the man in question pretends he doesn't see me at all. They're the ones I like best. After all, there's a whole lot more on show when I'm not seen.

This evening I position myself on a bench near the centre of the park. High hedges surround it on three sides, so it is secluded; perfect for viewing the leafy arbour opposite. The park is busy tonight, so it's not long before the shrouded seat is occupied.

Sean is a regular night visitor to the park, and popular with the guys. I don't know what his real name is. He's young – early 20s, I think – and has a smile that should have women falling over him if he was at all inclined that way. Tonight he is dressed in a T-shirt several sizes too tight that displays his lean, well-defined torso. His golden hair has been given a just-got-out-of-bed look with styling gel. He kicks a stone away before he takes his seat. Like me, he sits with his legs drawn up, although his posture is more studied and leaves his physique on display.

The first few men pass by with barely more than a glance in Sean's direction, and I fear it is not his night. Then, just as I push my palms against the bench to rise, one takes an interest and stays.

This man is older than Sean by a good six to eight years, and looks like he spends most of his life in the gym. His arms are like corded steel, and even through his shirt I can see his muscles flex. He sits in the middle of the bench, just a few inches away from Sean. Sean doesn't look up; he just lets his knees flop out to the sides, parting his thighs and putting more of his crotch on show. The impressive bulge beneath the zip obviously catches the other man's attention, for he leans closer and says something to Sean.

I strain to catch those words, since his voice is barely a whisper. 'Wanna fuck?' is all I make out.

Sean tilts his chin upwards a fraction, the merest flicker of a smile on his lips. 'OK.' They walk off together, with Sean taking the lead.

In the bushes, Sean's hands clasp lightly around the other guy's bare hips as he carefully tongues his thickening cock. He licks the shaft as I would an ice cream, starting from the base and working up in long drawn-out strokes that finish with a swirl about the tip. Watching him, I can almost feel the guy's dick in my mouth; taste the slightly bitter tang of salt, sweat and soap.

Sean works his own fly open with one hand and roughly shoves the cloth down his thighs, exposing his pale perfect cheeks to my hungry gaze. He kneads his butterscotch skin, eager for contact, then urgently clasps his half-hard shaft, which thickens as he pulls. I can feel the tension in his grip. The overpowering desire for contact that has him stumbling to his feet. Pre-come still glistening on his lips, Sean kisses the older man, pushing his tongue deep like he can't get enough. Strong arms crush him in a tight embrace and their hard cocks stab urgently against their stomachs. Sean wraps his hand around both shafts and works them together. His pace borders on frantic now and his features heighten with colour at the exertion. The other man slows him and takes charge; he spits into his palm and then draws his foreskin over the end of Sean's cock so they become one.

'Yeah, man.' Sean gasps his approval.

It's too much for me. My pulse is racing. I wriggle one finger inside my clothing, and lift my hips urgently against my hand. The caress of my fingertip brings welcome relief to my over-eager clit. Pleasure like pinpricks ripples under my skin and almost takes me to the brink. I try to pull back and lock my focus on the two hard naked bodies thrusting together only yards away, oblivious to the chill night air and their silent observer. But the force is too strong, and my fingers work independently of my brain, stroking quickly, wetly, until I am panting and teetering on the edge, ready to fall.

Sean comes with a gasp; the other man with a long drawn-out groan. Only then do I allow my head to loll back, my eyes to close and my mouth to open in a silent cry.

Ten minutes later I'm by the town clock, queuing for a cab and still cursing the bastard that stole the last one from under my nose. Still, I should be used to it by now; this happens every week and I've been performing this little ritual for months. It's strange to think it all started as a childish dare.

It was a girls' night out: Sally, Jade, Kirsten and I, all traipsing back from the pub, just about staying upright. The boss had let us off at midday to celebrate the successful end of a major project, and we'd been drinking the night away. Finally, at closing time, we'd left the bar behind, with vague plans to carry on the party back at Sally's place.

'Let's cut through the park,' Kirsten had suggested, definitely worse for wear, and always up for crazy stuff when she was drunk.

'Bad idea,' said Sally and I.

We all knew better than to go wandering about the dark lonely groves at night. It was a mugger's paradise and I think I said as much.

'Chicken,' Kirsten said and, to my surprise, Jade backed her up.

'You're not gonna get jumped in there, there's too many people about. It's where the guys go ... You know –' she said, elbowing me in the ribs, '– to get laid and stuff. The gay guys.'

'Really!' Now Sally was interested.

Meanwhile, Kirsten had an odd smile on her face. The kind I just knew meant trouble but, before any of us had the chance to stop her, she was off, running between the park gates and hollering at the top of her voice. 'I want to see some cock!'

Sally and I looked at each other, then at Jade. We couldn't leave her, and so off we all went after her.

Jesus, what a nightmare, chasing after a drunken woman when I could barely walk straight myself. To make things worse, Jade was right: there were figures in the bushes; men of every shape, size and colour. All far more interested in each other than four screaming women.

I lost sight of Kirsten and the others along a particularly shrouded pathway that had thick rhododendrons growing on both sides. The rustle of the leaves brought me to a sudden halt halfway along. Off the path, to the right, two men leaned against the mossy trunk of a gnarled oak. They were locked in an embrace with their cocks sliding between one another's thighs and their trousers coiled at their feet. I stood riveted to the spot by this vision, watching the nearer man's pearly cheeks dimple as he thrust, and listening to their rasping breaths and the slick slide of flesh against flesh.

After a long moment, my sense of propriety caught up with me through the fog of alcohol. I turned away, not sure where to look after my first wide-eyed gape. I was half-hoping that one of the girls would appear so we could break the raw edge of tension and drive them away with some childish remarks, but I couldn't even hear their voices on the breeze. Maybe they were enraptured by similar scenes in other parts of the park.

Curiosity and the rhythmic sounds of sex soon drew my gaze back to the half-naked bodies of the two men. Their motion had become more frenzied. The man with his back to the tree clenched and unclenched his hands, digging and kneading his fingers into the bottom of his partner. My breath caught in my throat. I'd never witnessed anything quite so intriguing or erotic.

I'm certain that if I were a man I'd have been hard as

rock that night. As it was, I just felt unbelievably horny. I watched until they both came, and then returned to the park gate, flushed, to find the others debating whether to search for me. When I finally arrived home, I spent the next hour frantically masturbating, trying to chase the demons from my head.

No one said anything about their own adventures in the park, either that night or the next day at work when we were all nursing sore heads. To me it felt like a dream, and I didn't want to break the spell by sharing the experience. Besides, I didn't think anyone else had seen what I'd seen and, if they had, would they feel the same way about it?

Images of the two men rutting haunted me. For over a week I fought the compulsion, until eventually, one evening after work, I found myself back at the park. It was as I remembered, with men in pairs, or sometimes even in threes, looking for a quick fix or an illicit thrill. I found myself following a stray – that's the name I've since given those first-timers who wander into the park looking for something, yet terrified of finding it. They probably haven't even come out to their closest friends, but their hunger and need drives them recklessly into the arms of strangers. I noticed this one because he was even more nervous among the dark leafy avenues than I was. Just by chance he hooked up with the owner of the dimpled bottom that I'd watched with such fascination during my first visit.

'What's your name? I'm Jason,' he asked the newcomer. Later I learned that Jason was something of a regular in the park.

'Andy,' came the hesitant reply.

'OK, Andy. So, what do you like?'

Andy glanced back over his shoulder, as if he expected

to find an audience. 'I don't know. I'm not sure. I've got a wife ... a family.'

'Well, I don't think they'll be watching you from the bushes.'

'You're probably right,' he said warily. They weren't, of course. But I was, and I wondered if he could somehow sense my presence. Jason gave him a friendly smile and put his hand on the other man's shoulder. It seemed to reassure him, but I suspected it was mostly to get his attention back; it worked. Their eyes locked.

'So, do you want to do or be done?' Jason asked.

I waited for the reply with my heartbeat hammering so loud in my ears I thought I wouldn't hear him, but after a short nervous pause, he whispered, 'I want to be done.'

Once in a while I get treated to a scene like that; it's a moment of honesty when someone comes to terms with who they are and, when it's over, they've learned something new about themselves. It reminds me that there's more to these men and their frenzied couplings than just the urge to fuck. Like me, they have lives outside of the boundaries of the park.

The streets are narrow where I live. From my bedroom, I can see into the wide upper windows of the five houses opposite. On most, the thick curtains are drawn. Not so on number four. Instead, thin roller blinds cover the panes and I know from experience that with a little light behind them they become quite transparent. So you can imagine the pleasant surprise I got when my new neighbour turned out to be Jason, the man I'd seen so often cruising in the park.

Jason arrived home an hour ago along with a guest. They've spent the last hour downstairs, talking and

swigging beer from bottles, with their hands uncon-
sciously clenching around the glass necks, no doubt
imagining how it will feel to touch each other's cocks.

Now one of them has made a move, pinning the other
in an arm lock. The ensuing scuffle brings them closer.
Shoves and fake punches turn into caresses. Questing
hands move roughly over the bare skin of their backs.
Their lips meet, and they kiss in the long, slow way they
do in black and white movies. Upstairs beckons. They
waltz into the bedroom, glued to one another and blind
to where they are going. Still bound together, they fall
onto the bed. Jason untangles himself and throws the
pillows off, making an uncluttered surface on which to
fuck.

There are no details through the blinds; no colour, no
flesh tones. You can't see the flush before orgasm or the
tiny details that make up the contours of a smile or
frown. Instead, there are two perfect male silhouettes
framed by the broad bay window.

My imagination fills in the missing details as I watch
Jason unzip his companion. He tangles his fingers in the
bush around his cock, the hairs tickling against his palm.
I smell the sweet scent of skin when he presses his lips
to the head; taste the warm salty taste of pre-come as he
kisses up the stem.

Jason grips his partner's legs and scoops them over
his shoulders. It looks as if he is licking his partner's
balls, washing the fuzzy sac with his tongue before
tracing it down towards his anus. I watch his shadow
dab at the puckered hole and poke inside. At the same
time, I lift my nightshirt and push my hand between
my tightly clenched thighs. Unlike my visit to the park,
I don't hurry. I let the need build slowly, not touching
my clit until I reach fever point, and then I pat it gently,
tormenting myself, not letting myself come.

Across the street, the guys' lips move in speech. Jason moves out of the frame, perhaps to a drawer, then returns and sheathes his cock in latex and lube. With excruciating slowness, an inch at a time, he then pushes deep into his partner's behind. Once in all the way, he moves with his hips, pumping in a careful figure-of-eight motion. I picture the way the muscles of his bottom hollow with each stroke and his jaw clenches, just like when I've watched him in the park. The other man's prick points upright, like a rocket ready for launch. Jason grasps it in one large hand, squeezing it in time with his thrusts.

My own bed rocks in time with their motion, accompanied by the squeak of a loose floorboard. The sound rises, growing increasingly high-pitched, as I pursue my crescendo just as the men pursue theirs. Tendrils of lava swirl around my clit and make it prickle as if a thread were drawn tight. I wet my finger, stroke faster now, but both men beat me and I lose my momentum once they have come. Edgy and distressed, I collapse into the covers, hoping to find relief in the sleep that I know won't come.

At 3 a.m. I'm still awake. My bed is a tangled mess. I dig my elbow into the pillow in a futile attempt to create a comfortable spot, but the mattress is full of lumps. I close my eyes, but the manic itch between my thighs won't let me relax enough to sleep. Across the street, a lamp flickers on. I turn to my side and watch the repeat. This time, Jason is rimmed and fucked.

As I watch the silhouettes press together, I picture the glow upon Jason's cheeks, the beads of perspiration peppering his back, and watch his cock dance, beating against his stomach as they crouch doggy style.

I picture myself as the rumpled sheet beneath them.

Their weight presses down on me. They claw at my surface; twist sections into their palms. Jason's expression is one of rapture – total ecstasy. I want to reach up and lick the line of perspiration from above his lip; to nip at his neck and chin. His eyes are wide, and bright ocean-green. His mouth is soft, his kisses wet. My tongue tangles with his, dances a heated tango, while his cock finds comfort in my cunt. I fumble my vibrator from the drawer and twist the knob to full power, then rub it back it and forth in my moisture before pushing it in deep.

I close my eyes. Jason whispers to me. His words are like his kisses, fleeting and hard to hold on to. I strain to catch each murmur of affection, each gasp as he drives himself deep. His back is bathed in sweat and his movements are entirely down to instinct. My orgasm starts in my toes. It rushes all over my skin. My muscles clench around his prick as I pant out every moment of pleasure.

When I open my eyes, I am shocked to find the two men are watching me. They have pulled up the blind, and are peering straight into my room at my widely parted thighs and the life-like dildo I have buried there. Alarmed, I pull up the covers right over my beetroot-red face, but a moment later I emerge again, too intrigued to stay hidden.

To my relief they are both still there.

Jason waves; they are both grinning. Tentatively, I wave back and they seem pleased. Jason beckons me to come over. I look down at the empty street between us and shake my head. In sign I explain that my bed is warm, but the refusal prompts a second suggestion. He indicates that they will come to me. Although I wildly gesture back and shake my head, it is too late. They pull on clothing and moments later I see them cross the street.

When they knock upon my door, it makes me rise with a start. They rap three times before I summon the courage to answer. I peer around the edge of the door at them, still dressed in only a flimsy nightshirt. Jason is more delicious than ever close up. He is tall with light brown hair that is cropped very short, and I discover his eyes are grey-blue not green. His friend, who stands possessively beside him, is dark, has a heavier build and a five o'clock shadow around his jaw.

'Hi,' they say.

Dumbstruck, I stand motionless, and let my eyes flicker between the two men.

'Can we come in?' Jason asks. 'By the way, I'm Jason. This is Mark.'

I nod mutely, then push the door wide and stand back from the threshold to let them cross. 'I'm Jo,' I manage to mumble once they are in. 'Would you like a drink?'

We settle uncomfortably in the lounge, sipping cold beers from the fridge. I'm not a very good hostess. I don't know what to say. I've never been very good with words. Jason tries to draw me out, but it is Mark who breaks the tension. He grabs Jason and pushes his tongue deep into his mouth in a wet noisy kiss. My heart nearly stops when I see this. Then it beats wildly. I stand up as the two men roll off the sofa on to the floor and, suddenly, I have two guys making out in my front room. My nervousness falls away; instinct takes over and I'm immediately caught up in the scene.

To my surprise, it isn't the colour that I notice first; it's their scent. Normally, I'm too distant to even catch a hint of it. It is the heavy blend of two testosterone-soaked horny men, a musky undercurrent that is both sharp and sweet. I drink it in like an intoxicant, until I'm almost ready to swoon.

Mark pulls off Jason's T-shirt. They both wriggle from

their jeans. Neither man is wearing underwear. I circle around them like a photographer eager for the best shot. I've never been so close before. I want to see every angle, notice every blemish and remember every tiny thing.

Jason straddles Mark, and lowers himself on to his upright cock until their bodies meet. I realise that they probably broke off what they were doing earlier to watch me. For some reason, that knowledge pulls the cordon of lust inside me that bit tighter, and I run my hand down my thigh and under the hem of my night-shirt. I notice immediately that Jason's attention is now locked on to me.

'Show me,' he begs. 'Take it off.'

Willing to oblige his whim, I do just as he asks, and the satiny sheath goes sailing across the floor. Emboldened by his stare, I lift my breasts, pushing them together so the nipples peak between my fingers. Jason's cock swings a fraction higher at the sight. Mark merely grunts, which might signal acceptance or just resignation.

Jason's cock is long and thick with a cute, kissable cherry-red top. It slaps against his stomach as he bounces on Mark's prick, leaving sticky dots, and I just know he's aching to be touched. Too involved to just stand back now, I reach over and trace my fingertips down his length.

'Oh, man!' he cries. He licks his lips. I remember how Sean licked the guy in the park and I want to do the same for Jason. I run my tongue over my lips, kneel by his side ready to descend.

'Wait.' He stops me just an inch above his cock. 'I want to turn over.'

I can't resist. I stick my tongue out and give him a sly lick before shuffling back while they twist around. Jason takes up his new position on his knees with Mark between his feet. Mark has friction burns on his shoulders that I touch with a mixture of curiosity and sympathy. I lick his shoulder, across the red graze, then down the length of his spine, before wriggling between their legs to lie beneath Jason. His straining prick bobs just above me; I lift my head and swallow him in one delightful gulp. I've waited too long for this.

'More?' I ask when I come up for air.

He nods his head frantically.

'Hurry it up,' Mark says. Through Jason, I can tell his thrusts are becoming more urgent.

'Not yet. Jo needs a little encouragement.'

'Don't worry about me,' I try to say around his prick, but somehow Jason manages to support himself on one hand while he sweeps the other downward over my stomach to my clit. Immediately, I feel my muscles flutter. Clearly, Jason's known a woman or two. The aching sweetness soon spreads. I grind myself against his hand, lost to everything but that sensation and the one in my mouth.

Mark comes with a roar that sends Jason over the edge. He comes in my mouth while still frantically trying to bring me off. That show of consideration is what finally makes him succeed. I let his prick slip from my mouth just before my orgasm shakes me.

Now, when Jason brings men home, he sometimes leaves the blinds up. He's been over several times since that night, mostly with Mark but once without. I've not been back to the park. Today he sent a note; he has something special to show me. At the appointed hour, I twitch the voile curtains open, take up my place and look out.

The Stranger Nine Declare

My boyfriend Neil had just finished securing me to the bed when the doorbell rang. I couldn't move. My hands were cuffed behind my head and the cuffs were attached to a rope which was fastened around the bedposts. My ankles were tied with more rope. I was spreadeagled; opened wide. Neil didn't do things by halves. The last thing I saw before he blindfolded me was his grin. He ran one hand over the length of my naked body and went to get the door.

I didn't hear him close the bedroom door behind me. This was unexpected. If anyone came into our flat, what if they saw me in here? I heard him open the front door, then, 'Hey, man!' It didn't sound like he'd been expecting this guy, whoever he was. I heard the two men exchange pleasantries – it sounded innocent enough. I strained to pick up every detail of the conversation. Neil started to speak lower, and then the tone changed. The other guy had been sounding like he would leave in a minute, but now it sounded like Neil was suggesting something else.

I waited.

The front door closed. After a moment, Neil came back to me. 'Sorry about that, baby,' he said. 'A friend of mine. He was just returning a book. Now, where were we?'

I hated it when he'd say, 'Where were we?' It made me feel like I was in a cheesy film. But I knew there was something more important to worry about. I knew full well that the other man hadn't left. I could feel his presence in the bedroom. I knew he was staring at my naked body right now. I was powerless to move from his gaze, and I couldn't even see him.

'Who is he?' I asked. 'Why'd you bring him in here?

'I didn't bring him in here, Sandra. He left. Didn't you hear the door?'

'Jesus, Neil. Don't bullshit me. What are you playing at?'

'She's a feisty one,' said the other voice, sounding amused. Now let me tell you, I *hate* being called feisty. I've always found it a very patronising word. But again, it was an irritation that was the least of my concerns right now. At least now he had admitted he was here, Neil couldn't bullshit me any more.

'Allow me to introduce my girlfriend, Sandra.'

Neil didn't bother to introduce the stranger. The stranger said, 'Pleased to meet you, Sandra.' And, 'You have great tits. May I?'

I was about to retort indignantly when Neil said, 'Sure, go ahead,' and I realised that the stranger hadn't been asking *my* permission. I felt his hands on my breasts. He stroked them slowly. Then he pinched my nipples. Then he squeezed a breast in each hand. Then he squeezed them from the sides so that they were pushed together, and bent his head to my chest and sucked on both nipples at once.

I was aware that Neil was standing in the background, breathing a little heavier than normal. He liked watching the stranger play with me. He liked the idea of prostituting me.

'Can I have a go?' the stranger asked. Again, he was asking Neil, not me.

'You can't fuck her,' Neil answered abruptly. There was a pause. Then he said, 'She's pretty good at sucking, though. You should try her out.'

'Sure!' The stranger sounded happy. I heard him unzip his trousers. My heart was thumping. I didn't even know this guy and he was about to put his cock in my mouth. Not only did I not know him, I didn't know what he looked like. I didn't know who he was, or how he knew Neil. I could walk down the street and he could pass me by with the knowledge that he had seen me naked and I sucked him, and I wouldn't know him from Adam.

The thing was ... I kind of *liked* that idea. Against my better judgement, I was getting wet, and I wondered if the stranger knew this. Although it had been kind of low of Neil to bring him in here without consulting me first, I trusted him enough not to let anything bad happen to me.

Or so I hoped.

So, I knew if I was a good girl I should be protesting right about now, but I didn't. The only thing I opened my mouth for was to taste the stranger's cock. He knelt astride me and fed it to me. I licked at it tentatively to begin with. It tasted a little different to Neil's. It wasn't a bad taste, just kind of more salty. The inherent wrongness of the situation I was in turned me on more. I wished Neil would put his fingers inside me while I was doing this, but I was vaguely aware that Neil was most likely beating off in the chair by the door. I opened my mouth wider to take just the tip of the stranger's cock inside. He moaned.

'God, you're right. She *is* good,' he said to Neil. He played with my tits and then thrust deeper into my mouth. I sucked on it, getting more and more desperate and horny. How could I get someone to attend to *my* needs? I tried to lift my head off the pillow so that I could get closer to his cock, and he held his hand beneath my head to help me. I licked up and down the shaft and then wrapped my lips around it sideways. I licked his balls. They were hairless. 'Oh, God, yes,' he said. 'Do that again, slut.'

Shouldn't Neil be telling him not to talk to me that way?

Oh, well. I liked it.

I sucked his balls with more force. And then he came. I closed my mouth just in time because, to be honest, I don't like to taste it. He shot all over my face. I could feel that it had hit my hair and the pillow as well. It dripped from my face down and round to the back of my neck. I lay my head back, my jaw exhausted. The stranger sat back astride me, panting.

The phone rang.

'I'll get that,' Neil said reluctantly. I heard him zip up. I'd been right. He left the room.

The stranger got up off me, reached for the tissues on the bedside table, and cleaned himself up. He didn't say anything to me. And I didn't dare say anything to him.

Then he said, 'You look so filthy. My come is all over you.'

I had never been spoken to this way before. I wondered if maybe the fact that he knew I didn't know who he was allowed him to be freer with the way he spoke to me.

As he mopped me up, he whispered, 'Did you enjoy that performance? You like being treated like a slut, don't you?'

I didn't answer.

'I know you do.' I could hear a smile in his voice. Then I felt his fingers slide into me. I sighed, relieved that I was finally being touched. 'You see? You're so wet. I know you like it.'

I moved my hips to let him know he was right. I hoped he wouldn't stop. 'So now I know what you feel like on the inside,' he said. Then he moved his head close to mine. 'I'm going to fuck you,' he whispered in my ear. 'Your boyfriend doesn't want me to. But I'm going to fuck you some time. Wouldn't you like that?'

I didn't dare breathe. I did want that, but I didn't want to give anything away. I didn't want to be disloyal to Neil. (Neil, who had just invited a random guy to put his cock in my mouth – I didn't want to be disloyal to *him*.)

'I can tell you like it rough,' the stranger said. 'It's OK, you don't need to say anything. Some time, I'm going to stick my cock in right here, where my fingers are. I'm going to fuck you like a whore. You're going to beg me not to stop.'

I allowed myself to breathe again. Heavily. Damn right I would beg him not to stop, if it was anything like the way he was fingering me. But right now, I think we both had this sense that he shouldn't be doing this to me – not if Neil hadn't allowed it. If Neil came back into the room and saw what was going on, he'd be pissed off.

I heard the little bleep as Neil hung up the phone, and I released a sad little moan as the stranger pulled out of me. 'Don't worry,' he whispered, 'I'll be back for more.' Then Neil came in and the stranger thanked him very much for letting him use me. Neil laughed and said no problem, any time, you can have my girlfriend suck you off any time. I heaved a sigh of relief inwardly, because I wanted him back, but at the same time I was saying to myself: have I just lost my mind? I don't even know who the hell he *is!*

Neil showed him out, and this time when the front door closed, I knew the stranger was really gone. Neil came back into the bedroom, got out of his clothes, got on top of me, and fingered me for a second. Then he shoved his cock straight into me. He fucked me hard and fast. While he fucked me he said words he had never said to me before. Whore and bitch and slut and cunt. It was almost funny how he had so obviously been inspired to talk like this by his friend.

It didn't take long for me to come. Neil fucked me for another minute and then I felt him twitching inside me and he came too. Finally he spoke.

'How did you like that?'

'It was great.'

'I mean tonight. Sucking off another guy.'

'It was weird. But . . . yeah, I really liked it. Did you?'

'Yeah. I really liked seeing you doing that with someone else. It made you look so dirty.'

He enthused for a while longer about how much he enjoyed watching me with the stranger. He never once told me the stranger's name, and I never asked.

'We'll be seeing more of him,' he said with a laugh. 'Well – *I* will. You'll just be sucking him. With the blindfold on.' Then Neil untied me and I went to have a shower.

If this was going to be the set-up, well, surely there was no need for the stranger's identity to be hidden from me? I mean, he wasn't going to be somebody important who'd be involved in a scandal. He was just one of Neil's friends. I didn't recognise his voice, so I was pretty sure I'd never met him before. I figured if they kept me blindfolded whenever he was around, it would just be to add to the mystery, to the illicit thrill. So they could watch me and I could wonder who it was who was doing these things to me. So they could treat me as more of an object.

And, to be honest, I wasn't complaining. In the weeks that followed, whenever I met a friend or acquaintance of Neil's, I sized up the way he talked, the way he smelled, and the way he behaved with me. I thought, does this guy know something I don't? Has he ever put his fingers inside me? Has he ever called me slut? I could go crazy if I kept thinking like this. I managed to satisfy myself that none of these men could be the stranger. The stranger only saw me when he visited; when I was tied up and told to take him in my mouth.

The next time I encountered the stranger – I can't say I *saw* him – it was a couple of weeks later. When I'd got home from work, I'd gone into the kitchen to start making my dinner, but Neil had been in there, and he was already aroused. He kissed me, and his huge erection pressed against me.

'Let me have some food first,' I said. 'I'm starving.'

'Tough,' Neil retorted. 'We're on a tight schedule here. Take off your clothes.'

I *was* starving, but I always liked to take orders from him. As soon as he told me to do something, I would be turned on. So I stripped off while he closed the curtains. Then he made me get down on my hands and knees. He handcuffed me and he affixed the blindfold. He was just sliding the handle of a wooden spoon in and out of me – Neil loved putting things inside me – when the door-bell rang.

'He's late,' said Neil, and went to answer it, leaving me with the realisation that all of this had been set up. My clit throbbed. The two of them came in, the stranger bringing with him the cold air from outside. I heard him take off his coat. He didn't bother to greet me, as I knelt expectantly.

'Have a seat in that chair,' Neil told him. 'She can suck you off while I fuck her.'

I was no longer spoken to directly. I was *she*. I was third person. This time, it sounded like they were both taking their clothes off. The stranger sat in a chair, which he positioned in front of me. I sensed that his legs were spread out on either side of me.

Nothing happened for a moment.

Neil slapped my ass. 'Go on, slut, suck his cock.'

As I moved myself forward on my hands and knees so that I could get my mouth to the stranger's crotch, Neil opened my legs wider and I felt his penis pressing against me for a moment before he shoved it all the way in. The stranger held my head to his crotch, and he sighed as he responded to my lips and tongue. I moaned as Neil's cock went deeper. This seemed to turn them both on, as the stranger plunged into my mouth harder and Neil fucked my cunt faster. Soon we were moving rhythmically, all three of us, as they pumped me at both ends.

I imagined that this was really some sort of repressed homoerotic situation: that secretly Neil and the stranger lusted after *each other*; that they weren't actually having sex with me; my body was just a vessel in between. I liked the idea of this. I liked to imagine that they would use me like this until they had the courage to admit their hidden desires. Then they would pounce on top of each other for some hot man-on-man action. And I'd be left to writhe forgotten on the floor until my blindfold had fallen off and I could watch and enjoy.

But, much as I liked that little fantasy, I didn't believe it to be the case. Neil and the stranger were just two straight boys who enjoyed treating me like a piece of meat. Anyway, there was one thing wrong with that fantasy: I would see the stranger. Much as I was intrigued, I knew deep down that I didn't really want to see him. This was for a simple reason. It was just because he might not be my type. I was picky. He made me feel so wet, so dirty, and so horny that I didn't want to discover he was ugly. I didn't want his looks to spoil how he made me feel. Neil was gorgeous and he was the only man I actually needed to look at.

Over the next couple of months, the stranger called round regularly. The three of us did everything we could think of that didn't involve the stranger touching me *down there*. And I guess it was partly because of Neil's silly rule about this that I wanted that more than anything – especially to take his cock inside me. And the stranger wanted it too. He reminded me of his promise whenever Neil left the room for a moment. He whispered in my ear and stroked my clit and called me whore in a way that made me want the freedom (no restraints) and the permission (Neil's go-ahead) to jump on him and let him inside.

Meanwhile, they played with my body. Neil would fuck me bent over the kitchen table while the stranger looked on. I would suck the stranger while Neil fucked me, with his cock or his fingers or my vibrator or anything lying around – it didn't matter. We tried every position we could think of. I was stripped and caressed and groped. I was handcuffed in the shower and made to suck them off in turn while the water drenched me. I was chained up and told to play with myself while they discussed my body parts as if they were separate to me. Sometimes they'd just sit and drink a couple of beers and laugh together while I put on my show for them, and then suddenly I'd find myself drenched as they poured the alcohol over me: the stranger would lick it off my tits while Neil lapped it up from between my legs. And then I'd be fucked at both ends again.

One night, Neil was about to take a shower when the doorbell rang. 'Stay there,' he said to me. I was never allowed to answer the door in the evening any more in case I came face to face with the man whose cock I was so used to tasting. I waited patiently in the kitchen. I heard his voice. It was him all right.

'Look, I'm about to take a shower,' Neil was saying.

'Hey man, I don't want *you* to suck me,' replied the stranger. He sounded so mellow, and so self-assured. Technically, he was talking Neil into allowing something to happen that Neil didn't want to happen. But never mind. It was all fine with me.

Neil thought for a minute and then said, 'OK. Wait there.' He came back into the kitchen, stripped me completely, and sat me down in a chair. He tied my hands behind it, tied my ankles to the legs of the chair, and put the blindfold on me. Then he let the stranger come in, and left the room himself.

I didn't say a word. I wanted the stranger to do so many more things to me than had been allowed so far, and now it seemed that we had the privacy for it, but I still felt wrong about it because I knew it was something Neil didn't want to happen. Even though, I mused, Neil had just gone off to take a shower, leaving an unknown man to have his wicked way with his girlfriend. Dear God, he could do *anything* to me! Logic was a funny thing.

It didn't seem to be the stranger's plan, anyway. He seemed pleased to see me tied up in this position. He got down on the floor on his knees, and then his tongue flickered across my clit. I leaned my head back and exhaled. Gradually, he worked his tongue inside me, joined by a couple of fingers. He licked and licked, and then he paused to suck my clit until I nearly cried out, and then he went back to licking. I heard the running water of the shower. I came. He licked me clean again. Then we heard the shower switch off and the stranger stood up. I heard him gathering his things.

'She just can't get enough cock! Thanks, man,' he said

to Neil on his way out. I sat, still tied, still blindfolded, still naked. I was amazed. It was like our little secret or something. Me and this man I'd never seen, but whose body I knew so well – we had a secret.

But I was getting the feeling that Neil wasn't liking the situation so much any more. Maybe the novelty had worn off for him or something.

The next time the stranger came round, before we started anything, he asked Neil straight out: 'How come you won't let me fuck her?'

I was kneeling on the floor, naked as usual (sometimes I wondered if the stranger would recognise me if I had clothes on), my hands chained between my knees. I caught my breath. What Neil said now would make all the difference.

'Come on, man,' Neil said. 'She's my girlfriend. I get to fuck her. You don't.'

'Oh, right. She's your girlfriend. What about all this calling her a whore, then?'

'That's different.' I could hear Neil getting uncomfortable.

'It's *not* different, Neil. You're just all talk.'

'No I'm not.'

'Yes you are.'

I kept my mouth shut. Nobody consulted me as to whether I would like the stranger to fuck me. They argued, but the stranger knew not to go too far, not to spoil his chances altogether.

'Look, man, you get a pretty good deal out of this,' said Neil. 'I let you come in here all the time and she sucks your cock for nothing. You're lucky. You don't have to go out with her or anything, and you don't have to pay.'

What was *that* supposed to mean? I wondered indignantly. Neil sounded almost jealous of the stranger's set-up. 'She doesn't even know who you are!' Neil continued.

'Yeah. So why not just let me fuck her? I mean, jeez, what difference does it make?'

'Look, it matters. Leave it. I just don't want some other guy fucking my girlfriend. I bet you wouldn't like some-one fucking yours, either.'

So the stranger had a girlfriend? For a moment I lost myself in fantasies of what she was like and what they did together. I wondered if she was ever tied up. I wondered if she took orders. I wondered if she sucked his cock as well as I did – would he still be coming here if she did? Maybe they just had boring missionary position sex. Or maybe she was a total slut. Maybe she would spread her legs for anyone. Maybe she couldn't get enough. Maybe he would bring her here and she would sit on my face while he pushed his cock deep into my cunt. We could have sex while the boys looked on and then joined in. I wondered if I would rather see her, or be blindfolded still. I thought about Neil fucking her. If we could have a trade-off and I could fuck the stranger, I wouldn't mind.

The stranger was still cajoling Neil, strategically. I realised that Neil was now stumbling. He reminded me of how I used to be when I was younger and guys would try and talk me into having sex with them when I didn't really want to. Up until now I had never heard a man being put in this position. The stranger was coming across all logical, reasonable, pushing for what he wanted, dismissing Neil's reasons for saying no. For a minute I felt sorry for Neil. Then I didn't. I just wanted this fuck.

Look, before you think I'm this shallow, cold-hearted, fickle kind of person, you should probably know that

Neil and I did not have that good a relationship anyway. Sure, the sex was great. But he didn't love me, and I didn't love him, and at least we didn't pretend. We lived together because we couldn't afford to live separately. We didn't communicate all that well. And now I was getting annoyed that he had decided to give my body to this stranger when it suited him, but not to give it fully. I was the submissive in the chains, and it wasn't really my place to complain, but I wished now that I had some say in the matter.

The stranger finally talked Neil into having a game of Tekken with him. The winner would then fuck me right then and there. My body went into a new kind of alertness. I tensed up, goosebumps forming all over me. I couldn't believe that a video game was going to decide my fate. Something about that felt so deliciously sordid.

Of course, Neil only agreed because he was very good at Tekken. I was well aware of this.

They pulled me into the living room with them and set up the machine. I sat in the far corner, still on my knees, still chained up. They could glance across at me in between rounds. They had stopped talking now; the heated debate was over. They each smoked a cigarette, opening the window to let the smell out. I stayed in my corner feeling the smoke and the breeze rush over me. I shivered slightly. I started to touch myself as subtly as I could. I couldn't help myself any more. My hands were between my knees so I inched them back between my legs. Nobody said anything. I didn't know if they were watching me or not.

They played. I couldn't work out how well each one was doing. Both Neil and the stranger seemed to come out with an equal amount of 'Fuck!'s and 'Yes!'s. Apart from that there was only a frantic pushing of buttons.

I'd never heard anyone play so fast. You'd have thought Neil's life depended on it. It was kind of funny really.

I heard Round 3 being announced. This was the decider. They must have both done about equally well up until now. Nobody bothered to keep me informed of the score. I only knew at the very end; somebody shouted 'YES!', and it wasn't Neil.

'That's it, man,' said the stranger. 'You played a good game, but I'm going to fuck your girlfriend now.'

Neil didn't answer.

'I think she wants it, man,' said the stranger. 'Did you see her playing with herself before we started the game? She's really up for it. But don't worry. I'll be good to her.'

Neil grunted and I heard him light a cigarette.

'OK, so she may not be able to walk for a week. But you'll still be able to fuck her. I mean, man, she's a slut. That's what she's for – you've said so yourself. You shouldn't take it so hard.'

'Fine,' said Neil. 'I'm going out.' I heard him get to his feet.

'Aw, Neil! You should stay and watch! Don't you want to hear her moan when I stick it in her?'

Neil didn't say another word. I heard him stride across the room. Then I heard the front door slam.

There was silence for a moment.

'I shouldn't have rubbed it in so much, should I?' said the stranger. Again there was a smile in his voice. I didn't respond. 'But come on, I had to. You know how much I've wanted you. And there you go. You're mine now, slut. Are you ready?'

I nodded.

The stranger pulled me to the centre of the room. He made me get down on all fours, but told me to stretch out further than I had ever done before. 'Hang on,' he said. 'Where is there a condom?'

'In the bedside drawer,' I said. I was grateful that he had asked. I had been wondering how to negotiate that from my powerless position.

He left the room and came back. I heard him remove his clothes, and then I heard the rustle of a condom wrapper. A moment later he was crouching behind me.

'Open wide, slut,' he said.

He'd seen Neil take me in this position before, but the way the stranger did it was different. First he slid his fingers into me to check how wet I was. Then he wrapped his arms around me and held me by my tits. He licked down the length of my back. He squeezed my ass cheeks. Then he very slowly slid his cock into me. Inch by inch. All the way, up to the hilt. For a moment we stayed like that, not moving. Then he began to move it. I felt his cock deep inside me; felt how wet I was; felt my ass slapping against his hips.

The stranger pushed my head until it was down on the carpet, which in turn made me raise my ass higher in the air. I thought of myself as being just a rag doll for the stranger to fuck. He rammed it harder and harder into me, faster and faster. He held me by my tits one minute and my hips the next, and he whispered in my ear: 'I told you I'd fuck you some day.'

'Please,' I whimpered, 'please don't stop.'

It was everything I'd wanted. This man, whose name I didn't know, who could be the most repulsive man on Earth for all I knew, was good at treating me the way I wanted to be treated. Neil didn't want him to go all the way, but it had been too late: the stranger had come to look on me as his property, too. And I was. He was taking possession of me right now. He pumped his cock into me and I spread my legs wider for him. My head rested on the carpet just in front of my cuffed hands. I stopped begging him not to stop and settled for moaning instead as he filled me up. He panted. He liked what he was doing to me and he liked that I liked it. He told me that I was filthy and deviant, that I was such a good little whore, that he wished he could keep me and just use me for fucking all the time.

Vaguely I heard the front door open again, but then I forgot about it as I felt the spasms start within me.

'Do you like it, slut?' the stranger said, getting ever faster. It was like my moans spurred him on.

'Yes,' I gasped. I'd never felt anything like this before.

'Whore –'

I think he was going to say something else there, but I came. And came. And came. I cried out. My head buzzed. And then I collapsed on the floor and lay there wondering if I would ever have the good fortune of feeling this way again.

After a few moments the stranger turned me over. I thought he wanted me to suck him or something now, and I was so exhausted I didn't know if I'd be able to. But he surprised me. He lowered his face to mine and kissed me, really tenderly. I had never had contact with his face before. He was clean-shaven. His tongue slid in and out of my mouth. Maybe it was partly because of the orgasm I'd just had, but it felt amazing. It felt like some kind of dreamlike experience. And when he stopped kissing me, he finished with just a little peck on my lips. It actually felt affectionate.

Maybe he'd grown fond of me after I'd served him obediently for so long. I guess it could make sense.

Of course, Neil didn't like seeing me being fucked by another man and enjoying myself so much. The fact that he kissed me like that at the end must have really rubbed it in. The stranger was not invited again, and did not call around again. I think they must have exchanged strong words when I was not present.

Neil and I had embarked on the downward spiral. We stayed together for another couple of months, but then a friend of his said he had a room available and Neil moved out straight away. Some would say you shouldn't invite a stranger into your bed because it will just break you up. I think we would've broken up anyway. And I didn't regret for a moment having had the stranger.

Time passed. Neil didn't matter any more, but I still thought of the stranger sometimes. He had been an erotic experience the likes of which I had never encountered before or since. I mentioned him once when I was playing drinking games with a bunch of girlfriends, but they looked at me with horror as soon as I started to describe the situation we had, so I never dared to tell much of the story at all. They wouldn't understand.

It had been a while since I had had a dental check-up. Clearing out some old junk and papers that Neil had left behind, I found an appointment card for a local dentist and decided I might as well register there. I found the place during my lunch break, sat in the waiting room and read mundane magazines; then I was ushered through.

'Hello, Sandra.' The dentist shook my hand. 'It's nice to meet you.' He was around my age, a bit taller than me, dark hair, glasses. I wasn't really thinking about whether he was attractive or not, but he was OK. It was just his smile that unnerved me a little. Something seemed oddly familiar, and I couldn't put my finger on it.

I lay back in the chair and closed my eyes, blinded by the light shining in them. He lowered the chair. Was he supposed to lower or raise it? All of a sudden I couldn't remember.

'Open wide,' he said. I heard the soft sound of a zip, and then, under his breath, I heard him finish the sentence: 'slut.'

Ice-Lollies for a Hot Climate
Francesca Brouillard

The marble floor is peppermint cool to my feet after the sun-scorched tiles round the pool. I stand for a moment to adjust to the darkness of the room.

Sweat trickles down the backs of my knees and from under my breasts. It drips down to the skimpy line of my bikini pants – I have removed the top. My nipples, I notice, are swollen from the sun. They are so pointy it looks as if extensions have been stuck on top; they remind me of old *National Geographic* photographs of native women. They look so fat and juicy I want to squeeze them between my fingers; I want Simon to suck them and make them go pert and crinkly. Simon tells me I shouldn't spend so long in the sun, but he's working all the time and there's nothing else to do here.

In the first few weeks after we'd come to Spain, I lay listening to *Teach Yourself Spanish* tapes, but now they bore me. Besides, the only people I ever seem to meet are the architects and engineers from the project Simon's working on and they all speak English. Now my eyes have adjusted, I can see Simon sitting at his drawing board. He looks so cool in his fresh white shirt. No damp stains round the armpits. A crisp clean man in a linen suit. My elegant, clever husband.

I go to stand by him and watch him work for a moment, his slim hands making precise lines on the paper. His forehead is creased slightly in concentration and I can see the pale outlines of veins in his temples.

Simon makes love with the same attention to detail he applies to his work. Everything is meticulously prepared and carefully executed, from the cologning of his body to turning down the sheets. It is never a spontaneous or impetuous act but one that has been planned with precision. It's what attracted me to him in the first place, that almost clinical detachment he has. It seemed so sophisticated to me then, in my twenties, this very adult approach to sex; treating it as something almost sacred, to be ritualised and choreographed.

All that casual sex and jumping into bed drunk after parties seemed suddenly puerile. Here was a man who took sex seriously. Candlelit dinners, music, crisp, fresh sheets and the act itself, always preceded by a suitable variety of foreplay. He's never gone in for anything particularly risqué but, whereas with some people you feel a limited sexual repertoire is due to lack of imagination, with Simon you always have the feeling that he's tried everything and these are the techniques he considers to be the best. He has the air of a quietly self-assured expert.

So, at twenty-seven, I decided I'd outgrown fun sex and wanted someone suave and sophisticated, with a mature attitude.

At the moment, though, what I want is for him to notice me; to turn round with his special silver pen that's making such neat lines on the paper and draw circles round my nipples. I want to watch the sharp tip press into the soft flesh of my breasts and make a perfect black line round each swollen aureole, then another, smaller circle round the tips. I imagine him pushing the pen up inside me so I can feel the cold stainless steel, hard and cool as an icicle. I want it to pierce the suffocating ball of heat in my sex and let it flow out between my legs like a molten glacier of lust.

Instead he looks up and smiles. 'You look terribly hot, darling. Why don't you go and take a cool shower, hmm?'

'I thought you might like to . . . you know . . .'

'Not now, love. I'm terribly busy. I promised to have these drawings ready for Señor Castalles by Thursday.'

I go and lie on the bed and look at the ceiling. Inside I burn up with wasted lust.

It's Saturday evening, the one time of the week we're supposed to be able to spend time doing something together and, instead, I'm on my own at a bloody party I never wanted to come to while Simon is off talking to some local bigwig about the Barcelona project. We're only renting the villa here while he's on the project, but apparently it is still important that we join in the local life of this dull, rural community.

One of the waitresses is being very attentive towards me. She probably feels sorry for me. Poor lonely English woman stuck in this tedious backwater with no friends or company. Still, she can save her pity. At least I'm not stuck here forever. She's wearing some sort of traditional, rustic costume – presumably issued by the restaurant for 'authentic atmosphere' – but it's rather tacky.

She must be local by the look of her. I remember when Simon first came back from sorting out the villa, he described the girls in the village as being 'positively bovine'. He reckoned they were 'heavy boned, heavy breasted and had childbearing rumps.'

This one's a bit like that.

'More vino, señora?'

'No, thank you. I'm fine.'

But she doesn't go away; she smiles at me and starts running her fingers over my blouse, feeling the fabric.

'*Es bonita!*'

She fingers the edge of the neckline, then starts running her hand down the front, stroking the material.

'Is silk, yes?'

I nod, feeling uncomfortable. I'm embarrassed by her proximity and the intimacy of her gesture, but don't know how to stop her without seeming rude. I also feel guilty about how I've just been judging her.

'Very nice. Expensive.' Her rough stroking movements now reach my breast, and almost brush my nipple. I pull away slightly. She laughs.

'Mine is cheap. Feel.'

Before I can do anything, she takes my hand and rubs my fingers over her blouse.

Her hand is surprisingly soft and small. She draws my unwilling fingers down from her shoulder towards her breast in a rough, careless movement. She only wants to demonstrate the coarseness of her blouse, but I am scarcely aware of the fabric, all I can think about is what lies underneath – the hot flesh beneath my fingers.

I'm suddenly cross at Simon. How could he have let me get into this situation where one of the waitresses, just an ordinary village girl, is able to embarrass me by making me stroke her blouse.

Then I feel ashamed of myself for being so English and uptight. Why should I be freaked out at the touch of another woman? It's just a cultural thing. We don't go in for much close physical contact at home, I suppose. She's only wanting me to feel her blouse, after all; what am I getting so tense about?

I try to relax.

'Such poor quality.'

Her hand continues to run my reluctant fingers down her breast till, with a sudden shock, I feel the firmness of her breast sink under my fingertips as I touch her nipple. I withdraw my hand sharply but she just smiles at me.

'You don't like the feel? It's too rough, I think.'

Again she rests her hand on my breast, feeling the silk, but with such openness I can only feel cross at myself for being so jumpy. She's just innocently admiring my top. I felt I'd behaved rather rudely, pulling away like that.

'I can try it on?'

'Well, perhaps some other time –'

'I've never worn silk before. Only cheap clothes. Cheap fabrics.'

I don't know what to say. It's a ridiculous situation, the waitress asking to try on my blouse, yet I feel mean and guilty.

'We can try now if you like? I have a room upstairs. We can be very quick.' Her dark eyes are wide in appeal.

I look around desperately, trying to catch Simon's eye, but he's nowhere to be seen. I nod reluctantly.

Taking my hand in hers, she leads me across the room and up a short staircase which smells of wood polish and stale wine. She opens an old plank door on a corner of the stairs and we go into a tiny bedroom.

In contrast to the drink and smoke of the bar, this room is fresh and feminine, littered with clothes, bottles of perfume and cosmetics, books and a scattering of shoes. Against a wall, a crumpled unmade bed is strewn with papers and files and what look like newspaper cuttings.

While I am taking this in, she is already unbuttoning her blouse and taking it off. Beneath it she is wearing an under-cup bra which supports her breasts yet leaves them bare, which is evidently why I could feel her nipple so clearly through her blouse.

I look away embarrassed but she doesn't even attempt to turn her back. I'm shocked by the sight of her plump bosom and enormous nipples. Even given the generous proportions of her breasts, the nipples are huge, like saucers, and a deep, rich brown with the satiny sheen of melted chocolate. Against the pale creaminess of her breasts, they look magnificent.

I'm transfixed; they seem to cover almost a third of her breast.

'You like?' she asks and I feel myself blush in confusion, but when I look up I see she is holding her blouse out to me.

'Er, no thanks.'

I realise she is waiting to try on my top, so I slip it off quickly and hand it to her. It will be far too small, I'm sure, but she pulls it over her head and wriggles into it. I'm left feeling rather naked in just my skirt and bra and I fold my arms across my chest.

The silk is taut across her breasts and the most intimate details of her nipples are clearly revealed. She looks at herself in the mirror, disappointed.

'Too fat, see. Much too fat.'

'No you're not. It's just ... well, the blouse is just too small for you, that's all.'

As she tries to take it off, it gets stuck. Her head is trapped inside and the broad hem has become wedged. I go to help her and realise I'll have to try and tug it over her breasts. I'm frozen with embarrassment. However I tackle the problem I'll be forced to touch them.

'Please help me!' she cries.

I pull rather uselessly at the neck, then try and tug it up at the sides.

'Stop! It is my – what you say – my tits is stuck.' She giggles.

My hands are damp and I feel a churning in my stomach that disconcerts me. I push her breasts up, one at a time, to try and squeeze them out from under the blouse. They are warm and heavy in my hands; solid yet yielding. My thumb sinks accidentally into a nipple and a shock like electricity runs through my body.

A cold flush creeps up from my ankles causing goose pimples to break out on my thighs and breasts, tightening my nipples. I've got to get out of here.

The blouse is suddenly yanked free and her breasts slide trembling through my hands back onto the precarious perch of the under-cup bra, where the nipples, glistening with sweat, seem to stare at me. She is laughing now, unabashed by her jiggling bosom and, happily, unaware of what it is doing to me.

I feel flustered and somehow foolish. I pull the blouse, still warm from her body, back on and, mumbling an apology, exit abruptly.

I seek the privacy of the bathroom; I need to compose myself. Locked in the safety of a cubicle, cooled by the rim of the toilet seat under my thighs, I discover my pants are damp and that I'm sticky between my legs. I mustn't think about it; must forget the entire incident. It's too unnerving.

I sit in my underwear in front of the mirror, running a brush mechanically through my hair and trying to work out what I feel. I'm bored, angry and still vaguely disturbed by the memory of the party last week, but, more specifically, I'm cross at Simon. He's gone off and left me for yet another week of meetings, and arranged for

Yolanda, – the waitress – to come and stay. The bloody cheek of him.

'It'll be good for you to have a bit of company,' he said. 'I know you get lonely here when I'm away and this'll give you a chance to find out more about the culture and the locals.'

It turns out she's the cousin of someone on the project and she's keen to have the opportunity to speak some English. He could have at least consulted me before inviting her. I've not told him about the incident at the party. He'd say I was being foolish; imagining things that weren't there. Maybe he's right but it still makes me feel awkward in her presence and I find I keep going over it in my head.

I hear the slapping of wet feet on the marble. Yolanda appears behind me. I watch her in the mirror. She's wearing a yellow crocheted bikini I've lent her, which is far too small. The two triangles of the top offer no more than nipple cover, and the tiny bottoms almost disappear up her backside, but I suppose it doesn't really matter in the privacy of our pool. At least she seems delighted with it.

She also is watching me through the mirror. Without taking her eyes from mine, she reaches up and removes the clip from her hair, letting the tangled mass fall around her shoulders in dark waves; then, her eyes still on mine, she pulls the knitted string of the bikini top and lets it drop to the floor.

Once again those enormous nipples – like burnished copper teacups – have me transfixed, drawing my eyes down to meet their brazen stare. I watch their heavy bounce as she walks slowly up behind me. I'm unable, even if I dared, to look her in the face again. She rests her hands on my shoulders and I tense up. Her fingers start kneading the base of my neck. I watch her breasts through the mirror as they roll slightly with the movement of her hands, the two huge eyes of her nipples trembling just above my head.

And all the while I know she is watching me.

Although our bodies aren't touching, other than where her hands are on me, I can feel the heat of her against my back. I shut my eyes and try to concentrate on the massage; if only I could ignore the proximity of those breasts I might be able to work out what to do. Surely this is a come-on, but how should I deal with it without feigning outrage or looking hysterical?

Am I even sure I want to deal with it?

Her hands slip down my back and I hear as much as feel the click as she unfastens my bra. With the same circular massaging movements, she slides the straps off and lets the bra drop into my lap. She continues massaging my neck and shoulders then, almost imperceptibly, her hands edge closer and closer to my breasts. I begin to sweat in anticipation of what might happen next. If I do nothing now she will know I am completely in her control.

The soft squeezing hands work their way down to my breasts till she cups them in her palms and begins kneading them. I open my eyes and she is staring directly at me through the mirror. She smiles. I realise my passivity implies consent. Yet consent to what exactly? Is this still within the realms of a friendly massage or is it more?

I say nothing.

As she continues rubbing my breasts she pulls me gently back against her. I can feel the damp bikini pants against my back and the soft rounded warmth of her belly pushing into me – comfortable, reassuring. I let my eyes close again and give in to the soothing movements of her hands on my breasts.

After a while I sense her shift and, although she doesn't cease massaging, I feel her body sliding down mine. I open my eyes and, as I watch, she eases her torso down my body till her breasts rest on my shoulders. I stare straight ahead, avoiding her eyes, looking only at the reflection of my own head held between those breasts. My stomach is churning but I am no longer able to identify my emotions. There is apprehension certainly, yet also excitement and something else I don't want to put a name to. I know she is watching me closely, willing me to meet her gaze, but I won't. I can't.

With an entirely unselfconscious gesture, she puts her hands under her breasts and adjusts them so they rest more comfortably on my shoulders, cushioning my head and framing my face.

It is impossible to pretend the situation could still be ambiguous. This is a blatantly sexual gesture and one I am helpless against. I can't tear my eyes from those smooth chocolate-tipped breasts pressing into my face. Close-up, the nipples seem even larger and beautifully satiny. I can make out all the detail and texture: the circle of bumps like pimples that surround the aureole; the indentation in the tip of the teat.

Being enfolded in this intimate embrace is terrifying yet thrilling. The gentle weight on my shoulders and the warm pressure against my cheeks relaxes me and I suddenly want the warm softness of her breasts to envelop me completely.

I've never felt attracted to another woman before but, trapped between those silky breasts, I find myself becoming aroused. Those voluptuous nipples so close, so tempting. I would only need to twist my head slightly to be able to touch one with my tongue. Just to lick it. Taste it. No more.

I swallow and shut my eyes to lock out the vision. Then my head turns. There is no intent on my part; I want to resist but my lips open instinctively and I feel my tongue pressing against the resilient teat.

In a smooth, easy movement, Yolanda twists her body round, raises her leg over my lap and straddles me, her feet on the floor either side of my chair. She takes her breast in her hands and holds it so the nipple slips sweetly into my mouth. My body begins to melt as I feel my nose press into it. I want to suck the whole fat nipple into my mouth till all the flesh has disappeared. I want to sink my teeth into its softness and chew on it, run my tongue over it and squeeze the juices out.

As I draw her deeper into my mouth her hands close around my head and pull me to her. The hot wet triangle of bikini and the plump roll of her stomach press into my belly and her thighs, pushing heavily down my own, make the edge of the seat dig in to my legs.

My hands begin to explore the curves and creases of her body. It is soft and rounded, not at all like a man's, yet her back is surprisingly strong and firm despite her plumpness. I knead and squeeze the flesh on her sides, pressing my fingers into the hidden folds. Then I slide my hands down to the smooth flaring of her hips, where the strings of the bikini cut in like cheese wire. I tug at the half-buried knots till the flimsy pants come apart and can be removed. Suddenly I'm aware of her pubes tickling my belly and a new heat coming from her.

In response she pulls the now-puckered nipple from my mouth and, before I can take a breath, replaces it with the other one, fat and succulent like an exotic fruit. I bite gently into it and my cunt fills with juices as if Simon had come inside me. The wetness makes me want something in there, something I can feel my muscles tightening on, a resistance to my contractions. Wrapping my arms around Yolanda, I squeeze my hands in her fat dimpled buttocks and pull her to me till I can feel her stickiness.

Any inhibitions I may have had dissolve at this moment. I am consumed by an almost animal lust.

With unexpected abruptness, Yolanda pulls away from me and her nipple, glossy with saliva, is tugged from my mouth. My lips reach greedily for the other one but, laughing, she pushes my head away and pulls me to my feet.

'Come,' she says, moving over to the bed.

For the past seven years I've known only Simon's body. He has a slight, spare build, not over muscled but nevertheless quite good for a man in his forties. It's the sort of body that goes with Simon's sort of sex: neat, carefully maintained, and nothing out of the ordinary. In comparison, Yolanda's body is extravagant, indulgent and sensual. Everything about her is ripe and voluptuous and full of promise.

She flops back onto the bed and pulls me on top of her. I feel my breasts press into hers and the hard ridge of my pubic bone sink into the softness of her belly. Her hands immediately slip under the lace edging of my pants and begin to caress my behind. Dipping my head, I put my lips to hers in our first kiss.

It is so different from kissing a man. Her smooth face, the skin silken where our chins and cheeks brush and the soft full lips tasting faintly of lipstick. Even her tongue exploring my mouth is somehow more sensuous and languorous than a man's.

I suck at her tongue and feel our saliva mixing, smearing my face, trickling down my chin, dripping onto her throat. It feels naughty, as if we are wallowing in our own illicit juices.

Simon would hate this wetness. He would wipe his chin and turn me over so I couldn't drip onto him. Even the stickiness from his own ejaculation has to be dabbed up discreetly so as not to mess the sheets.

The probing of her tongue makes me hungry again for her nipples. I slide down her body and the luxurious breasts loll to each side of her. I gather one up in my hands, moulding it till the nipple forms an enticing cone that I feed into my mouth. As I suck I knead her breast and squeeze hard, almost roughly, till suddenly I feel the nipple swell against my lips and melt sweetly on my tongue as milk unexpectedly floods my mouth. A part of me is shocked. I hear Simon's voice in my head expressing disgust. It's unnatural, he'd claim. Depraved. Exchanging female bodily fluids; women suckling women...

Then a hand touches the back of my neck, caressing my hair. I suck again and feel my mouth fill with a warmth that flows seductively through my body, both calming yet arousing.

Sod Simon! Sod his patronising views and his talk of 'bovine' women. I want to be smothered by this indulgent, opulent body and transformed by her self-assured, liberating sexiness.

Suddenly Yolanda rolls me over and pins me to the bed with her weight. Strong arms hold mine down and powerful thighs trap my hips. Although I am helpless I still try to move under her with a desperate feverishness. She is laughing at me.

'So much passion in such a little body. You crazy woman!'

Her pubes are tickling my belly and I can feel the wetness of her cunt. As she laughs her breasts jiggle heavily and the dark chocolate nipples come tantalisingly close. My mouth waters, greedy for the salty, milky taste of her. I raise my head but she pulls back and I only brush the tips with my lips.

'You are too hot! Now stay here and I get something to make you cool.'

I close my eyes while she is gone. What am I doing? She's right, I must be crazy. I'm a happily married woman with a husband many women would die for. I've never been attracted to women before so why am I doing this now?

I hear her feet on the marble tiles and feel a throbbing between my legs.

This is madness. Pull yourself together, Lisa. Keep your eyes shut and tell her it's all a mistake. Tell her to go home.

Her hand touches my knee. I clench my thighs. The hand slips gently between them and glides up towards my crotch. Inside the taut lace of my pants I feel my blood pulsing.

Perhaps she can sense my tension; maybe she even suspects my qualms. Instead of touching me as I am expecting, she starts massaging my thighs. Bit by bit I relax. My knees roll apart, and I feel her fingers curl under the elastic of my pants and tug gently till I raise my hips allowing her to remove them. My eyes are still tightly closed as if, in this way, I can absolve myself of any responsibility.

Delicate female fingers peel open the lips of my cunt with meticulous care. Suddenly I am pierced by a burning-freezing sensation that almost shocks me into screaming out. The hot coldness touches my outer flesh first and then shoots up inside me. My muscles contract, trying to eject the sensation, but, instead, they seem to draw it deeper inside me.

Yolanda laughs. 'This will cool you down, you hot woman!'

I can feel her pushing something into me and I realise now it is cold, not heat, that is burning me. She keeps pushing till I can feel her knuckles against the inside of my thigh.

'It is my passion indicator. You feel it?'

There is a weird sensation as she seems to twist the thing inside me.

'It's an ice-lolly! Orange, my favourite!'

Yolanda then hoists herself up my body till I feel the weight of her breasts spreading generously over my ribcage and her body half covering mine. Deep in my belly the cold ache of ice seeps into my womb as her body presses down on me. Her hot mouth covers my breast and her tongue teases the nipple to a pebble. I am conscious that she can almost get my entire breast in her mouth while I struggled to accommodate merely her nipple.

I watch her squeeze my breast between her hands so it stands erect, almost phallic. She lifts her head and starts licking the tip. The pressure of her hands crushing my breast is uncomfortable but the sight of her moulding my flesh like that is hugely erotic and, when she nips the nipple, pink and swollen, a tingling sensation runs right down to my sex.

She sucks the whole mound of my breast into her mouth then draws it slowly back out, squeezing with her lips as she does so. She does it again, faster, sliding her mouth up and down the distorted flesh as if it were a cock she was giving mouth to.

I let out a groan. Yolanda's hand reaches between my legs and something is withdrawn from inside me. She holds up a lolly stick, wet and orange, to show me.

'My passion indicator.' She laughs. 'You have reached meltdown, you are so hot!'

Yolanda takes up my other breast and subjects it to the same moulding caress, squeezing tight around its base till it rises like an obscene cock, flushed and swollen. Then, with relish, she performs her bizarre breast-fellatio till I am almost crying with the pain and attenuated pleasure of her attentions.

Finally she releases my breast, marbled with love-bites, and runs her tongue down my belly as she wriggles down the bed. When she starts to pull my thighs apart I realise with a shock that she is going to go down on me. I try to push her away.

'No! Please ... Yolanda.' I'm embarrassed at the thought of another woman exploring me down there. It's too intimate. Her own familiarity with that area makes me more shy than if she were a man.

'You mustn't ...'

She raises her head and looks at me with an expression of comic disappointment.

'But my ice-lolly!'

I begin to laugh and, as I do, I relax and my knees roll apart. I feel the warmth of her lips on me.

I suppose I've never considered before what sort of things women might do to each other sexually, but I've always assumed it would be gentle touchy-feely stuff, all stroking and petting. Yet what Yolanda does to me right now is far from that. She pins me open with her thumbs and sucks me into her mouth, tugging greedily at the delicate folds of tissue as if she wants to devour me. There is no cautious probing or fingering – just her overriding desire to break down my inhibitions and release my passion.

Her soft lips rub and chew while her tongue pushes into the dark, slick heat. This is nothing like the polite oral sex performed by Simon in his more adventurous moods; that clinical tickling of my clitoris with the tip of his tongue while his fingers dabble inside me. No, this is a hot-blooded, unrestrained, lust-driven mouth job.

I moan. She takes my flesh between her teeth and starts sucking rhythmically. My clitoris begins to throb with each tug and I feel myself flood inside.

As her rhythm increases my back arches like a bow and my body tautens in a muscular spasm that bends me off the bed. The sensation between my legs becomes almost too much and I scream for relief. In opening my mouth a contraction is triggered that begins in my sex and convulses outwards in waves of exquisite pleasure, as if the entire electrical circuitry of my nerves has been connected to Yolanda's mouth.

The explosion leaves me in a limp, exhausted limbo; my body is weak and curiously weightless. I don't want to open my eyes. I don't want it to be over. I want to stay surfing the knife edge of that wave, riding higher and higher till I plunge back into the whirlpool of passion and feel her suck me under again.

I am brought back to the present by soft lips pressing against mine. I open my mouth and suck in her tongue, tasting the saltiness of my own juices mingled with the synthetic orange of ice-lolly. It has set off a warm churning in my belly. I reach down for her breast and she slides over me until the fat juicy nipple drops into my mouth and the creamy breast presses into my face.

I push my hand between her legs into stickiness and feel her plump folds close around my fingers.

My explorations are brought to a sudden, sickening halt by an unexpected, but all too familiar voice.

'Well, well. So this is what my little wife gets up to while I'm away, is it?'

I struggle to sit up but I seem to be all tangled up with Yolanda and the sheet. Oh, God, Simon! What's he doing here? Why is he back?

Yolanda rolls off me with irritating indifference. She appears untroubled by the arrival of my husband and content to lie languorously beside me (on *his* side of the bed), unembarrassed by her nakedness or the situation. I, to the contrary, am suddenly shy at being naked before my husband and am painfully aware of the lovebites on my breasts and the sticky orange stains leaking down my thighs.

My mind is both a whirr and empty. Fleeting thoughts explode like fireworks then disappear. What should I say? Do I apologise? I'm tempted to utter those stupid clichés like, 'this isn't what it seems', and, 'honestly, we're just good friends'.

My face muscles twitch and I'm afraid I'll break into hideously inappropriate laughter. Then I become obsessed by the state of the bed; the shocking stain, the stray pubic hairs, the sticky patches. To my fastidious husband this is perhaps a more appalling sight than his wife in bed with a woman.

'Quite a surprise I must say!'

How can he seem so calm? Is he going to explode in a rage? Might he turn violent?

'Not exactly what I had in mind, Lisa, when I suggested you might benefit from company.'

It's ridiculous. I feel like a chastised schoolgirl. I can't even think of an answer. Then Yolanda replies:

'You like what you see then, Señor Simon? Is it true you Englishmen like to have many, many women?'

Oh no, now she really is going to make things worse. She is propped up on one elbow, smiling and totally self-assured. Her breasts hang heavily and I notice one nipple still glistens with my saliva. Why am I looking at them?

Simon studies her for a moment but I can't make out his expression; it's too bland and innocuous for anger yet there's a glint of something in his eyes.

'Most men, I suspect, would like to *know* many women, Señora, but as for having to *live* with them . . .'

Here, he looks pointedly at the soiled bed, the floor strewn with underclothing and the telltale orange lolly stick now stuck to the bedside table.

'It would appear that more women seems also to mean more mess; a most regrettable circumstance. However . . .'

Slowly he starts unbuttoning his shirt, not taking his eyes off Yolanda, then – and this completely shocks me – he lets it drop to the floor. I look in disbelief at that crisp, spotless shirt, lying in an untidy heap, but he's not stopped. He is unfastening his belt, unzipping his trousers.

'However, Señora, since you and my wife have already concluded the preliminaries . . .'

Now he bends down to undo his shoes and step out of the trousers, which he kicks to one side.

'I had perhaps better abandon my principles, try to ignore the rather unsavoury bedding, and join you.'

As he stands up naked I see he already has an erection and feel myself blush. The bed rolls slightly as Yolanda shifts across and my husband, apparently oblivious of the garish orange patch, gets in between us.

Excitement tingles in my stomach when Yolanda reaches out to take his cock in her hand and he pulls me down to suck my marbled breast.

* * *

My relief that the situation has been diffused is tainted by disappointment; I realise I had been looking forward to making love to Yolanda and going even further than we already had. My imagination had been toying with the different ways I could pleasure her and planning where I would start.

I catch her eye and we both smile. Then she mouths something at me. I frown and concentrate on the silent word her sensuous lips are forming. With a sudden thrill I realise it is a promise. 'Later.'

What Is It About Workmen?
Alison Tyler

What is it about workmen that makes me want to take off my clothes? To peel down and parade insolently through my beach-front condo in nothing but a fuchsia G-string and a pair of skyscraper black heels. To toss my long, ginger-red hair and pout my full lips as if that's exactly how I behave when I'm all by myself. I flutter. I pose. I sigh deeply as I run my fingertips along the waistband of my naughty panties. What is it about workmen that brings out the exhibitionist in me?

I know they're out there, on the scaffolding directly outside my window, and yet I impishly pretend as if they're not. I just go about my business, striding into the room with a fluffy green towel in my hand instead of wrapped securely around my body, my wet hair rippling past my shoulders, my nipples hard from the cold spray I blast at the end of every shower.

What is it about knowing those men might get a peek?

I've had plenty of time to try to answer that question, because workmen and I go way back. We feed each other; fill each other up. It started with the crew of tanned young men at the job site across from the beach house the summer after high school graduation. I hadn't noticed they were there until they gave me a standing ovation as I stepped onto the wraparound deck in my two-piece black bikini. They must have seen everything.

With their second-storey vantage point and my care-lessly open curtains, they must have watched me for the hours that it takes a teen to ready herself for the beach. And I'll admit this, my bright flush of embarrassment was gone long before the heat of arousal. From that first time of being seen, I was addicted.

Then there was the construction crew out the window of the Manhattan hotel I stayed in at age twenty-two. Who knew it wasn't safe to walk around nude with the shades open in a hotel on the 36th floor? I'd never been to a city like New York – a place where you could actually be cloud-level and still have a construction crew peering in through the windows. The men smiled and waved for the four days I stayed. We got to know each other. They were my fashion consultants, holding up a hastily hand-written sign that said, 'We like the blue one!' when I'd changed back and forth between two different sundresses – unable to make up my mind. And when they saw the suitcases on my bed on my final afternoon in town, they yelled out in unison, 'Please don't go!'

But this was different. I couldn't pretend the rules weren't the same because I was on 'vacation time'. Because nobody I knew would see me. Because I had been caught unaware. These guys were out there every day. I had to pass by them on the way to work in the morning, hurrying by their trucks in my sleek black suit and upswept hair. From the corner of my eye, I had just long enough to notice how fine they looked in their scuffed boots and well-worn jeans.

Once at work at the Culver City Studios, I couldn't get them out of my head. I read scripts for a living, rework-ing plots and analysing structure but, when I'd close my eyes to better visualise a scene, the structure I would imagine was the scaffolding attached to the condo.

'Get it together, Cat,' I'd tell myself. 'Think plot. Think

character.' The mental coaxing didn't help. The plots I put together involved me up there on the wood beams with them, holding onto the thick metal railing, letting the warm salt breeze dance up under my skirt to reveal – oh, my – I had forgotten to wear my panties.

'Cat,' my boss said early one afternoon, coming in unannounced and catching me mid-daydream. 'What are you reading? It must be amazing. You've got such a look on your face . . .'

'This has to stop,' I told myself after she left. Yet how could it?

I ran into the workers at six o'clock as I came into my building in the evening, the day's wear on me, my chic blazer off, hair down. I tried to pretend I didn't see them, but I'm a script girl, not an actor. Faking it has never been my strong point. As I pressed the code panel by the front door, I cocked my head up, watching as they dismantled their tools for the day.

Could I? Would it really matter?

Yes, it would. Another neighbour might learn of my exhibitionist thrill, blowing my cover as an upstanding young woman of high morals and fashionable tastes. I'd be labelled. Shunned. Or, at the very least, teased mercilessly. So where do I get my boys from usually? The studios surrounding my office. The screenwriter hangouts. The cafés and galleries and chi-chi restaurants. Not, let me add for emphasis, from the road crew.

That didn't stop me from choosing my favourite. He had a goatee framing a chiselled face. Black hair, deep liquid-blue eyes, burnished golden skin. That goes without saying in the heat of Southern California where his job was to re-shingle the condo complex. And muscles. Oh, man, the muscles on him. I wouldn't have been able to wrap my hand around one of his biceps, but the concept of trying made me so hot. I fantasised about it all the way down in the elevator the next morning. The vision of pushing open my window and climbing out there with him on the scaffolding. Of having him press me up against the glass and taking me from behind. Taking me out there in the open where anyone could see. Lowering my slacks. Slipping aside my ribbon of panties. Fucking me with the sound of the ocean crashing.

'Stop drooling,' my neighbour hissed fiercely to me as we left the building together and ducked under the ever-present scaffolding. They'd been working for two weeks now – two weeks of pure torture for me. 'You'll give them the wrong idea.'

'Or the right idea.'

'Come on, Cat,' Giselle grimaced, her Botoxed brow remaining unblemished. She shook her head fiercely as she made her way to her convertible sports car, then released the alarm with an almost violent push of a button. 'You don't want to encourage someone like that,' she called out to me before driving out on Ocean Boulevard towards Wilshire.

Encourage someone like *what*? I thought. Like a man? A handsome man? One who always tilted his head and looked at me thoughtfully, as if he could read each dirty desire flickering on the mental movie theatre behind my green eyes. I was on fire. He would quench my thirst.

Desperate for some non-Hollywood-tainted advice, I got on the phone at work and called my best friend from college, a preschool teacher who now lives up in Seattle. But before I made it past the part about workmen in our building, she launched into her own story. 'Our school is under construction, too,' she sighed, 'and at first I was so freaked out by all the noise I thought I'd go crazy. But it's turned out to be a good thing. You won't believe this, but the kids have actually bonded with the workmen.

We started by sending down notes on a long piece of green yarn. Then we made Rice Krispie treats last week and lowered those down as well. The workmen send up notes to us to thank us. It is so cute –'

That *is* so cute, I thought. What cute thing might *I* send out the window on a lacy green string? A treat other than one made of cereal, that was for sure. A treat like a pair of my prettiest panties, or one lone silk stocking ... or was that too obvious? Maybe something edgier: a set of regulation handcuffs? A black velvet blindfold? What are the social rules for engaging in this sort of tête-à-tête? I didn't have a clue.

But I did have a plan. I came home early from work one Friday and took a shower to wash away the pressure of the week. Then, working within myself to find the level of confidence required for this sort of erotic endeavour, I slid into the type of lingerie that I always assume French women wear on a daily basis. Stunning sheer black underwire top. High-cut panties trimmed with tiny red roses. I redid my make-up, as if I always wear plentiful mascara and deep wine-coloured lipstick when lounging around the house, and then, heart racing, I pulled the blinds.

I knew he'd be there. I'd paid careful attention to the regions that the crew was working on, and to which part in particular seemed to be his turf. As expected, there he was – facing exactly the wrong way. Christ, how was I supposed to get his attention while pretending not to want his attention? My mind reeled as I worked to fix the plot of my movie gone awry. Then suddenly it hit me. Music.

Quickly, I sprinted to my CD collection and scanned the choices. Oh, God. Sade? Annie Lennox? The Cowboy Junkies? Pink? So 'L.A. girl'. So not what I thought a construction worker might like. Where were my Guns n' Roses albums? Where was all the Aerosmith? The Rolling Stones? What music were they listening to on their boom box out there? Hip-hop? Rap? Panicked, I ripped through the collection until finally I found a Led Zeppelin CD, left over by a long ex-boyfriend. After perusing the selections, I blasted 'Black Dog'. Then I opened the window and waited.

It seemed as if I heard his heavy boots moving closer in only a moment or two, but to go forward with my plan, I couldn't check to be sure. I simply made my way across the room, as if I walk around looking like a movie star every day. As if, in fact, I was a movie star. Starring in my own very special movie. The one about the randy red-headed exhibitionist who likes to walk aimlessly around her apartment in her naughty lingerie. Sipping a glass of white wine. Touching things. Arranging items this way, then that. Moving slowly, without a care.

But this movie had more of a plot, say, than that of a music video. There was the 'cute meet' with the handsome builder, who accidentally catches a glimpse of the stunning starlet and can't keep his eyes off her. He knows it's wrong to watch, but that means nothing to him. Who pays attention to rules when swallowed down by lust? So he stands there, under the hot late-afternoon sun, and prays that she won't go into another room.

But she does.

She walks out of the living room and down the hall, knowing that if he's onto her, he'll follow outside on the scaffolding, hurrying to catch up with her. He'll know just where she's headed, and he'll be waiting.

All right. So *that* was the movie plot. The only way for me to know whether I had an actual audience of one was to fling open the full-length curtains in my bedroom. Had he followed me? Had he seen? I didn't even want to think about how I'd feel if the scaffolding was empty.

The knock on the window came before I could touch the cord on the curtains. It was a soft knock – a gentle rap – but it was him. I could tell. Quickly, I opened the ocean-blue curtains and slid up the window. As I stared at him, closer than we'd ever been yet, I realised that I'd written a movie without dialogue. Yes, I'd mentally gotten us up to this point – and far beyond it to powerful clinches on my sheet-strewn mattress – but I'd never thought to script what I might say if we truly met face-to-face.

Obviously sensing my insecurity, he took over. He simply tipped his head at me, as he'd done since his first day on the job, and then casually asked, 'Can I borrow a cup of sugar?'

'Excuse me?'

'Isn't that what someone's supposed to say when they want to meet a new neighbour.'

'But you're not really a neighbour.'

'And you don't really cook. At least, not dressed like that. Though you do dust very artfully –'

'Do you want to come in?'

'Like you wouldn't believe.'

With his words, the movie picked up again, with the two of us in instant motion. He climbed through the open window into my bedroom, and then he kissed me. His hands cradled my face before tipping my head up so that our lips met. I could taste the glimmering summer sun on his mouth. I could feel his firm hands roaming lower on my body, his fingertips calloused and warm. Each place he touched felt on fire. I wanted his hands everywhere, caressing each part of me. Thoughts rushed through my head at a speed too fast to decipher. There were almost too many things to do at once. Kiss. Touch. Stroke.

'God, you're sexy,' he sighed into my hair, 'and so naked, so exposed.'

I realised as he spoke that I liked how unequal we were right now – with me almost nude in my lacy lingerie and him still fully dressed in his work clothes. My outfit was far more risqué than any bikini; something a girl might model on special occasions for the most exceptional lover. It turned me on to be practically undressed in front of a stranger, especially one I'd fantasised about for weeks. His hands cupped my ass through my panties, and I heard him sigh as his fingers probed lower to find the wetness soaking the fabric. There was no way my body could keep that arousal a secret. But he had his own secret for me.

'It's not really fair,' he said, smiling. 'It's as if I've been winning at strip-poker without ever drawing a card. Let me even the score.'

We broke the connection just long enough for him to take off his pale-grey shirt, and I stared at him in awe. I hadn't known about the tattoos; the colourful drawings in ink that adorned his upper arms and his chest, some disappearing over to the canvas of his back. I traced my fingers over his skin, admiring him with my hands until he couldn't wait any longer and he pulled me tightly to him so that we were back together again. Skin to skin.

'You looked so pretty walking around your living room,' he said, tilting my head up so that he could look directly into my eyes.

'You liked that? The naughty French maid thing turns you on?'

'Depends on how naughty the maid is, I guess.'

'Pretty naughty,' I told him. My eyes flickered at him. I could feel the messages I was sending and I wondered whether he could read them.

'I couldn't keep my eyes off you,' he confessed. 'The way you moved your body to the beat of the music. That subtle sway in your hips.' As he spoke, he rotated my hips so that they pressed against him, and I could feel the hardness of his erection against me, pressing through the worn denim of his jeans. 'And I liked the way you sipped your drink, slowly, really savouring it.'

Now, I waited, sensing somehow where he was going with this line of thought.

'What else do you like to savour?' he asked, his voice low.

'What have you got?'

His hands were on my shoulders as he pressed me down, so that I could undo the button fly of his jeans and pull out his cock. The feeling of his rod beneath my fingertips made me tremble and made him moan. I brought the tip to my lips and started to kiss him, sweetly at first, but he was directing the show.

'Come on,' he said, 'suck it –'

'You'd talk like that to a maid?'

'A dirty one. And you *are* dirty, aren't you?'

I couldn't answer that. My mouth was already too full of his cock, drawing it deep down my throat, then letting is slowly slip free before capturing him between my lips again. I was ravenous, and it was too difficult for me to pretend to be shy any longer with the evidence of his arousal right there. Demanding my attention. I sucked him until he groaned and pushed me back.

'Stand up,' he said, 'please –'

But before I could, he was lifting me, spreading me out on the bed, pressing his mouth to my pussy through the barrier of my panties. That feeling was almost unreal.

The wetness of his mouth against my own hidden moisture, separated only by that sheer layer of nylon. His tongue made slow circles that caressed my clit and teased my pussy lips. Then he lapped in great greedy strokes up and down, using the perfect amount of pressure to take me higher. I gripped onto the bed with my hands, fists tightening on the duvet, arching up against him, near-desperate to climax. He had other plans.

'I have to be inside you,' he said, amending his statement immediately. 'I mean, I have to fuck you –' and as he said the words they needed to come true fast. We both understood that, and he moved us so that we were up against the windows – exactly as I'd pictured in my fantasy – except we were on the inside this time. My palms pressed flat on the glass, my body arched. He took me from behind, sliding aside my sheer black panties in order to get inside me. His chest was firm against my back, his jeans still on but open. I could feel the faded denim against my thighs, that deliciously soft fabric, so worn it was white instead of blue. And we fucked. Christ, just perfectly fucked.

He brought his hands up to cradle my breasts, pinching my nipples through the fabric of my sheer demi-bra. The roughness of the way he touched me, coupled with the refined quality of my lingerie, took me even higher. I imagined the two of us out there on the scaffolding, with him so deep inside me, and me holding tightly to the railing, leaning forward, feeling the ocean air whip over my body.

'Oh, God, do you feel good,' he said, his face pressed against the nape of my neck, his hands still working my breasts, teasing them, thumbs and fingers working together to surround my hardened nipples.

I could see our reflections in the glass. That was me – the wild woman with the crazy mane of red hair and the glowing green eyes. And that was him – the star of all my fantasies, holding me tightly to him, fucking me so hard you could see each thrust in the way my lips parted, in the way my body trembled. Then I saw through our reflections and out to the sunset fading out towards the Santa Monica coastline. With the golden hour upon us, the sky was striped in butterscotch-yellow and rose. The whole room became lit with this magical light, and I was lit as well – lit from within with the way that he worked me. His hands left my breasts, moved over my hips, across the flat of my belly, and then down, to flit against my clit until I could take it no longer. He slid his hands under the waistband of my panties and spread my pussy lips wide open. Then his thumb touched my clit, over and over, tapping lightly and carefully until I reached climax. I sighed as I came. Whisper soft, head bowed, feeling the vibrations ripple through me.

He thrust hard as my pussy gripped onto him, and his mouth found my shoulder and bit into me, searching for purchase as he came inside of me. The shudders seemed to last a long time, rocking both of us. He held me so tight, his arms so strong. 'Next time,' he murmured. 'Be loud.'

Next time, I thought.

'I mean,' he said, lifting me into his arms, '*this* time –'

And then, as if we'd gotten it out of our system and could relax, he carried me to the bed. He spread me out, kicked off his boots and jeans, and climbed on top of the mattress with me. I could see all of his tattoos now; the intricate designs that gave me more insight into who he was. I wrapped my hands around his arms, trying to connect but failing. Just as I'd imagined. He didn't know why I was smiling, but he didn't seem to mind. His cock was hard again, and ready, and he pressed forward, slipping in my juices, probing into me. I lifted upwards to meet him, then slid back down on the bed with each thrust. We didn't have to talk at all. We just knew. Knew to keep looking into each other's eyes, to keep the connection as we slid through that second rippling ride.

Our bodies moved in synch as we did the deed. He pushed into me, and I felt almost as if he were fucking through me, all the way from the split of my body and radiating upward. Each thrust connected me further to him, and I wrapped my legs around his waist to hold him closer to me.

'So sexy,' he said, looking into my eyes. 'I wanted to break the window to get inside to see you – when you drew open the curtains, I had such a fucking hard-on. I wanted to pull you out on the scaffolding with me. To bend you over and take you right out there.'

Oh, he was spelling out my fantasy, word for word. When I started to come, he turned my head so I was staring out the side window rather than the one facing the ocean; staring into the wall of windows in the sister-condo building next door. Who knows who's watching? I thought. And that's why he'd turned me. I understood that. He was showing me that we were the same in that way. Aching to see and be seen. But then he tilted my face back to his again, and we met our gaze and locked on hard. And maybe it didn't matter anymore if someone else was watching. Maybe this time watching each other was enough.

'Be loud, baby,' he said again, reminding me in case I could possibly have forgotten. 'I want to hear you.' I pushed up against him and closed my eyes as the moans escaped me. Although I'm often quiet in bed, this time I made the sounds of an animal; low rumbling growls that came from deep within me, then harsher groans. Quick and fast, the volume increasing as if someone was working an inner dial. One right at the center of my body. As I bucked and pushed against him, he came with me, and I knew what brought him over the edge was seeing me untamed. Seeing me undone.

After, he wrapped me up in his arms and held me tight. We faced the ocean view; watched together as the light faded all the way down to a ribbon of the purest red on the horizon. And then he whispered against my neck, 'Took you awhile.'

'For what?'

'To see me watching.'

'You were watching me?' I asked, stunned to think of that statement the other way around. Hadn't I been the one watching *him*?

'You know,' he said, somewhat shyly. 'My friends have been ribbing me for weeks about showing off for you. Flexing whenever you walked by. But what can I say? Can't help it if I'm a bit of an exhibitionist, you know?'

'Yeah,' I grinned to myself. 'I know.'

Opening Ceremony
Jean Roberta

Pru's tall, slim body was coiled elegantly on the leather sofa in her new shop. Her grand opening was scheduled for the next day, but for now we were alone, like two actors on a stage before the curtain goes up. I couldn't help admiring the glow on my friend's dark lively face, or her elaborate hairdo. She had learned from a Nigerian woman how to wrap dozens of tiny braids in black thread that caught the light from different angles whenever she moved her head.

'Well, what do you think?' she asked.

'It looks good, Pru,' I assured her.

Pru's clothing store was decorated to look like a forest, and the effect of the murals on the walls and the indirect lighting was surprisingly convincing, despite the full racks of dresses, suits, blouses and pants that seemed to be blooming in the unexplored wilderness. The furnishings were in earthy shades of green, gold and brown. 'It looks like a sacred grove,' I ventured, running the risk of offending her.

Pru rolled her eyes, as I knew she would. She leaned towards me, and I caught a whiff of her musky perfume. Her blouse gaped to show the gentle rise of a small brown breast. 'Beth,' she laughed, 'you know I'm not superstitious, but I want this place to be blessed. I know what my mother would say: "Pru-dence, you must trust in de Lord".'

Pru and her mother had moved to the city from their native island of St Lucia years before. I knew that Pru's mother and aunts practised a combination of pious Christianity and kitchen voodoo that seemed very odd to me, and that Pru had rejected prayers and spells of every kind when she was a rebellious teenager with a quick mind and a burning desire for upward mobility. All the same, she knew that the success of her store would somewhat depend on luck.

I caught sight of us in one of the mirrors that reflected gleams of light around the room. My skin, tanned to a light peach colour, and my reddish-gold hair contrasted with Pru's. I was wearing an old T-shirt and a pair of jeans, which had both shrunk so that my shapely breasts (of which I was vain) and my hips and ass were gripped by the fabric. I wondered if Pru thought I looked tacky, and if she thought I had dressed this way to show off. I wondered if she might be right.

As if reading my thoughts, Pru uncoiled and stood up, then casually reached for my hands and pulled me to my feet. 'I want to see my merchandise on you,' she chuckled. There was something strangely shy behind her outer confidence, as if she wanted more from me than she could put into words.

Without asking my size, she smoothly pulled a draped turquoise silk dress from the rack and handed it to me. 'Try this,' she ordered. *She wants to change my image*, I thought with amusement.

She handed me a pale blue lace bra in my size, 36C (*but how did she know?*), a matching pair of panties, a cream satin garter belt and a pack of stockings. The shoes, a pair of turquoise satin pumps, were simple in design but too high in the heel to allow for easy walking. A hot blush spread all through me.

I had wondered for months if Pru wanted anything

more than friendship from me. After nights of fantasising hopelessly (or so I thought), I wasn't sure I could handle her obvious intentions.

'You know I don't wear dresses, Pru,' I mumbled. In spite of everything, I wanted to feel the silk on my skin and the skirt swinging against my legs. For Pru.

'Just go try it on,' she laughed, pushing me with surprising strength. 'Unless you want me to dress you like a baby.'

Alone in the cream-and-gold fitting room, I could feel Pru's presence nearby, as if she could see through the curtain, while I peeled off my everyday clothes and stood naked before the mirror. It was near the end of summer, and my body was clearly marked where shorts, swimsuits and halter tops had protected my white breasts and belly from the sun.

Feeling self-conscious but increasingly excited, I put on the clothes Pru had provided. Reaching over my shoulders to fasten the tiny blue buttons up the back of the dress, I watched the silk pull at my lace-covered breasts. Smoothing down the skirt and running a hand through my shoulder-length hair, I felt strangely proud of my ladylike appearance. I had worn clothes like this before, but not for another woman.

Her eyes were sparkling when I wobbled out of the fitting room on the killer heels. 'This is ridiculous, Pru,' I muttered under my breath.

She pulled me by the shoulders for a long, soft kiss. Thanks to my shoes, she didn't have to bend her head much to find my lips, and the warmth of her mouth on mine told me how much she appreciated my co-operation. Her skin felt as soft and comfortable as old denim. When her persistent tongue found its way between my teeth, I moaned.

I wrapped my arms around her long, slim back and

felt the hard edges of ribs under a thin layer of flesh. Her body was like her spirit: vulnerable but determined. *May the Goddess forgive me my past*, I thought, *and may this decent woman never find out*. A faintly spicy smell rose from her skin, mixing with the musk of her perfume. 'Pru, I want you,' I murmured in her ear.

Her ribs heaved in a silent laugh. 'Then why didn't you ask me before now?' she teased. ''Stead of always giving me those hungry looks?'

I was mortified. I had known Pru casually for years – we both went to the same bars and some of the same parties. I could name her last three lovers, but I had never thought I could get close to her until I had forced myself to join the conversation when I overheard her telling two friends about the store she was planning to open. My knowledge of design attracted her attention and she asked for my advice. My ego expanded, but I had never guessed that she was watching me watching her. 'I didn't think I had a chance with you,' I confessed, burying my nose in her warm neck.

Her long, probing fingers slid over my silk-covered breasts, making my nipples hard. Dipping her tongue into one of my ears, she grasped my bursting tits and began squeezing and playing with them. Hot moisture oozed into my panties.

We were standing in front of a hall mirror, and I could tell by her sudden change of position that Pru was watching her reflection over her shoulder. 'My mother used to say something about seeing an albino woman over your left shoulder,' she sighed, as if to herself. 'It's supposed to be good luck.' She pulled back and looked in my eyes to see how I was taking her remark.

'I hope I'm good luck for you, Pru,' I chuckled, 'though I suppose an ordinary white person is less exotic than an albino.'

'Everyone is exotic to someone else, girl,' she said, running one hand gently through my hair. I realised that she knew how it felt to be a coconut among apples, or a swan in a world run by geese, but my feelings stopped me from pursuing this thought. 'Let's use the sofa,' she purred.

I watched Pru's firm high ass as she led me by the hand to the leather sofa. She unbuttoned the back of my dress, and we reached for each other almost simultaneously. The sight of her willowy brown body with the two black nipples on her tight little breasts made me eager to touch her all over – but first I wanted the satisfaction she could give me. She gently pushed me onto my back as her deep-brown eyes burned into mine.

'What do you want?' Pru asked me in a low voice. She looked embarrassed, and I saw with surprise that she was nervous. 'Do you want me to be the butch and you'll be my woman? Or you want us to be equals and take turns? Do you want my tongue or what do you like?' The look of strain on her face showed me how hard it was for her to ask such honest questions. Her courage and her respect for me were breaking my heart.

'Pru,' I told her, 'I want us to take turns doing everything. I want you to suck my tits and my pussy and I want to learn your whole body by heart.' I stopped talking to kiss her, and this time I gave her my tongue. I felt slightly nauseous with guilt and fear, but I was not going to back down. Like her, I wanted to change my life.

Suddenly Pru slid down my body until her head was level with the soaking hair of my crotch. She parted my legs, and spread something smooth over my inflamed clit, then darted a pointed tongue over and around everything she could reach. Lightly holding my folds of tense flesh with her teeth, Pru began diligently sucking my pearl toward surrender.

She was teasing me out of my mind, and I wanted more. Just when I thought I would have to settle for what I could get, she touched me where I was hungriest. One, then two gloved fingers slid into my slick, steaming entrance, stroking and teasing me to frenzy. I didn't believe I deserved so much pleasure, but she was giving it to me and I didn't feel as if I had a choice.

I came as though a bomb had exploded in my clit. I clutched Pru in relief and amazement as she slid up my body to give me a long, deep, possessive kiss.

'Honey, you're so good,' I sighed. She laughed and ruffled my wavy hair.

Slowly, almost lazily, I pressed my hands down the round curve of her buttocks and across her smooth, flat belly to the springy black hair below. I was delighted to find her almost as wet as I was, and squirming with impatience. 'Elizabeth,' she breathed into my hair, which was now trailing across her breasts and hard torso as I moved downward, 'kiss me down there.'

When I arrived at the swamp between her legs, I gently pushed them further apart and savoured the sight and the smell in front of me. Her hips were rocking in a restrained but definite rhythm that pushed her hard clit in my face to a regular beat. Her hunger for me was like her hunger for beauty, wealth and space of her own. At that moment, I wished I could give her everything she wanted.

I could feel the energy flowing from her cleft. I began flicking her with my tongue, then fastened my mouth on her and sucked. The motion in Pru's hips changed to hard thrusting.

Something more was needed, and I managed to pull on gloves, one at a time, to explore her more thoroughly.

After some searching, I found the small, wrinkled entrance to her back passage and massaged it with one finger. In a few minutes, my woman was bucking and clutching my head.

As the tension in her body subsided, I pulled off the gloves and ran my hands down her long thighs. Sliding upwards, I sucked each of her shiny brown nipples, then paused to admire the contented look on her face. 'Beth, you a born lover,' she cooed.

I couldn't stand it. 'You could say that,' I muttered, tasting the salt in my own saliva. 'I've even been called a professional.'

Her dark eyes flew open. 'You a ho?' she demanded. 'You sell it to men?' I wanted to cry.

'Not now!' I assured her. 'Not any more. I never did that while I was going with a woman. I wouldn't.' *I'm so honourable*, I thought to myself sarcastically.

'Do cocks turn you on?' she enquired coolly. 'Or couldn't you find a job doing something else? You really like earning money on your back, girl?' Tears were stinging my eyes, and I wished I could disappear.

'I don't love it, Pru,' I said. 'I did what I had to do, that's all. I worked for two escort agencies for about five years, between regular jobs and my classes. Sometimes I pounded the pavement looking for real work but I couldn't find anything, and welfare always screwed me up one way or another.' I paused for breath, and switched to the present tense. 'My degree in Fine Arts just makes most employers think I'm over-qualified or too flaky for an ordinary job, and I can't get any more student loans until I pay back the ones I've already had. What would you do?' I wanted her forgiveness, but I was beginning to hate her for making me defend what I wanted to forget.

'Last time a man mistake me for a ho, I slap him,'

she spat at me. 'I would rather scrub floors than sell pussy.'

I felt dizzy, as though she had thrown me against the wall and beaten me up. I didn't want to hear whatever she might have to say about my sleazy life. I felt an overwhelming urge to fight back.

'How do I know about you, Pru-dence?' I hissed in her face. 'All you have done, and who with?' Her long, hard fingers were still grasping one of my breasts, unwilling to let go.

Pru began to speak, but I didn't really want to hear a roll-call of her past lovers. Not now. 'Woman,' I interrupted her, 'there's still a lot we don't know about each other, but I want to find out everything about you. I'm sick of the lies men always want to hear, and I don't want to play that game with women. Especially with you. That's why I told you the truth.' My eyes were starting to overflow, leaving embarrassing wet tracks on my cheeks.

Her her deep brown eyes revealed an uneasy mixture of anger and compassion. 'Are you ashamed, 'Lizbeth?' she asked thoughtfully. 'Are you sorry you let those men use you as a thing?'

Oh shit, I thought. *Fuck this.* 'I'm sorry there aren't more serious jobs for a person of my abilities, Pru,' I said aloud. 'I'm sorry the men who paid for the use of my body wouldn't hire me to work in their offices. I'm really sorry this world is mostly run by stupid men who don't know that women are human beings. But I did what I had to do, that's all. Don't tell me you've never had to sell yourself in any way to pay the rent.'

Pru's eyes clouded over briefly, as though she were remembering something. Suddenly she wrapped both arms around me and pushed me down underneath her. 'How did you do it, Beth?' she asked quietly. 'Did the johns come pick you up, or did you find them some-where? What did you wear?'

My face was burning. 'They liked me to wear garter belts, split panties, lacy bras – you know. Under sexy dresses. They liked colours like red and black, or any-thing that contrasted with my skin. And hoop earrings, strings of pearls, spike heels. You know the kind of thing, Pru. We never did anything in the office except make the arrangements. Usually the men would take me out for a drink first. They liked to think they were taking me out on a date.'

One of her gloved hands was trailing down my torso on a relentless journey to my nerve-centre. My flesh responded to her touch.

Pru thought of something else. 'You like this,' she accused me. 'You like me touching you, and you like it most in your pussy. How cold you hate it all the time when they fucked you? I bet some of them made it good for you. I bet they liked watching you come.'

I took a shuddering breath. 'How can I ever explain it to you, Prudence?' I pleaded. 'Usually it was no more exciting than washing dishes, and no, they weren't try-ing to turn me on. Sometimes I pretended they were women so I could get through it better. I thought of myself as an actress. I was doing it for the money, not for kicks.'

'Wouldn't your parents help you?' She was still scep-tical, but less accussing than before. One of her arms held me around the shoulders while the other hand teased my clit. She was rocking me, slowly and gently, while the leather upholstery creaked under us. My hands tentatively cupped her very firm ass-cheeks, wanting something solid to hold onto.

I forced myself to focus on her question. 'They'd've helped me,' I explained, 'if I'd gone home to live with them. In their house, by their rules. Will you go home to your mother if your store folds?'

Three long fingers plunged into me. 'My store won't close, girl,' she grunted. My muscles clenched around her as I jerked and then lifted my ass to meet her thrusts. I could feel her fingers moving over my cervix and exploring the walls of my wet cave. A residue of anger clung to her demanding hand. I could feel guilt rising from her warm skin like evaporating sweat, but she offered no apologies. 'I'm so into you,' she mumbled. 'Are you into this?'

'Yes,' I gushed into her face. 'I always want you inside me, Pru.' *Even if you despise me for it*, I thought. 'You're the one I want.' Pru buried her face in my neck, still pumping me full. Hot tears fell on my skin.

'Elizabeth, baby,' she whispered. 'Sweetheart.' She sounded like a suffering sinner, praying to the blessed Mary Magdalane. 'Don't hate me,' she sang quietly in my ear. Her desire for my pleasure and forgiveness moved me as much as the thrust of her fingers.

I came and came, holding her fingers deep inside me, never wanting to be empty again. I took a deep breath. 'Honey,' I sighed. 'This is the real thing for me. I'm telling you.'

She pressed her hot mouth to mine, spreading my teeth apart with her tougue. While her fucking hand stayed firmly in place, her other hand reached up to roll and squeeze one of my nipples until I groaned softly. She laughed. 'I don't want to pull out of you,' she purred into my ear. There was a question in her voice.

'Then don't,' I whispered back.

''Lizbeth,' she crooned, 'you not a street person. Forgive me, but that is one little thing I know about you. I don't know how you could walk into that business and expect to be safe. I know you got a brain but you weren't using it. I want you to stay alive, woman. I want to move you out of your apartment tomorrow, 'case some of those johns know where you live.'

My cunt clutched her fingers in a quick, irritated spasm. 'Christ, Pru,' I snarled, 'why can't you leave it alone? I left Carlo's agency in the fall and no one has bothered me since I got an unlisted phone number. No one is on my case except you.'

That Carlo expects you back,' she asked, or stated.

'Probably,' I agreed.

The look on Pru's opaque face was hard to read, though her softly stroking fingers sent a message of need and promise into my guts. A warm current of anger still hummed through her skin. She was also confused. 'Baby,' she begged, 'do you still have the lingerie and jewellery you used to wear for men? Would you wear them for me? Would you let me take you out for a drink and then take you home? Just me and no one else?'

'Oh, yes, Pru,' I breathed into one of her small ears. 'I'll wear anything you like.' A monstrous orgasm was forming in my overstimulated pussy. I felt delirious. 'You can raise my skirt under the table in the restaurant and fuck me against the wall in the washroom,' I promised. I wasn't sure I really wanted her to take such liberties in public, but I was pushing myself over the edge, encouraged by Pru's lecherous fingers. Her heavy breathing kept pace with mine. 'Just – don't – blame me,' I panted. 'Or condescend. Or deny my feelings.'

Pru groaned and clamped her mouth on one of my nipples. I knew my fingers would leave marks on her clenched cheeks as I writhed and wailed in concert with her. One of my bare hands slid around her hipbones and reached for her agitated clit. 'Come to me, baby,' she moaned, stroking me in a way that drove everything else out of my mind. My cry, mixed with the sound of Pru's voice, echoed off the ceiling.

As we both sank back into normal consciousness like windblown kites drifting to the ground, Pru seemed to shrink into herself. 'I don't want to hurt you, Beth,' she mumbled almost inaudibly. She stroked my back persistently. 'I'm not one of the assholes who wants to use you.' Her shame seemed to be stuck in her throat. Her eyes pleaded with me. 'I'm scared for myself, Elizabeth. I got loans up to my eyeballs and they all got to be paid back sometime. If this store doesn't make money, I'm screwed.' She sighed in my arms. 'I guess we're all scared of ending up on the street, angel woman.'

In the crazy flashes of light that bounced off the mirrors, I shifted her until I was lying on top. 'Mmm,' I hummed, grinding my crotch into hers. 'You'll be all right, Prudence,' I soothed her. 'Just don't ever tell me I'm a ho and you're a virgin saint.'

'You could work for me for a salary,' she suggested quietly, looking at the painted trees on the walls and the jiggling lights from the mirrors. Business was never far from her mind, and she had obviously been considering my assets for weeks. 'You know how clothes are made, even though your taste is in the gutter.' I rose on my elbows in indignation, and she pulled me back down, laughing. 'Girl, you'd have to work,' she went on. 'It's hard to get a new business off the ground and I can't afford any lazy woman in my life.' I laughed with her.

'I can work, honey. I love your store and I want it to be here a long time.' The smell of our satisfied bodies seemed to fill the space.

I could feel Pru's nervous exhaustion. 'But can you mix business with pleasure by working with me all day is what I'm asking, sweet woman? I don't know if you want to be my employee. I don't know if I could handle being your boss. You could be my partner, but you'd have to buy into the store. This is a serious entanglement we're discussing.'

Like a devout child of the Goddess, I was struck by enlightenment. I knew then that Pru had been wanting me as long as I had wanted her, but she had been afraid of everything she didn't know about me, and she hadn't known how to find out. I caressed her troubled face. 'Pru,' I told her, 'don't worry about it. I won't know whether I can take orders from you until I try it. If it works out, I could become your partner. If we can't work together, I still want to give you what you need. Let's see how much of our lives we want to share.'

Pru relaxed with a deep sigh, lazily running a hand down my back. 'I'm not sure I can keep my hands off you,' she chuckled.

'I bet you'll love helping women in the fitting rooms,' I joked.

She laughed and slapped my behind so that my cheeks quivered. 'You naughty girl,' she scolded. 'You need a good spanking. I don't intend to molest my customers.'

'No, honey,' I protested, sliding against her skin. 'I don't believe in molesting anybody. I just want to help women get what they want whether men like it or not.'

'Mmm,' she agreed, squeezing the back of my neck. I suddenly felt tired, and wanted to fall asleep in her arms. 'Hey,' she snickered, stroking my face. 'Don't close your eyes, woman. You want the customers to find you here like this tomorrow?' I laughed, forcing my eyes open. 'Let's go eat something.'

Reluctantly I pulled myself off her and stood up, stretching. 'Well, we broke in the store,' I told her, reaching for my jeans.

'Baby, no. If you're dining with me, you can't wear those things. Wear the dress I gave you.'

Trying to wipe the smile off my face, I retrieved the lingerie and the dress.

'That's better,' she said.

'Just one thing, Pru,' I said humbly, looking into her eyes.

'What's that, sweetheart?' she urged me.

'I can't walk in heels like this. They'll ruin my feet.' I didn't like the look of disappointment on her face, but the pain in my feet was worse. 'Could I save them for special occasions? With you?'

Pru laughed with delight and wrapped her long arms around me, pulling me close to her. 'Sure, Beth,' she breathed into my hair. As soon as she let go, I found a more sensible pair of low heels in the shoe display. I loved the look of admiration on her face as her eyes travelled from my shining hair to my neatly shod feet and back up my body. When we turned out the light and locked the door.

Late Night Shopping
Jade Taylor

To be honest, he wasn't really my type.

I usually went for big stocky men. The type who were builders, gym instructors, casual labourers; any profession that developed those meaty forearms, wide shoulders and wide chest. The type of man whose physique showed that he could crush me as soon as look at me, lift me up in huge arms then pin me down and take what he wanted. And there was nothing more I wanted than to be dominated by these men; to have them hold me helpless while I submitted without protest.

A bit of rough was my favourite fantasy; the one I fulfilled most often. I loved my casual flirtations with danger.

But Adam was different.

It's difficult to explain, and I know it's strange, but there were times when I met someone and I knew that I could not go on without sleeping with them. I could find them anywhere – libraries, the pictures, even in a doctor's waiting room. These obsessions were nothing like the no-brains-all-brawn type I had so often. They could be anyone, any age, any occupation; all the markers we rate as important were meaningless when I was struck by these compulsions.

There were no limits when it came to this passion. There had been married men that I had met in nameless hotels and watched as they showered the scent of our sex away, hoping their wives couldn't detect the odour of a sexed-up woman upon their bodies. There had been two friends' fathers: one in the conservatory as his family and friends celebrated his fifty-fifth birthday while he tried to fuck that fact away; and another whom I had held all night as he wept at the shame of what he saw as our 'incestuous liaison'. There had been women, including one friend's sister, one friend's mother (her father hadn't been my type), and even my ex's new girlfriend – the one he had left me for. That had been fun. He had thought it mature to all remain friends, and it had been easy to flirt with her, tease her casually and make her wonder what it would be like with a woman. I told her that another woman would know how to touch her, how to please her as a man never could, until she finally let me kiss her and then told me she would leave him for me. I fucked her in his bed, revelling in her softness, the sweet scent of her pussy, licking her clit in a way I knew he never would, showing her what she was missing with him. After it was over I couldn't help but phone my ex up and tell him how I had made her come so many times; how she had moaned my name so loudly.

He'd always wanted me to tell him about my experiences with women, so I guess he finally got what he wanted.

I'd even managed to seduce a vicar – the ultimate in seduction.

If it was wrong to have them, the desire only increased. The more wrong it was the more right it felt.

I let the big stocky men take me without any chase; let them do what they wanted, their solid bodies suppressing my free will. I would do as they told me, suck them hard, and fuck me any way they wanted. I would not say no to anything they desired.

But the obsessions I chased without thought, allowing nothing to shake me from my pursuit. Convention, morals, friendship – they could all be cast aside until after I was satisfied.

Nothing mattered but getting what I wanted.

And I wanted the young Adam more than anyone else I had ever met. I suspected this was because I thought he was a virgin.

I wasn't certain, of course, but there was something about him – something inherently awkward in his movements that had suggested inexperience to me, if not innocence.

It was that which had first caught my attention.

And that first time I saw him I knew I had to have him. All I wanted to do was take him home with me, strip him off and show him all the tricks I had learned.

Instead of being submissive I wanted to dominate him, hold down his wrists as I rode him into ecstasy, and know that he would be so grateful.

How could he resist?

At first I thought that he may be too young, and tried to curb my desire. But after seeing him at work in the supermarket over a few consecutive evenings, I caught him with stubble on his face, looking at once so much older, and I knew he was the right choice.

In fact he was damn near perfect.

He had short dark hair, intense blue eyes, and shoulders and chest as broad as any older man's. Sometimes, when busy, he undid the top button of his shirt, showing thick chest hair that I couldn't wait to run my fingers through. His bottom was tight with youth and strength, and this was another thing that attracted me, as he bent down to put out the vegetables.

There was never any question that I would not have him, and now, finally, was the time to make my move.

It's 9.50 as I walk in, ten minutes before the shop shuts. There are no other customers about, and very few staff. I flick my hair as I walk past him, knowing my golden highlights will attract his eye, wanting his attention completely.

As I feel his gaze upon me I stretch to reach the top shelf. I've dressed carefully for this occasion, and the short skirt I've picked out specially performs its purpose as it slowly rides up my thighs. I know that if he is looking now, and I am sure he is, he can see the dark absence where my panties should be.

I turn and smile as he whips around, pretending that he wasn't watching. 'Can you help me?' I remain on tiptoe, making sure he notices as I reach further for the strawberries.

'Sure,' he says, standing slowly. He's blushing furiously, and I know now that he's been looking for sure. I don't move as he approaches, forcing him to stand close to me as he passes them down. I sigh softly, breathing in his scent – he smells so masculine for such a young man. As I move away I seize the chance to brush my breasts against him, nipples hard even before they come into contact with his burning skin.

'Thanks,' I say, then run my finger casually down his chest to tap his name badge. 'Adam.' His face flushes further, and he turns away as if angry about my intrusion on his space.

He returns to his work, studiously ignoring me as I fill my trolley, taking every opportunity to bend, stretch, anything to show him what he could have. The thought of him watching already has me wet; the thought of him ignoring me because of my effect is even more stimulating.

I rush around the shop in a heady daze, determined to be finished just after ten o'clock, not wanting to draw anyone's attention to me but Adam's.

The cashier is a young hard bottle blonde and, rather than the usual supermarket mantra of smiling and saying hello, she scowls as I begin to unload my shopping. For a moment I think it's the time – that she's cross because I'm making her finish late – but her behaviour tells me different. Without even trying to hide it she looks me up and down, and then glances back to where Adam is working. I can't help but wonder if she has some teenage crush on him, or maybe she is his girlfriend and has seen me flirting. I unload my shopping carefully, not wishing to flash at her and anger her further, seeing no reason to irritate her.

It will be enough when I have him.

I ask for a packer, and she scowls then tuts loudly. She shouts loudly for Adam, and he avoids eye contact as he shuffles across reluctantly.

'Aren't you helpful?' I say, resting my hand on his arm, feeling the flex of his muscles as he packs my shopping hastily. 'Would you mind helping me outside?'

He blushes again, but nods mutely.

'Isn't he great?' I ask the cashier. 'I wish you'd let me take him home with me!' I laugh, she scowls, and Adam looks like he's about to explode.

We are alone outside, all the other customers have left, and, as the trolleys are chained up, I'm certain that the trolley man's left too.

The chill of the night is a shock after the warmth of the shop, the cold air initially like an invasion. Then, as my body slowly grows accustomed to the change, the wind feels like cold fingers, teasing my cunt with delicate tenderness.

'How old are you, Adam?' I ask, praying that he is over sixteen, and knowing full well that if he isn't I will be back when he is.

'Seventeen, nearly eighteen. Why?' he asks sullenly, and I guess he has problems with seeming younger than he actually is.

'Just wondering,' I reply carelessly. I don't care if he's sullen, I don't care about anything as long as he wants me. His temperament only makes him more appealing; something to overcome before I can satisfy myself with him.

As he follows me to the car I relish the anticipation coursing through my veins. I'm feeling so horny, so hot inside, I almost push him to the ground there, tempted to rock us both to orgasm in the disabled parking spaces by the shop, the store's lights illuminating us in a strange imitation of candlelight.

Somehow I resist, and lead him to the car, opening the boot without a word.

I'm not so careful this time as I bend over, wriggling my hips as I do, knowing the tightness of the skirt means it will ride up. I can hear his breathing now, not with the exertion of lifting, but the exertion of restraint.

As he puts the last bag in the boot I turn to him, knowing the skirt's around my waist, showing him the dark curls of my sex.

To his credit he maintains eye contact, but his nervous swallowing gives it away.

'Thanks, Adam.' As I say it, I slip my hand down, fingers opening my lips, showing him the pink moistness waiting for him. My hands are cold, and I want his hard hot cock to warm me up.

'All part of the service,' he replies, his voice barely more than a whisper. He swallows again.

'And is that the end of the service?' I demand, stepping closer, my skirt still around my waist, and our bodies almost touching.

His hands twitch nervously, and his left hand carelessly catches the lips of my sex. I can't help whimpering, I want him that much. As he realises what he's done, he coughs nervously and steps back, but I step forward with him.

'Don't you want to touch me properly?'

He starts stuttering, but the words die in his mouth.

'What's the matter, Adam? Are you a virgin?'

He shakes his head furiously, unable to even try to speak.

'Don't worry, Adam, I'll show you what to do.'

I reach out for his hand, and place it between my legs.

'Isn't that better?' I ask, slowly rubbing myself against him. He doesn't move, but he doesn't pull away. I move closer still and now he moves his wrist so that his hand stays touching me. I press myself up against him hard, my breasts mashed against his chest as I feel his heart beating faster. I move my lips millimetres from his, wondering how long he can last.

'Don't you want to touch me properly? Don't you want to know what it feels like?' I ask teasingly, rubbing my lips softly against his neck, knowing from his breathing that he wants this as much as I do.

'Someone might see us,' he half-protests, pulling back as he glances around the deserted car park.

'Let them,' I reply, and it seems this gives him permission to act. His mouth meets mine, teeth clashing briefly with the force of the kiss. His hand remains still as his tongue explores my mouth. I know I am oozing moisture onto him, and I don't care.

Suddenly he pulls away, watching me as he now *finally* moves his hand. The heel of his palm slowly strokes my hot flesh, and I wantonly rub myself against him, desperate for him to touch my clit. He seems to sense this and his fingers gently part my lips, revelling in the wetness as they slide around me. I realise Adam isn't as inexperienced as I thought, as his fingers tease my clit, circling around it and then tapping it so softly that his fingers barely touch me.

'I know what to do,' he proudly tells me, teasing me gently.

'I'd noticed,' I reply, gasping as he slides a finger inside me, then back to my clit, then two fingers, then three, stretching me, making me wish he'd fill me up with his cock.

Adam kisses me hard again, leaving my lips feeling bruised when he stops. Now he is in charge, grabbing me by the wrist as he pulls me forward to sit on the bonnet of my car. He quickly opens my blouse and pulls my breasts free of my bra. My nipples are swollen, and he touches them with an expression that is almost reverential. He lowers his mouth to my breasts, licking and kissing across them, but avoiding the nipples. I'm too impatient for teasing, and push a nipple into his mouth, demanding that he suck it. I reach down for his other hand and place it on my other breast, and he pinches me until I cry out in pleasure.

He straightens up, his hands all over my breasts as he bites my ears, my neck, hardly knowing which part he wants. Now he is almost lying on top of me, grinding his hardness against me as he grows more desperate.

I pull his head away from me, and wriggle away across the car bonnet, until his face is between my legs. I pull him towards me, but he pulls away, shaking his head.

'No, I don't do that!' he protests, trying to move away from me. I figure he's never done it before, but that's no excuse. I grab his hair and pull until his face is almost touching me.

'You do now.' For a moment I think he'll refuse, then he begins tentatively licking me, making me moan loudly. He learns quickly, and licks harder, swirling his tongue around my clit now, making me feel like there's nothing else in the universe except my sex and his tongue. Without even realising what I'm doing, I stroke my nipples, pinching myself as the tension grows.

His tongue circles my clit as he slips a finger inside me, and then slides another into my asshole. I'm surprised he's so knowledgeable about what to do to me, but I can't formulate thoughts clearly; I'm writhing beneath him, trying to force his fingers in deeper, pushing myself onto his tongue, desperate to come. I see that he's watching me, and as our eyes meet I can't contain it any longer. I explode, moaning loudly, ripples flowing through me as I clamp my thighs around him, holding his head in place as I shudder beneath his tongue.

I've never come so hard before, and can hardly believe this innocent-looking boy has been the one to take me to such heights.

Adam falls back, seemingly in shock. I move over to him and kiss him hard, tasting myself on his lips. I kiss his neck softly, then bite him hard, wanting to leave my mark on him. Then I roughly open his shirt, rubbing my hands across his hairy chest, then moving to lick his nipples. I slide my hand inside his trousers, ready to make his dreams come true, then I realise they're sticky; he hasn't been able to last as long as I'd hoped.

'What a disappointment!' I say. He looks humiliated, but I don't care now – I've got what I wanted. I straighten my clothes quickly, get into my car and drive away, my insides still quivering.

* * *

I don't shop there for weeks, embarrassed that I behaved so wantonly, and that my seduction went so wrong. I was supposed to be the one who taught him how to please a woman, not give myself up to him so easily. I was supposed to fuck him like he's never been fucked, not let him lick me better than anyone ever has and then get so excited he comes in his pants.

Finally I return to the scene, at midday, figuring that he will be at college.

I'm wrong.

He sees me before I see him, and I feel his hot eyes on my back before I realise he's there. Our eyes meet by the washing powder aisle. It's like a jolt of electricity flowing through my body; I'm shook by this physical reaction to his presence.

I've already seduced him; he's not supposed to have any effect on me anymore.

I'm tempted to walk straight out, but can't give in to the feeling, seeing it as failure.

I never fail.

Adam walks over to me, standing so close I can feel his breath upon my neck.

'So, the bitch is back,' he says, and the coldness of his voice excites me as much as the hardness of his cock did.

'Why wouldn't I be?' I ask, voice full of mock bravado, knowing this façade could easily crumble.

'After what you did I thought you'd be embarrassed.'

I laugh, and he's shocked. He may be tougher than I thought he'd be, but he's nothing compared to me. 'Me ... embarrassed? What about what you did? I never regret anything I've done.'

'And what if I were still mad at you? What if I wanted to get my own back?'

I laugh again. His face is still close to mine and he's breathing fast with anger, but as I step closer to him I casually brush my hand against the front of his trousers, and feel the erection straining to be free. He may be mad, but he's also horny.

'You wouldn't,' I reply, certain that he wouldn't have the balls to do anything – not at work, and probably not ever.

'My girlfriend dumped me because of you!' he whines, the petulant teenager showing through once more.

'The girl on the till?' I laugh. She's only a teenager; he must know that I have much more to offer. 'And that's a problem?'

'You could have lost me my job too!' he exclaims, showing how important his girlfriend was. 'You were almost naked, lying on the car bonnet in the car park where anyone could have seen!'

I feel myself growing wet as he reminds me, thinking of his tongue in my mouth, his mouth on my breast, his tongue on my clit.

I usually lose all interest once I've had each obsession; all interest lost after I've got what I wanted.

But Adam is more unusual than I thought.

I want him again.

'And you didn't want it?' I ask, moving my face closer to his, aware that we probably have an audience, but wanting to push him; wanting to see what he will do when I push him too far. 'You could have said no.'

He grabs my wrist so hard I wince and people turn to look as he pulls me close, so hard I stumble into his chest. 'Follow me.'

He pulls me towards the back of the shop. Now there are lots of other staff around and, as we pass, it seems all are watching. He is not supposed to show me up like this, but I follow him without a word, wondering when the roles changed; when he became my master.

He takes me to the back door of the shop where the

deliveries come in. There's a man there, stacking crates. He's older than Adam, but it's obvious they're friends as Adam drags me over to him.

'This her?' he asks, and Adam nods.

'Can you fuck off for a bit?'

The man steps closer to me, and I know I'm supposed to be embarrassed that Adam has told him what happened, but instead I flush with pride.

The man puts his hand on my face, and I smile, watching Adam grow jealous as this older and more experienced man looks me up and down. He likes what he sees as he runs his hand down my neck, then across my breasts, feeling my nipples harden beneath his touch.

I can't help but love being treated like a whore.

'Well, she certainly looks like she wants it,' he says, laughing.

Adam roughly pulls the man's hand off me. 'Go on, give us twenty minutes.'

The man is still laughing as he walks away and Adam pulls me outside.

'So I could have said no?' he growls, grabbing me and quickly pushing me against the wall, taking my wrists and pinning my arms above my head. He pulls my skirt up and my pants down with almost clinical efficiency, making me writhe in his grasp as my imagination runs wild. If any deliveries come they're going to see everything. The shop is full of staff and customers, and although the area seems secluded, we're not that far away from other people.

I don't know whether the thought of them seeing me is scary or exciting.

Adam licks his fingers and roughly pushes them inside me. He needn't have bothered with lubrication;

I've been dripping wet since he first grabbed me, his face impassive, and his erection straining in his trousers.

'It's an easy word to say,' I tell him, my voice hoarse with desire.

'Say it then,' he demands. 'Show me how easy it is.'

He's changed, he's harder now, and I like the way I've changed him.

I want to say it, want to fight back, but know I would be betraying my body; that he would pull away and leave me aching.

He pushes himself against me, cock rubbing against my stomach and lips millimetres from mine – *my trick*! I move forward to kiss him, but am still pinned against the wall by my wrists, and he pulls away *just* before our lips meet.

'If it's so easy, say it.'

I can't reply.

'Then don't you think you owe me an apology?'

'You enjoyed it as much as I did,' I reply, my voice now barely more than a whisper.

'But you called me a disappointment,' he teases me, trailing his lips over mine again.

'You were. You came in your pants!' I lean back against the wall as I try to resist his teasing, wishing my lips weren't so sensitive, wishing every fleeting touch wasn't setting me on fire. His tongue flickers out, touching mine briefly, but he pulls away again when I try to kiss him.

'You didn't seem that disappointed to me,' he laughs, rubbing his cock hard against my belly, but still firmly holding my wrists.

'Let me go now, and I'll make it up to you,' I plead, and I can't help but sound like I'm begging. I can cope with being dominated by my big men, but I am supposed to dominate Adam, and can hardly believe the way things are going.

'How?' he asks, his lips on my neck, his breath hot in my ear.

'I'll kiss you, I'll suck you, I'll fuck you, I'll let you do anything you want.'

'This is what I want,' he tells me, pushing me harder against the wall, feeling the gravelly surface scratching my bottom, hurting and turning me on at the same time.

'I want to do to you what you did to me.'

He pulls my T-shirt above my head, leaving it tangled around my wrists to add to my restraints. Now he doesn't tease me, but instead sucks as much of my breast as possible and bites the nipple hard, as if to punish me. I feel pain, but also pleasure, and whimper with the combination.

'And I want to see if you can say no.'

He grabs my shoulders and pushes me to the floor, then opens his trousers quickly and sticks his thick cock into my mouth. I nearly gag at his first thrust; he's big and he forces himself deep into my throat without restraint, grunting with each movement, selfish in his excitement. I don't care; I want him to come in my mouth, and suck hard, wishing I could touch myself without him noticing. His breathing becomes erratic and I tease my tongue under the rim of his cock, tasting pre-come. Suddenly he pulls away and hauls me up, holding my wrists firmly above my head again. He puts his fingers inside me, roughly opening my lips, spreading my wetness and teasing my clit. He moves his hand from my wrists now, but I still keep them there, as if still pinned against the wall, my will no longer mine, this total submission turning me on as much as his touch. His hand now pushes my abdomen against the wall, preventing me from moving forward as I try to grind my clit against his unwilling fingers.

'Please,' I moan. 'I'm sorry.'

'You should be,' he tells me sternly, still roughly rubbing at me.

I'm desperate to come now. It feels like an ache deep inside me, and I know that even if he doesn't touch me I will still come soon. My breathing goes shallow, and he pulls away.

He turns me round, and bends me over roughly as I grab at the wall for some support. Then he is inside me, filling the ache that he has caused, his deep thrusts making me shake with desire.

'Touch me,' I beg, my voice now guttural with desire.

'No,' he tells me, grabbing my hips and thrusting faster, coming as I speak, leaving me groaning in disappointment as he pulls away.

I turn; watching what he will do next. His trousers are around his ankles and his dick is still twitching. Without thinking I sink to my knees once more, and take him in my mouth. He tastes of me and his salty come, and I lick away the stickiness. His dick grows hard again, and he plunges deeper in my mouth, grabbing the back of my head, trying to control me as I easily tease him to another juddering climax.

Now he doesn't move away; instead he pulls me up and kisses up my stomach to my breasts, teasing me as he did the first time. He pins me to the wall once more, kissing me hard, his fingers running up my thighs. They slide between my legs again, but this time there is no teasing. Instead his fingers are instantly at my clit, stroking it hard until I come. I am writhing hard as my arms scrape against the bricks. He doesn't stop as I try to pull away, overwhelmed by sensation, but continues, making me come again and again as he covers my mouth with his to stifle my shouts.

This time it is me who collapses to the floor as he lets me go, my legs no longer strong enough to hold me up. And this time it is he who walks away.

I had turned a boy into a man, but it was he who taught me more.

As the aftershocks slowly subside I smile. That'll teach me to judge by appearances.

I'd learned my lesson well.

Mooncakes Kimberly Dean

Beautiful, but lonely . . .

A long time ago in the mystical land of the Orient, a powerful general named Yi saved the earth. As a reward, the Imperial Majesty gave Yi the magic pill of eternal life. Yi took the pill home, but hid it from his wife, Chang E. One day while Yi was away, Chang E's curiosity overcame her. She discovered the pill and swallowed it. In a flash, gravity let go of its powerful hold, and she went flying towards the moon. Eternal banishment was the price she paid for her inquisitiveness. Yi tried to follow, but typhoon winds swept him back to earth. Now, forever, Chang E watches over the world from her heavenly prison. She rules the night sky as the Moon Goddess – exquisite, yet untouchable – except for one night of the year.

Moonlight punched holes through the cloud covering and illuminated the secluded Northwest countryside. Tia Chen pulled her wrap more tightly around her shoulders and tried to fight off her uneasiness.

'Where is he?' she muttered. She'd called for a tow truck thirty minutes ago.

The clouds in the midnight sky bunched together and darkness swept across the valley. Tia shivered. Of all the places for her car to die . . . Seattle was a busy, crowded place, but she lived in the relatively remote suburb of Woodinville. On a dark night like this, the road home took on an eerie, lonely cast.

'Please,' she whispered. She tried the engine one more time, but got the same response – nothing. She sank back against the leather seat. She didn't know what had happened. There'd been no warning. There'd just been a sudden noise before she'd lost all power.

The moon peeked through the cloud cover again, and she glanced up at it. She knew exactly how the Moon Goddess felt – isolated and *alone*.

A sharp light suddenly bounced off her rearview mirror, and she shut her eyes to block out the glare. The sound of a tow truck, though, was unmistakable.

'Oh, thank God,' she said. Relieved, she reached for the door handle and got out. The light from the tow truck hit her square on, and she lifted her hand to shield her eyes.

'Hello?' she called.

A man stepped into the light, his shape a dark silhouette. He began to walk towards her, and Tia's feminine instincts went on alert. He had one of those tough, testosterone-filled strides that only street fighters and motorcycle thugs could carry off.

She took an unconscious step back. 'Easton Auto?'

The man stopped two feet in front of her. 'You need a ride.'

It wasn't a question. She didn't like the implications – especially when she could feel his gaze running down her body.

'My car,' she said uneasily. 'It's broken down.'

The man circled her and gave her backside a once over. 'Let me take a look.'

He'd turned so that the headlamps lit his face. Suddenly, Tia's feet were rooted to the ground. He was even rougher than she'd imagined. He wasn't handsome; dangerous would be a better description. His nose had been broken at least once, and a small scar ran through his right eyebrow.

By all rights, she should be hopping into her car and locking the door. Instead, she felt an unfamiliar sensation unfurl in her stomach.

That scarred eyebrow lifted. 'Pop the hood?'

He'd caught her staring. Hurriedly, she reached into the car and pulled the lever.

'Your timing belt snapped,' he said almost as soon as he got a look at the engine.

Tia cautiously rounded the car. 'Is that bad?'

'It's not good.'

She chewed her lower lip and moved closer. 'Will it be expensive?'

'Well, now,' he said slowly. 'That depends.'

'On what?'

He looked at her again, and Tia had to fight to hold her ground. The moonlight caught his eyes at just the right angle that they sparkled.

He had the eyes of a wolf.

'It just depends,' he said in that same, molasses voice. His gaze slid leisurely down her body. 'You're cold. Go hop into the cab of my truck, and I'll take care of things here.'

Tia glanced down. Her face flamed when she saw that her nipples were standing like two little tent poles under the velvet of her dress. Embarrassed, she pulled her wrap more tightly around herself.

'I was a bridesmaid at a wedding,' she said, as if to explain her hard nipples. She rolled her shoulders and tried to fight off a shiver that had nothing to do with the chill in the air. 'I think I'll take you up on that offer. Let me just grab some things from my car.'

She turned away, but the man moved right along with her. 'I'll help you.'

Tia backed away stiffly as the man took over. He picked up the leftover wedding cake from the back seat, and she grabbed a few things before following him to the tow truck. She kept a safe distance, but her gaze couldn't help but wander down to his tight ass. His walk looked even better from behind.

He put the cake in the cab and then turned sharply. Her heels skidded on the gravel shoulder of the road. He was too close.

'What are you doing?' she squeaked when his hands closed around her waist.

'It's a big step.' He lifted her and settled her on the seat.

It was intimidating how easily he manhandled her, but with her hands full, there wasn't much Tia could do. She smiled her thanks, but her smile turned brittle when he didn't back away.

His wolf gaze focused on her face. 'So who got married?'

One of his hands left her waist, but moved only as far as her thigh. His thumb rubbed back and forth on the burgundy material, and her quadriceps bunched. Instinctively, she tried to close her legs, but his touch remained gently firm.

Unable to stop him – and ashamed at her lack of effort – she looked straight out the window. 'My sister,' she said brightly.

Overbrightly.

He didn't move.

'Don't you like him?'

'Who?' Tia asked. It was hard to concentrate with his hand burning a hole through her dress.

'Your new brother-in-law.'

'Of course I like him. He's great.'

'Were you screwing him?'

Her head snapped to the side, and her mouth rounded in horror. 'Absolutely not!'

'Did you want to?'

'How dare you.' She pushed at his hand. He'd just crossed the line from being bad boy interesting to downright dangerous. 'Let go of me!'

His thumb continued its lazy caress. 'I'm just trying to figure out why your sister's wedding would make you so sad.'

Surprise made Tia stop. How had he known the wedding upset her? His wolf gaze pinned her, and her shoulders slumped. 'It was my *little* sister.'

His stare was so intense, goosebumps popped out on her skin. After a moment, his hot gaze slid down her body. He examined her chest with as much concentration as he'd given her face. Tia squirmed. She'd liked the sleek form-fitted bridesmaid dresses, but the low-cut back hadn't allowed for a bra. She'd been somewhat self-conscious at the wedding, but with him, she felt as if she were flaunting her breasts for his approval.

And he was giving it.

'I wouldn't worry, China doll,' he said.

He squeezed her thigh, and she nearly came out of her seat. Without another word, he backed off and shut the door. Tia's heart thudded in her chest as she watched him move back to her car.

'Oh, God,' she groaned. His touch had made her realise how long it had been since she'd had a man between her legs and how much she wanted one there. Now.

She reached up to rub her temple. What was she doing? She wasn't the kind of person who took risks like this. What was wrong with her?

The driver hopped back in the truck and moved it. She kept quiet as he worked, but her brain was skittering all over the place. By the time he'd hooked up her car and settled behind the steering wheel again, her nerves were stretched thin.

'So where's home?' he asked.

'Home?' she said sharply.

'You don't have a car. You need a ride.'

Tia fought not to squirm. She was vulnerable, and he knew it. 'That's not necessary. Just take my car to the shop, and I'll call a cab.'

He didn't even bother to respond.

She bit her lower lip. 'Take a right at the next crossroad.'

The trip took less time than she would have liked. He pulled up in front of her house, and she reached for the door before he even came to a complete stop. She didn't want him helping her down. Up was enough.

It was a big step. Her skirt pulled tight, and the slit gaped widely as she settled one high heel on the ground. The driver rounded the truck, but came to a dead stop when he saw her. Looking down, Tia realised that her leg was so exposed, he could see the lace band of the stocking around her thigh.

An inch more and he'd be able to see the crotch of her underwear.

She quickly climbed down. 'Please call when my car is fixed.'

She reached for her things, but her spine went ramrod straight when his body brushed against her back.

'I've got it,' he said gruffly.

He was too close. Tia grabbed what she could, turned on her heel, and hurried up the front path. The quicker he left, the quicker she could get her emotions under control. She unlocked the door and moved directly to the kitchen. She was setting down a box when she heard the door close behind her. She turned in time to see him slide the cake onto the table. Reaching out, he slid the butter dish to the side to make room.

'Well, thank you again,' she said tightly.

He didn't move.

Tia felt a shiver go down her spine. Why hadn't she turned on a light? She'd been in such a hurry. Light would have been good right now.

She took a shaky breath. The moonlight was dangerous. It streamed through the window over the sink and illuminated him. He was a rough and tumble character – one she'd never want to run into in a dark alley.

But she'd met him on a dark road, and she hadn't run away.

She stood immobile. His dark blond hair glistened in the cool moonlight rays. None of the men she'd dated would have let their hair get that shaggy ... but for some reason, her fingers itched. The overalls he wore were definitely not attractive with their grease stains and holes ... but they were intriguing. What would she find if she slid that zipper down, down, down ...

'Your cheque,' she said, snapping out of her reverie.

Her legs trembled as she scurried out of the room. She found the chequebook and was reaching for the lamp when his hand suddenly closed around hers.

'I wasn't at that wedding,' he said in a voice close to her ear, 'but I bet you put your sister to shame. Believe me, China doll, nobody was feeling sorry for you.'

Tia's breath caught. He'd read her like a book.

She tried to sidestep, but he stopped her with a hand at her waist. He'd trapped her. With one, simple move, he'd caught her between his body and the hassock in front of her living-room chair.

'With you wearing that dress, people had other thoughts on their minds.'

He gave her silk wrap a tug. It slipped from her shoulders and fell to a puddle on the floor. Except for the curtain of her hair, her back was left naked and exposed. Tia's muscles went rigid when he brushed her hair over her shoulder and trailed a finger down her spine.

'There wasn't one man in that church – priest included – who wasn't wishing he could have a piece of this.'

His hands were fast. She didn't have time to even flinch before they slipped under the velvet and encircled her. His hands settled possessively onto her breasts. 'Probably some women, too,' he whispered into her ear.

Heat slammed into Tia's belly.

'What are you doing?' she gasped. She tried to catch his hands, but his strength made her struggles laughable.

'Giving you what you need,' he said. His head dipped into the curve of her shoulder.

Her breasts were small, but sensitive. If the cold air hadn't made her nipples perk up, his rough hands were more than capable. He cupped her tightly and began squeezing, demanding more reaction out of her flesh.

Her pussy clenched when his tongue snaked across the pulse at her neck. 'Let me go,' she demanded.

'Not tonight.'

The world tilted. Suddenly, Tia found herself on her knees with the stranger's weight bearing her down onto the hassock. Her heart leapt into her throat. Panic mixed with excitement. She knew she shouldn't let this happen, but a traitorous trickle of moisture wet her panties.

'You need this bad,' he whispered into her ear.

With a quick flip, he pulled her dress up and to the side. The long slit allowed her no modesty. Tia closed her eyes tightly as he leaned back to look at her. She could only imagine the picture she painted as she kneeled in front of him. The elastic of her hose suddenly pinched tighter around her thighs and the crotch of her panties seemed extra thin. It was the only barrier that separated them.

The trickle became a stream. He was right. She did need this.

'So sleek,' he said in that low voice. She gasped when he cupped her mound. He squeezed, and her back bowed when his thumb pressed into the crevice of her ass. It rubbed against her anus, and her hips bucked. 'Ah,' she cried out.

'And responsive,' he noted. He spread his fingers wide against her back. His heat nearly branded her as he gently pressed her back down.

Tia's breath went shallow when he caught the elastic waistband of her panties. Ever so slowly, he pulled them down. Cool air lashed against her pussy. His knees pressed against hers, forcing her legs wider. The silk bit into her thighs, and a small sound escaped from the back of her throat.

She opened her eyes and tried to get her brain to stop swimming. She was in her own living room, laid over her own ottoman like a sacrifice, with a total stranger about to fuck her.

She'd never been so turned on in her life.

'So exotic,' he whispered as he combed his fingers through her hair. 'Do you know that when you stepped out of your car and into the light, I got a hard-on so fast, I could hardly get out of my truck?'

A zipper rasped, and Tia looked back. He was shrugging out of his overalls, but his gaze was centred on her pussy.

That look alone made her cream.

'You're lucky I didn't bend you over that car and take you on the side of the road.'

The overalls dropped to his knees, and he whipped his T-shirt over his head. His chest was a riot of muscles.

Her fingers ached to touch him but, in her submissive position, she couldn't reach him.

He pulled his briefs down and his cock bounced as the material caught its tip. It surged back upright, proud and ready for action.

She scooted back on the hassock to get closer. She was ready for that big dick. She'd been ready since he'd squeezed her thigh in the truck.

'Slow down, little China doll,' he said.

'Hurry,' she said through her dry throat.

'Slower is better.'

His hands began squeezing and caressing her ass. Tia braced herself against the hassock and settled her forehead against her forearm. Her reactions threatened to overwhelm her. The moonlight gave the room a cool, blue-white glow, but she felt red hot.

'Such a pretty pussy.' His thumbs caught her lips and spread them apart. He was looking right into the heart of her. 'Baby, this is what the men at that wedding were thinking about. They didn't give a rip that you're older than your sister. Their brains were filled with thoughts of this.'

She groaned when he jammed two thick fingers into her.

'They were wondering how tight you are.'

He leaned over her again, and his bare chest rubbed against her back. The contact was electric.

His fingers scissored inside of her. 'They wanted to know how wet you get.' He nipped her earlobe. 'How eager.' 'I'm the only one who had the balls to find out,' he whispered.

She jerked when his fingers moved to the bud of her anus. In shock, she craned her neck to look over her shoulder. She tried to squirm away, but he was rubbing something smooth against her most private spot.

The butter from the table. He'd brought the butter from her own kitchen table! 'No!' she cried when she realised what he intended to do.

'Yes,' he said firmly.

Her hips swivelled hard, but he had her under his thumb. Literally. He continued to lubricate her. No matter how she moved, she couldn't get away from that disturbing touch.

Without warning, the pressure against her tiny opening increased and his thumb slipped inside. Tia cried out. His fingers tickled her wet pussy and, to her dismay, she felt herself clench him tighter.

'I knew it,' he said.

That insidious thumb pulled out of her, and she risked another glance over her shoulder. He was rubbing the slick yellow butter onto his pulsing cock. His *big* pulsing cock.

Her heart slammed against her rib cage. How had she let things go so far? How had she gotten herself into this situation? Why hadn't she taken better care of her car?

He was ready before she was. His wolfish gaze caught hers. If he saw her trepidation, he said nothing. He just caught her cheeks and spread them wide.

Tia couldn't bear to watch. It was more than enough to feel. She pressed her face into the hassock and held on for dear life.

The bulbous head of his cock touched her. The heat made her swallow hard. When the pressure began, she closed her eyes tight.

'Tonight, you need something special,' he said.

He nudged her knees wider, and the elastic of her panties bit into her legs. The pressure increased, and her senses zeroed in on the spot his cock was trying to invade. He kept seeking entrance – pushing, nudging, probing. Finally, her body's defences gave in.

He shoved into her, and she let out a choked cry. Air left her lungs in short gasps. It was too much. She couldn't take him. The pressure was too intense.

The muscles in his thighs bunched, and he pressed harder. The butter eased his penetration, but Tia felt panic creeping in. It was too much. It was unnatural. She felt overfilled.

He gave a hard thrust, and her control splintered.

'Ohhhh,' she gasped. Waves of pain and pleasure made colours dance behind her closed eyes. She squirmed with discomfort while raw need clawed at her.

The need was too dark. She was afraid of it. Her hands flailed as she reached back to push him off of her. 'Oh, oh! It hurts. You're too big.'

'Just let me get it in,' he crooned.

'No, I can't – Ohhhhhh.' He'd tilted her hips and slid in deeper. The darkness grabbed Tia and wouldn't let go. It pulled her in, and she stopped fighting.

'There, that's better. Just a few more inches. Come on, babe. You're eatin' me up.'

He was watching her take him in the ass! The intimacy was almost too much to bear.

Tia's fingers dug into the hassock. He was so big. The pain. The heat. She was about to come apart.

'Damn,' he groaned. 'China doll, you were made for this.'

His balls bumped against her pussy as he reached the hilt. Tia tried to remember to breathe. She was impaled on his cock, but her thighs were sticky with her excitement.

He let out a grunt, and his hips surged.

She came right up off the hassock. The friction! It was like he'd lit a match inside her.

'Let's do this,' he growled.

He pulled out, and she moaned. Before she could catch her breath, he thrust back in.

He didn't give her time to adjust. He didn't give her time to adapt.

He just started fucking the hell out of her.

Tia cried out. The pain was biting, but the sinister pleasure was more powerful. It hit her in waves, and she knew she was going under.

His hips swung back and forth in a wide arc. Desperately, she reached back to catch his thighs. She wanted more.

'Christ!' he growled. 'You're hot for it.'

Tia couldn't talk. Sensation overwhelmed her senses. All she could do was fight for completion. It was there, waiting, just beyond her grasp.

He was working deep. His fingers bit into her buttocks as he spread her wider. The heat and pain made tears press at her eyes, but her hips began moving against his, eagerly taking his harsh thrusts. She was so close. So close.

Desperation tightened her chest. Her ass was aflame, but she couldn't come. Her pussy was crying with frustration. 'Please,' she begged. 'Help me.'

He was past words. All she got was a grunt as one of his hands squeezed between her body and the ottoman. He cupped her mound and ground the heel of his hand against her. It caught her right where she needed it, and the spark sent electricity throughout her body.

The explosion rocked her, but another quickly followed it. Then another. They came at her, one right on top of the other, until she couldn't tell her body from his. Day from night. Pleasure from pain. When her senses finally cleared, she found them both collapsed onto the hassock with his chest clinging to her back. His breath rasped in her ear, and his limp cock rested snuggly inside her.

'God,' he panted. 'I think we both needed that.'

Tia couldn't find her voice. Her brain was still numb, and her ass –

They both jerked when the phone rang.

Her face flamed with embarrassment. Dear Lord, who could be calling *now*?

'Aren't you going to answer that?' he asked after three rings.

'No,' she said, horrified. She could think of nothing more mortifying than talking to someone while he was still where he was ... doing what he was doing.

She spluttered when he picked up the phone and handed it to her. 'Hello?' she said, an octave too high.

Her throat nearly closed off when she heard the voice on the other end of the line.

'Hi, Mom,' she said weakly. Humiliated, she reached back and tried to push the man off of her.

He ignored her, and licked the back of her neck.

A shudder ran right down her spine. 'I had some car problems,' she said into the handset. 'I had to get a tow.'

'And a nice, thick cock.'

Tia slapped a hand over the mouthpiece. She couldn't bear the idea of her mother finding out she'd just been screwed by a tow truck driver. Butt-fucked, no less.

'I'm fine, Mom,' she said.

'Fine?' he said as he nuzzled her ear. He thrust slowly, and her eyes widened. He was getting hard again. She could feel him swelling inside her.

'Mom, it's late. I've got to go.' She needed to end this call. She needed to get this stranger off of her and out of her. She needed to get him out of her house!

He wasn't about to be put off so easily.

'Ooo,' she moaned when he lifted her hips so high her knees left the floor.

He ground himself into her.

'Keep talking or not,' he told her. 'I'm in the mood to fuck.'

Tia felt her ravaged backside come under siege again.

'Yes, yes,' she said, not knowing who she was talking to. 'The Har ... vest Moon Fest ... ival. Your house. I'll – Oh, God! I'll be there.'

He was rubbing more butter onto her.

'I know,' she choked out. 'Uhhh. On Wednesdaaaaay.'

'Your car is taking a long time to be fixed.'

Tia looked sharply at her mother before turning back to the lantern she was lighting. 'I know,' she said in a neutral voice. 'Do you need yours back?'

'No, I'm just worried how much that shop is going to charge you.'

Tia moved on to the next lantern. She was worried about a lot more than that. She hadn't seen her car or the tow truck driver since the night of her sister's wedding. She still didn't know what had happened. They'd had blistering sex, and then he'd walked out without a word.

For days now, she'd been confused, flustered, and disappointed.

Not to mention embarrassed.

She'd had anal sex with a total stranger. Twice. And she didn't even know his name.

Call the shop? She didn't think so.

A knock on the door ended the uncomfortable conversation. 'Someone's early,' her mother said as she glanced at her wristwatch.

She went to answer the door and Tia moved to the

table to finish preparations. She was taking the plastic wrap off a plate of mooncakes when she heard her name. She glanced over her shoulder – and froze.

It was him. The tow truck driver who'd screwed her brains out was standing next to her mother in the doorway. His wolf eyes glittered as he looked at her.

'Speak of the devil,' her mother said. 'This gentleman is here to deliver your car.'

Tia opened her mouth, but no words came out. She simply stared at the bizarre scene in front of her. Horror was her first reaction. If her mother knew ... or had the slightest idea what she'd done with this man ... Her second reaction was arousal. That devil had left her wanting – and from the look on his face, he knew it.

'I could have come down to the shop,' she said.

'We strive for personal service,' he said without missing a beat. 'Why don't you come out and I'll show you what we did?'

Tia's palms dampened. She couldn't be alone with him. She didn't trust herself.

'Go ahead,' her mother said. 'I can finish up here.'

Tia found herself caught by the arm before she could think of a good excuse.

'I parked it back here,' the tow driver said as he pulled her towards the alley that ran behind the house.

Her legs turned wobbly the further away they got from the streetlights and lanterns. It was dark back there, except for the moonlight – and that made her edgy. The moonlight had gotten her into trouble before.

'How did you know where my mother lived?' she hissed.

'I followed you.'

She was turning on him when his hand whipped out and caught her by the back of the neck. His lips came down hard on hers.

'God,' he said when he came up for air, 'I can't believe I made it four days.'

His mouth caught hers again, and his tongue pressed deep. It was a hot, desperate kiss that made Tia's pussy tingle. It was enough to shake her control. She wrapped her arms around his neck, and he shuddered when their bodies came together.

'That's it,' he said against her mouth. 'On the car.'

She grabbed at his shoulders when he lifted her. 'Wait! I can't. Not here.'

'Yes, here.' He settled her on the hood and started pushing up her skirt. 'I can't hold my wad much longer.'

'Stop!' she said as she pushed at his hands. 'There are people around.'

Guests had started arriving. She could hear them mingling in the back yard.

'Then you'll have to be quiet,' he said as he worked the material up to her waist.

Tia batted ineffectually at his hands as he stripped off her panties and tossed them aside. He pushed her legs apart, and her hips reared off the car when he reached deep between them to touch her in that not-so-secret spot.

'Did you miss me?' he asked.

'Ah!'

'Were you sore?'

'Yessss.' She gripped his forearm hard, but his fingers still played in that sensitive area.

'Good,' he grunted in satisfaction.

'Good?' she snapped. It was good that he'd left her raw and tender?

'You had a lot on your mind. I wanted to get your attention,' he said in a low voice. His hands moved to cup her ass. He lifted her hips off the car and high into the air. 'Just like now.'

Tia looked frantically through the trees when his head dipped between her legs. What if somebody caught them? His tongue rasped across her pussy, and her back bowed.

'Oh, God,' she moaned as reaction jolted her.

'Do I have it?' he asked.

Have her attention? He owned it. She draped her legs over his shoulders and reached for him. Who cared about a crowd of people a hundred feet away?

'I'll take that as a "yes",' he said as she wove her fingers through his hair. He pressed his mouth harder against her. 'You taste like you look – like an exotic treat.'

Tia couldn't stand it. His tongue delved into her, and her head rolled against the car. Her pussy had been ignored the last time he'd taken her. It badly needed tending.

He was thorough. He licked, prodded and stroked her until his mouth was sticky. When he tongued her clit, she whimpered loud enough for the talk in the back yard to quieten.

His face was tight as he lowered her back to the car. 'We'd better make this fast.'

His hand went to his jeans. It didn't take more than two seconds for him to pull out that big dick. Still holding her by the ass, he spread her legs nearly as wide as they would go. With a tug, she slid down the car and right onto his hot cock.

Tia's neck arched. Her hands searched for something to hold onto, and she caught the windshield wipers. Her fingers turned white as he began pumping into her.

He filled her up. He was long and hard, and her toes pointed with delight.

'So this Autumn Moon Festival,' he grunted between thrusts. 'It's the Chinese night for fucking, right?'

'What are you talking about?' she groaned. She didn't care much why he was screwing her. She was just happy he was.

'This legend thing,' he said as he pushed a hand under her blouse. 'Old man Yi did enough service time to be awarded a palace on the sun. The yang to Chang E's yin.'

Her butt bounced on the hood of her car. He didn't even try to be gentle with her, and it made her all the hornier.

'Harder,' she begged. She tugged at his T-shirt and her nails dug into the muscles of his back.

'As an added bonus, he also got a talisman that allows him to join his wife on one night every year,' he said. 'This night.'

'That's why we celebrate,' she groaned. 'She welcomes him with open arms.'

'And open legs,' he grunted.

He pressed hers back against her chest. When he thrust into her, it felt as if he went twice as deep.

Tia felt the muscles in her belly going tight.

'Come on, China doll. Give it to me.'

It took only a few deep, hard strokes before she came unglued. Her mouth opened in a scream, but his hand quickly silenced her. He kept thrusting until his own climax was upon him. Then he had to bury his face in the curve of her neck to muffle his own shout.

Tia wrapped her arms around him when his weight bore down onto her. 'That's not exactly how the legend goes,' she panted.

'Sure it is,' he said as his lungs worked like bellows. 'That sexy Moon Goddess isn't glowing because they're playing patty-cake up there.'

Tia found herself smiling. He'd actually taken time to research her heritage. It made her stomach warm and her tired pussy clench him tighter.

He lifted his head to look down at her. His eyes glittered, and she felt a tug at her heart. She was pulling him down for a kiss when she heard a rustling noise in the bushes. 'Oh, my God. Someone's coming.'

'Let 'em look,' he said. The wolfish glint was back in his eyes.

'Is everything all right back there?'

Tia's eyes rounded with horror. 'It's my mother!'

'Christ, doesn't that woman have any sense of timing?'

'Hurry! Get off of me!'

'Don't you mean "out"?' Begrudgingly, he lifted himself. He showed no sign of urgency as he slowly pulled his cock out of its warm home.

Tia bit her lip as she gave him up.

'Tia?'

She paled at the sound of her mother's voice getting closer. Quickly, she pushed her skirt down. She slid off the hood as he zipped up his jeans. Her panties! She reached for them, but he swooped them up and slipped them into his pocket.

'Back here, Mom,' she called as she tried to smooth her wrinkled clothes.

'What's going on back here?'

'Nothing.' Tia spotted her lipstick on her lover's mouth. She reached to wipe it off, but quickly caught her hands behind her back when her mother stepped out from between the trees.

Mrs Chen's sharp eyes took in the situation. 'We heard noises.'

The tow truck driver wiped his mouth with the back of his hand. 'That was me, ma'am. I was showing your daughter some added features of her car.'

Tia blushed, but hoped the moonlight hid her secrets. Her mouth dropped, though, when she saw the contemplating look enter her mother's eyes. Had she seen? What, exactly, had she heard?

'We're having a party,' Mrs Chen said. 'Would you like to join us, Mr . . .'

Tia's mouth opened and closed like a grounded fish. She didn't know his name! She'd let him screw her three times, and she didn't even know his name!

'Rick Easton,' he said. He held out his hand. 'As in Easton Auto.'

Her head snapped to the side. He owned the place?

'Mr Easton,' her mother repeated as she shook his hand. She unabashedly examined him from head to toe. Finally, her shoulders squared. 'Are you here to court my daughter?'

'Mom!' Tia exclaimed.

Rick wasn't fazed. 'You could call it that,' he deadpanned.

Her mother held his look unflinchingly.

'Well, it's about damn time,' she finally declared.

Tia nearly fell over.

Her mother glanced at her and shrugged. 'You needed a man. There's no better night than tonight to get one. It's prophetic.'

Rick sent her an I-told-you-so look.

'I was worried about you after the wedding,' her mother said. 'You needed to find your yang.'

And Rick Easton fits that bill?

'Oh, this is wonderful,' Mrs Chen said, clapping her hands. 'I have to tell Mrs Li. She thinks all the festival is good for is the mooncakes.'

Tia watched in stupefaction as her mother turned and nearly skipped back through the trees. She couldn't believe it. Her mother approved, and Rick Easton wasn't a nice, Chinese boy.

'Mooncakes?'

He was right behind her.

She shivered. He wasn't even a *nice* boy.

'It's a treat,' she said.

'I know that.' He pulled up her skirt and cupped her bare ass. She went right up on her toes when he squeezed. 'Chinese moons are my favourite.'

Tia felt her body warm. Maybe her mother was onto something after all. Leaning back, she rubbed against the hard bulge behind the zipper of his jeans. She got a grunt of approval for her efforts.

'Rick Easton,' she said, making a decision. 'My attention is all yours.'

Horseguards Parade
Jill Bannalec

It was the last Saturday in November. A mild, wet, dismal day, but one that Caroline had secretly looked forward to for months. She and her husband Gary had planned a day in London: he sightseeing, she joining the crowds of Christmas shoppers, but later meeting up for a meal before taking in a show and getting the last train home. She gazed out of the rain-streaked windows of the train, watching the familiar landscape flash past, and felt her pulse rate increasing as her thoughts travelled back to that hot summer's day when she spent an hour or so on Horseguards Parade . . .

Sightseeing in London had been all very well, but eventually all of the museums seemed the same, and each beautiful building began to look like the last. It was mid-afternoon and, although they had paused for lunch during Gary's relentless pursuit to visit the places listed on his rather ambitious itinerary, his wife's aching feet and tired legs were on the point of prompting a strike. It was hot, and she longed to sit down, slip her shoes off and relax. The next visit, to the Regimental Museum of The Household Cavalry, sounded less than interesting – flags and silverware in abundance. Soon they were being dragged around the dusty parade ground by an animated guide who was waving his rolled umbrella in the air whilst giving the same monotone presentation in four languages, under a baking sun.

Caroline felt beads of perspiration on her forehead, even though she was wearing a light cotton dress and little else. She decided that enough was enough, at least for the time being.

'I need the loo,' she whispered in her husband's ear. 'I'll catch you up later.' He nodded, keeping his eyes on the guide's skyward-pointing umbrella as he led his party off the parade ground and into one of the surrounding buildings.

Caroline looked around. She needed the cool of the shade and a sit down, albeit only on the loo. She thought she had seen a sign for the Ladies a few minutes before, and attempted to retrace her steps. Unfortunately, as she approached a large, granite, single-storey building, she realised she was completely lost and decided to ask someone for directions. She cautiously walked inside, the only door visible being slightly ajar, and was immediately enveloped in beautiful cool air, at the same time recognising the musky aroma found only in a stable.

The quietness and familiar smell of the horses and their tack was so welcoming after the noise and bustle of the last few hours and, hearing someone somewhere in the distance, she ventured further inside. She approached a stall and was greeted by the not unpleasant sight of a guardsman wearing only jodhpurs and shiny, knee-length boots that matched the colour of his horse – which stood impassively nearby as he cleaned out the stall.

The guardsman's muscular shoulders rippled as he forked the dirty straw into a wheelbarrow, perspiration trickling down the small of his back. He talked quietly to the horse as he worked. The animal's ears suddenly pricked up as it sensed Caroline's presence. The guardsman, noticing the reaction, stopped what he was doing and turned around.

'I'm sorry, love, but you shouldn't be in here,' he said kindly, but with authority, while at the same time running his eyes over her body. The short flimsy summer dress barely concealed her, and he did not attempt to hide his interest in what lay beneath.

Caroline felt her temperature rise again, and tried to conceal her own interest in the handsome half-naked man a few feet away. She felt undeniable desire tugging deep inside her, and knew that her return to the museum would be delayed. She answered him in a disappointed, but coy voice.

'I thought as much, but I love riding,' she lied, 'and, to be honest, the tour was a bit boring. What's he called?' she asked, nodding in the direction of the horse.

The guardsman relaxed and smiled. 'Sultan – six years old and on parade at six o'clock.'.

'He's a big boy for six,' said Caroline, forgetting that she was supposed to know a bit about horses.

The man smiled again. Had he seen through her façade? She tried to keep the conversation going as he worked, enjoying the opportunity to closely observe the guardsman's honed sweating body, his firm hand dragging a brush over the horse's glossy hindquarters.

'He seems to be enjoying that,' she observed, but at that moment tried to eat her words as she noticed, to her horror and embarrassment, the rapidly extending equipment of the stallion. The guardsman laughed, following the line of her eyes.

'I see what you mean. But it's not what you think. I'd step back if I were you!' His warning was too late, as a flood of steaming liquid descended onto the hard floor of the stall, splashing onto Caroline's legs. She cursed, but the guardsman laughed even louder as she danced away, her high heels clattering on the stone cobbles as she tried in vain to avoid the sudden spray.

'You OK?' he asked, showing at least some concern. She nodded, blushing furiously, her calm, sexy persona shattered. He smiled again, his eyes roaming up and down her glistening legs. 'You don't honestly believe it was me that got him going, do you? It must have been you!' Caroline, standing in a shaft of sunlight, began to see the funny side of it.

'Rubbish! It would have got me going,' she heard herself say.

'Oh?' he asked, with more than a trace of mischief in his voice.

Caroline's growing feeling of excitement was becoming evident to both of them, as was his. 'You may be right,' she said, her eyes resting on the prominent and growing bulge in his jodhpurs, 'or is that a spare brush?'

His cock was clearly outlined, nestling down the top of his left trouser leg.

'What do you think?' he said. 'Now come here and let me get you cleaned up. You'll smell like a polecat after a few minutes in the sun.'

He disappeared briefly, returning with a bowl of clean, warm water and some soap. He beckoned her into an adjoining stall, empty and clean, with fresh straw covering the floor. He knelt down. 'Take your shoes off,' he said. 'I'll rinse them first and they'll soon dry.' He crouched down in front of her.

Her dress was so thin that the curves of her thighs and the join of her legs were clearly visible when she was outlined against the sun, streaming as it was through the window.

He positioned her in just the right place, his face a few inches from her waist, and began to gently soap her legs.

She bit her lip as she felt his firm hands encircling her calves, gradually sliding further up her damp legs. She felt herself swaying slightly, and held onto his shoulders.

'I think that's got it,' he said, towelling her dry. She looked down at him, catching his upward glance.

'I, I don't think so,' she said, a half-smile forming on her face. He dipped the cloth back in the water.

'You're sure?'

She nodded.

This time his strokes were more purposeful. She parted her legs as he moved above her knees, feeling the ever-increasing sense of arousal as he got higher and higher, holding the hem of her dress as high as decency allowed, then higher still as his fingers brushed against her pants – which were damp long before the cloth touched them. He put it down, and the palms of his hands insistently pressed against the smooth skin of her inner thighs, while his thumbs slid across the damp, stained surface of her satin underwear.

Her heart was beating fast, and she could not prevent herself from suddenly pulling his face into her, relishing his hot breath on her thighs, and then his tongue against her pussy. His hands grasped her buttocks, pulling her further onto him; then he slowly stood up, fastening her with his gaze, and placed her open, eager hand against his waiting cock. Caroline's fingers curled tightly around the stretched cotton before sliding down the zipper to find, to her pleasant surprise, that he was not wearing underwear. She held his warm, hard length in her hand, her curious fingers spreading a trace of pre-cum around the tip of his penis.

He moved behind her, his fingers gently tracing a line along her bare shoulders until she felt his prominent cock pressing against the middle of her back, where it left a dark, moist trail on the floral print. His body moulded against hers and he whispered quietly, as he had a few moments before to his horse.

'Do you want to rejoin the tour?' he asked, a trace of irony to his voice. She felt herself shake her head, and breathed deeply as his broad arms encircled her waist beneath her dress and his fingers sought out her nipples. She wore no bra, and they had already begun to respond to his foreplay. He squeezed and teased them to even greater prominence as she leaned forward, resting her elbows on the hay-filled trough on the wall, eyes focused on the reins that dangled before her. He slid his jodhpurs around his boots, her panties down her thighs, and his cock into her waiting, lubricated sex, lifting her momentarily off the ground with his first accurate thrust. She gasped in pleasure and appreciation as he filled her, taking his hand and rubbing it across her soaking pussy, coaxing his fingers between her swelling lips.

His forefinger sought out her clitoris, and her moans of pleasure made the horse lean over his stall door to find the source of the noise. She pushed eagerly onto the guardsman's length, gasping with pleasure, thinking that Sultan's cock had a serious rival!

They came together, muttering profanities as they climaxed. Her brief pangs of guilt were quickly replaced by pangs of longing for more as she felt him slide out of her and hang stickily against her buttocks. They stood pressed together for a few moments as they got their breath back.

As Caroline attempted to clean herself up, she watched as her guardsman, casually pushing his cock back inside his jodhpurs, made no attempt to avert his eyes. They each knew, though, that it was time for her to go.

'You'd best catch the rest of them up,' he said. 'Turn right, across the parade ground, and go into the Tea

Room. They always end up there after a tour.' Caroline looked towards the door, then back to him, and nodded, as if reluctant to join the real world.

He took her hand to his lips, kissed it gently, smiled, then turned and walked away, disappearing into the depths of the building.

Gary was waiting for her, finishing off a scone, complaining that she had missed all of the best bits, and that it had been a complete waste of time going.

'On the contrary,' she said, leaving him puzzled. 'I think I got my money's worth.'

That was six months ago, and as the train slowed down on the approach to Euston, Caroline recalled how she had readily agreed to Gary's request to visit the Royal Nautical Museum at Greenwich, providing he went on his own whilst she did some pre-Christmas shopping. They were both looking forward to the show that evening in the West End, and Gary was both surprised and delighted that she had shown such enthusiasm for the day and evening.

She had even dressed for the occasion, in a low-cut, black chiffon blouse and charcoal-grey wraparound skirt, under which she wore a black basque and stockings. A minute thong and a pair of high sling-back heels completed her outfit. A stylish raincoat afforded the necessary protection from the elements. They parted on the concourse, a brief kiss as they went their separate ways.

Gary could not help glancing after his wife as she melted into the crowds. She had not dressed so provocatively, he thought, for some time.

Caroline was banking on the regular routine of the guards being repeated, and her arrival at the stables was, this time, no accident – being timed to coincide with a re-run of her arrival in May. As she walked across the almost deserted parade ground, the tingling between her legs – which had started when she had slid the snug black satin thong over her hips and had continued ever since – seemed to be reaching a crescendo, to be replaced by a more intense and yet more dissipated longing. Was her guardsman going to be here? She entered the stable-block, her ears straining for any sounds to indicate a human presence. She could hear someone speaking in the distance.

She took a few steps towards the source of the noise and found herself in familiar territory, with stalls stretching away on both sides of the long building, each bearing the name of their occupant on a highly polished brass plate. A large blackboard on the wall recorded the movements of each horse, and a wheelbarrow stood nearby as before, loaded with feed. Sparrows, nesting somewhere in the wooden eaves, swooped backwards and forwards helping themselves. She became more aware of the voice, coming from a stall a few yards away.

She approached, and peered around the door. She was just about to speak when she was confronted by a spectacle that stopped her in her tracks, and froze the words forming in her mouth.

Her guardsman was stood at the far end of the stall with his back to her. He was stripped to the waist and his hips swung backwards and forwards as he drove himself powerfully into a naked woman, almost hidden to Caroline. She was leaning forward, her long black hair touching the deep straw that covered the floor as she supported herself on the iron feeding trough fastened to the wall. A sheen of sweat covered his powerful back and Caroline, transfixed, felt unable to look or walk away, but feared her discovery at any moment. The guardsman varied his strokes: short, gentle, tantalising ones, followed by deeper, longer, rougher ones, as the woman spread her legs further and pushed back onto him. He grunted with the effort and satisfaction, whilst the woman groaned with pleasure. Both seemed oblivious to her presence.

Caroline could not deny the sense of arousal that she was continuing to feel, and her hand strayed inside her skirt, her fingers pushing past her suspenders, slipping inside her already damp panties, her waiting clitoris responding to her touch. She moved her knees apart, sliding one, then two fingers between her moistening lips. The woman mumbled something and, letting go of the stall, slowly dropped down onto all fours. Caroline noticed that she seemed oblivious to the fact that her hands and knees had disappeared into the straw and general mess on the stable floor, and she momentarily squirmed in disgust, but could not avert her eyes.

The woman was unconcerned, lost in her sexual frenzy, while the guardsman parted her creamy buttocks to watch his cock sliding in and out of her slippery cunt. Her full breasts swayed with the rhythm of their coupling, as Caroline glimpsed the thick bushy hair that covered her pussy. Her own aching, jealous sex, already soaking, longed to swap places with this girl.

She shifted position slightly to get a better look. Her fingers had by now become slick with her own juices, and she watched, hypnotised, as they approached a climax. The girl's hands clenched, and her head looked backwards between her legs as she milked his cock. At that moment, the woman realised she was being watched. The next few seconds seemed frozen in time. Without the woman saying a word, the guardsman spun around, his hard glistening cock flailing in the air as he saw Caroline, who began to run. In her panic, though, she went the wrong way.

Even as she ran, and heard the stall door hurriedly unlatched behind her, she knew it was hopeless. She had become a voyeur and expected and deserved to be admonished. He caught her arm, firmly grasping it in a powerful grip from which she could not pull free. She was dragged back to the stall vainly protesting her innocence – that she was a lost tourist needing assistance – but he had already recognised her, and was one step ahead in the game.

The girl, who had pulled her pants on, was in no mood for forgiveness, and regarded Caroline with contempt as she was led into the stall.

'Had a good look? Well, you're going to pay for it!' she spat coldly, standing, hands on hips, still flushed and breathing hard from her exertions. Caroline stood in front of them both, hands guiltily behind her back, fearing the worst, and studied her captors. The girl was in her mid-thirties, big-bottomed, full-breasted, and about five foot three. Her knees and hands were filthy, and she was wiping them clean with a handful of straw as she, in turn, looked at Caroline. The man made no obvious sign of remembering their previous encounter. His familiar muscular chest and powerful thighs endorsed his life as a guardsman. He suddenly moved forward, pulled Caroline into the stall, and pushed her roughly to the far end where the woman stood, her face filled with thunder. The contrast between them was fascinating, and he studied them for some time.

Next to the woman, in her bare feet, with long tousled hair, exposed, flushed breasts and filthy hands and knees, stood this tall new arrival, fully dressed, make-up and hair immaculate, amidst the squalor of the dirty stable. The woman watched him comparing them with growing anger.

'What do you want?' he suddenly asked.

'Nothing. I'm lost. I better be going,' stuttered Caroline, in a mixture of fear and disappointment.

'Oh, no, not so fast,' snarled the girl. 'You don't do what you just did and get away with it.' She glanced at the guardsman for support, then pushed Caroline hard in the midriff, leaving a vivid dirty handprint on the material. Caroline looked down horrified, her mind trying to come up with some plausible explanation to give to her husband. The guardsman sensed her dismay, and intervened. 'Ladies, let's all calm down. Chrissie, go and get cleaned up, then I'm sure we can work something out to our advantage.'

'Chrissie' left, still glaring at Caroline.

As soon as she had gone, the guardsman moved closer to Caroline, staring at her sheer blouse, and the lace-edged cups of the basque beneath. He leaned against her, inhaling her perfume, noticing her breathlessness. She moved into him and sighed as his hands delved under her coat and slid down her thighs.

'Are these for me?' he whispered, as his fingers lingered on her suspenders.

She nodded hopefully. His hand moved inside the slit of her skirt, moving upwards onto her thong.

'And these?' Again she nodded.

'Then this is for you.' He guided her hand to his cock, still hanging semi-erect against his jodhpurs, stained by his and Chrissie's juices. She felt immediately repulsed by the feel of another woman on it, and withdrew her sticky palm, feeling the cock stiffen as she did so. They could hear Chrissie returning, and he backed away from her, quickly telling her not to worry, but to enjoy the next few minutes. She relaxed slightly, still afraid, but intrigued and apprehensive about what he had said.

Chrissie walked back into the stall, looking at Caroline and the guardsman with revenge in her eyes. 'I think we should have a bit of fun, eh, Chrissie?' he suggested, as if to a pair of concubines. Chrissie nodded enthusiastically, sensing an opportunity to get even, while Caroline still harboured doubts. Chrissie smiled at Caroline's apparent discomfort, and regarded her disdainfully. She was still seething from being interrupted.

'Take your coat, skirt and blouse off,' she instructed, and Caroline, glancing anxiously at the guardsman for reassurance, slowly complied. She placed them over the stable door, then stood nervously, hands clasped over her breasts, waiting to see what would happen next. Chrissie and the guardsman studied her, clad now only in shoes, stockings and underwear. Caroline felt a pang of fear as he made it clear that he shared Chrissie's annoyance with the way they had been spied on.

She owed it to both of them to make amends. 'I think she should be punished for what happened,' he said loudly, so that Caroline would hear, and Chrissie readily agreed. He pressed Caroline back against the stall, and she felt the cool, hard concrete against her near-naked buttocks. He took her arms and held them above her head. Before she knew it, Chrissie was beside her, tying her arms to the latticework with some old reins. She smelt the fresh sex and sweat on the other woman's body as she stretched past her, noticing the look of triumph and unsatisfied arousal in Chrissie's eyes. She struggled briefly as soft but strong brown straps were tied firmly around her wrists, but the guardsman was too strong. She protested, threatening to yell the place down, but he calmly reached behind her and took a bridle off the wall and held it in front of her.

The message was clear enough, and her heart beat faster as she saw the shiny steel of the bit. He recognised the uncertainty in her eyes and put his finger against her lips, whilst stroking the front of her clearly damp panties with the leather straps, blackened and shiny with age. 'Perhaps next time?' he whispered. Caroline nodded, and she stopped struggling, feeling a powerful pulse of pleasure between her legs.

Once her wrists were secured, she realised that her feet were being grasped and pulled apart. She almost over-balanced and saw, in horror, that her ankles were now also bound by similar leather straps that had previously been concealed under the straw which covered the floor. Chrissie came around and surveyed their handiwork, running her fingers slowly along the inside of the lace cups of Caroline's basque, brushing the edges of her nipples, feeling them respond to her touch.

'Aren't you the horny one,' she said, taunting her, and smiling with satisfaction. 'You like watching,' she said, with more than a hint of venom in her voice, 'so watch.'

She resumed her position of a few minutes before, looking directly at Caroline's face, then at her dampening panties. The guardsman, already erect, as much from seeing Caroline and her predicament as the inviting view of Chrissie's rear end, pushed himself into her, her well-lubricated body welcoming him. Chrissie smiled up at Caroline as his cock slid home. He looked across at her, hands on Chrissie's buttocks. 'Is this what you want?' he said, sliding in long and hard.

'Jealous, are you?' asked Chrissie, her face contorted by the pleasure his cock was giving her. Caroline briefly looked away, but was drawn back to the scene before her, a prisoner even without the bounds that held her.

She was becoming more and more aroused and frustrated as she watched, having made such careful plans, dressed so provocatively, and had got so close, but was now so far away. She longed to allow her fingers to give her some satisfaction and she clenched her eyes to avoid the performance on the floor of the stall. Her ears told her, however, just what was happening, as the guardsman's cock slid rhythmically in Chrissie's over-lubricated pussy, slurping noisily as it did so. Chrissie turned the rack in this exquisite torture. 'I can feel his balls slapping against my arse,' she mocked, and 'my cunt is so well filled, so wet. The juices are running down my legs . . . in and out. What a fat, hard cock, and it's all for me.'

The guardsman's gaze seldom left Caroline, his eyes roving over her as she stood, bound hand and foot, a spectator to the show they were presenting. He noticed her erect nipples, her more rapid breathing and, most of all, her engorged sex lips, which were becoming more and more prominent under the damp satin panties. Caroline hoped that his body was shagging Chrissie, but his mind was shagging her. Then he suddenly stopped and withdrew.

'Time to move on, Chrissie,' he said, and she slowly straightened up, her body covered with a sheen of their sweat, and smiled in agreement.

They both looked towards Caroline, and Chrissie moved threateningly close. Her adversary looked so out of place in the stall; so clean, so vulnerable and, although she did not know it, so appealing to them both. Chrissie knelt down. 'Payback time,' she whispered threateningly, and removed Caroline's shoes. Caroline felt the hay prick her toes and briefly wondered if her stockings would survive the ordeal, then decided she didn't care.

Chrissie leaned against her, reaching behind her to unhook her basque. Caroline was acutely aware of the mixture of smells on her body – sweat, horses and sex. After her initial feeling of disgust, she began to find it forbidding, but increasingly attractive and arousing. Chrissie noticed her reaction to her aroma.

'Like it, do you?' she mocked. 'You'd better get used to it, 'cos you'll smell the same before you leave.' Caroline felt a new rush of arousal coursing towards her loins as the words sank in, and hoped it was not obvious. Her reaction did not go unnoticed by the guardsman, who watched her salmon-pink nipples as the basque fell away. Her breasts sprang free as Chrissie stepped back, smiling at her predicament.

'Sort them out,' ordered the guardsman, pointing at Caroline's last vestige of decency: her pants. Chrissie needed no second bidding, and could not resist dragging her fingers across the wet material, using her nails to trace a line along the prominent groove of her cunt. Caroline writhed with a mixture of pleasure and disgust, but felt her arousal increasing until Chrissie, fortunately unseen, produced a knife from somewhere behind and slit the sides of the thong. The damp weight of it slid it down her legs onto the floor. Chrissie picked the panties up, sniffing them approvingly, and handed the tiny warm piece of material to the watching guardsman. He inhaled their powerful aroma, used them to clean his cock, then threw them to the floor.

'I see you're ready,' he said. Caroline's nakedness was complete, and her moist cunt, matted pubic hair, and erect nipples proclaimed her intense state of arousal.

'Now, miss,' he continued, 'you're going to get what you like, though not perhaps as you would choose. But beggars can't be choosers, can they, and I do believe you would beg for it if pushed?' She stood helplessly, wondering what to expect, her juices beginning to ooze beyond her pubic hair onto the inside of her thighs.

She closed her eyes and the warmth and sounds and smells of the stables filled her senses. It reminded her, and always would, of the sex she had experienced here before, and this time its familiarity promised something even more intense. In her mind's eye she pictured herself in Chrissie's position – naked, on all fours, being taken from behind. She again felt the urgent need to touch and stroke herself as she hoped he would soon be doing, and tried, half-heartedly, to pull her hands from the leather straps. Her frustration was obvious to her audience.

Ten miles away, as the crows in the Tower of London might fly if they ever felt so inclined, Gary had come to the conclusion that, whilst the Cutty Sark was interesting, he could not get the image of his wife in her stockings and basque out of his mind. He casually watched the attractive assistant who had just taken his money, and considered what underwear she might be wearing, gradually forgetting his wife as his mind delved further into the shapely brunette's potential wardrobe; his cock responded to his guiltless imagination. He fixed her semi-naked image in his mind's eye and, cock hard against his fly, pictured her bent over the counter being screwed by him. Then his mind cleared, and his thoughts returned to Caroline, lost in the throng of people, hopefully satisfying her endless appetite for shopping.

Meanwhile, a vengeful Chrissie had turned and crouched down, her wet sex deliberately positioned in Caroline's line of vision, and taken the guardsman in her mouth, sucking greedily and noisily, her hands cupping the bulging velvet sac of his balls. Caroline's torment and torture continued.

Chrissie gave his cock one final lick, from the tip to the base, then stopped and watched as he reached down and took some brushes from a bag on the floor. He smiled a threatening smile at Caroline. Taking a stiff bristle brush, he leaned forward, his cock still standing, wet and angry, and dragged the brush slowly down the inside of Caroline's thigh, applying gentle pressure at first, until she got used to the sensation. He then repeated the process, this time more firmly. The brush left a trail of tiny pink lines behind it, which slowly faded. It felt exquisite, like a thousand tiny nails being drawn over her skin. He reached behind her, pulling her away from the wall so that she had to bend her knees, and drew it down her back and over her buttocks, where he pressed more firmly. He took another, softer brush in his other hand, and worked them alternately across her skin, as if grooming his stallion. She bit her lip and enjoyed the sensual feeling of the brushes passing over her nipples and between her thighs. He continued for several minutes until she squirmed for more. Chrissie watched appreciatively with one leg raised onto an upturned bucket, her hand working expertly between her legs.

Caroline felt herself getting hotter. Her juices were flowing freely, leaving a silvery trail down the inside of her thighs and onto her stockings. Her pussy ached with desire and she longed for something, anything, to satisfy it. Help came from an unexpected source. Chrissie moved forward on all fours and Caroline watched with trepidation as she came closer and closer, until her face was inches away from her pubic bush. Then Chrissie dived between her legs and her tongue went to work. The feeling was unlike anything Caroline had experienced.

As the tongue flicked at her clit, Caroline thought that only a woman could really know how to do what Chrissie was doing. Her hips pushed against Chrissie's face, helping her tongue to reach further into her.

The guardsman, unknown to Caroline, released one of her ankles and a hand, but Caroline's mind was elsewhere. He then retied the straps. She did not object, until she sensed him behind her, and, turning her head, saw the riding crop. She gasped, and shouted in a fashion that was less than convincing to his experienced ears.

'No, no, not that – take it away, no!'

'You don't trust me?' he asked. 'But you did interrupt us.'

He moved behind her, glancing at the approving Chrissie, and lightly tapped her buttocks with the soft leather tassel at the end of the crop. Caroline flinched, attempting to pull her hands from the straps, and clenched her cheeks in anticipation of a firmer stroke. When it came, it did not hurt but was rather like the sensation in her hands when she was clapping. To her relief and surprise, she found it not unpleasant, and offered her buttocks for more. He expertly increased the speed, the frequency and the pressure until red weals were clearly visible across her backside. The sensation was again unlike anything she had ever felt. Her excitement was intense even though neither her breasts nor her sex were being touched. Some other, deeper desire was taking over, and her loss of control was puzzling but intoxicatingly enjoyable.

Chrissie looked on, slowly masturbating, getting some satisfaction from the beating being inflicted on her rival. Had she known how much Caroline was secretly enjoying it, she would have been less than pleased.

Presently, the guardsman stopped as trickles of moisture ran down Caroline's back, disappearing between her buttocks. She felt aroused to the point of orgasm yet still had an enormous appetite for his body which was, as yet, completely unfulfilled. She would not have to wait long, as the guardsman was of a similar mind. He untied all of the straps and she relaxed, her body glistening with sweat. But she wasn't ready for what happened next.

'Sort her out!' he shouted to Chrissie, who came forward and roughly pushed Caroline into the centre of the stall.

'Get down on all fours,' ordered Chrissie. She could not dissent. The animal environment was converting her, temporarily, into one herself. Her knees sank an inch or so into the hay and her hands likewise. The smell which lingered on Chrissie filled her nostrils – sweet, pungent, erotically charged. Her rear end pointed towards the guardsman, creamy white, though bearing the marks of her whipping, invitingly displaying her pussy framed in a mass of wet curls. Now it was Chrissie's turn to watch. Caroline felt his length probing for entry.

Caroline stared forwards into the stall at Chrissie's cruel but jealous eyes. She moaned softly as he finally slid into her, filling her sex that had waited so long for him and, just as she had seen Chrissie do, involuntarily grasped a handful of the hay as his cock moved deep within her. She was overcome by the situation, by her enjoyment, and her arousal had reached the point of no return.

He groaned with pleasure, speeding up the thrusts until he could hold back no more. His come flowed into her, his hips jerking spasmodically to force it home, and she felt her pussy contract in response. She responded in kind, and she jerked and flinched as her body acknowledged the pleasures that had been showered upon it. For several seconds they stayed still, getting their breath back on the stable floor, then he slid his hands along her flanks, stroking her temples gently, whispering reassurances, for her ears only. 'Thank you, my beauty. Thank you, but now you must go.' She nodded in agreement as he stood up, and she felt his lovely cock slide out of her for the last time. His tone changed abruptly.

'I hope that that has taught you a lesson,' he said.

'Yes,' said Chrissie. 'He's mine, and right now you'd better get back up the M1!'

Caroline's breathlessness prevented any words of reply, and instead she slowly stood upright, her pussy throbbing with pleasure. Her hands and legs were filthy, her stockings ruined, and her pants destroyed.

She stumbled past Chrissie with a struggle, since her legs were still wobbly. She pulled on her remaining clothes, put her shoes on, hands shaking, and wrapped her coat tightly around her. She felt glowing, triumphant. She had got what she had come for and more, far more besides, but she continued to put on an act to protect her guardsman. As she staggered out she said that she had never felt so humiliated, insulted, embarrassed, or so used – but muttered to herself as she walked out into the daylight, 'More's the pity'.

She hoped that any bruises would disappear quickly, and was grateful for an opportunity to wash and change and buy some new stockings and knickers – as close a match to her old ones as possible – at Euston station. She re-applied her make-up and liberally doused herself with perfume.

When Gary returned she looked reasonable again but had a tender backside and a seriously sensitive pussy. He was pleased that, despite the opportunity, she had spent, apparently, nothing. 'We'll have to come back another time,' he said, 'and give you a bit longer.'

Caroline smiled. 'OK,' she said, 'but I've been thinking. I know it's a bit out of the blue, but do you fancy going riding sometime?'

Gary's reply was fuelled by unfulfilled fantasies of his own, which he had never dared mention to his unsuspecting wife. 'Well, yes, all right. I'll make enquiries. I can't imagine you on a horse, though,' he lied, feeling his cock stir at the thought of his wife wearing jodhpurs astride some great beast.

Later, at the show, he was aware of an aroma that he could not quite put his finger on. He came to the conclusion that someone, not very far away in the audience, had, by a strange coincidence, been riding, possibly on Horseguards Parade.

Caroline struggled to watch the show, but her thoughts were elsewhere as she imagined how she might initiate her husband to similar in pleasures on home ground.

Sightseeing in India
Saskia Walker

A bead of sweat tickled a dusty smudge across my breastbone. I smiled down at it, self-indulgently. I didn't care; I was about to have the most longed-for bath on the planet. Four weeks of all the dust and grime that Nepal and India could possibly imprint upon my body was about to be gone, into blissful lukewarm water: I couldn't wait.

I turned to eye the bath tub. It was big, yes, but with the most pathetic-looking shower head forlornly drooping over it. Even that was a major symbol of luxury after the fortnight I'd just spent roughing it in the Vindhya Mountains. How I'd longed to get back to the junction town of Nagpur, which represented the height of civilisation, when confronted by yet another week of self-enforced suffering with insipid and/or sadistic guides, red dust, heat, insects, rumours of civil unrest and, more importantly, no bath!

I shivered slightly as the lukewarm water embraced my hot dry skin, and then slid deep into the depths of the tub. Ah, such luxury! It was going to be hard to climb out of this precious haven of moisture into the stifling air once again.

I lay watching the motes of dust floating on the hazy sunshine that fell from the high window. The dry season was at its driest; the monsoon would be on its way in a matter of weeks but, at that moment, I was immersed in complete bliss. Oh, how I was enjoying that bath. It was like having the most delicious meal after two months on a bread-and-water diet. It was like having sex, after ... after having none, in ages. Yes, I mused, sex. Sex after ... God, how long was it? Too long!

My fingers were already rippling the water in and around my pubes; I latched one leg over the edge of the bath, then the other. At home I have a big mirror leaning down from the ceiling at the end of the bath so I can have a long languorous session of self-indulgence. I watch myself seeking out every morsel of pleasure whilst imagining some poor slave-lover kneeling in front of me, hands bound behind him, unable to even get a touch of the cunt he is quite obviously desperate for. However, I wasn't at home, so I let my eyes close and my mind began to wander along with my fingers.

The train from Bombay had traversed a long flat plain where the earth met the sky in a dramatic sweep that filled my vision. The rocking motion had set me on edge. I pressed my thighs together, my sex flesh crushed and constantly moving with the rhythm of the train. My body had ached for release then, just as it ached now. Somewhere amidst the chatter emanating from further down the train a woman's voice had flown up in song and the sound of finger cymbals danced towards me, softly entwined with the scents so distinct to the East: sandalwood, tamarind, coriander. The exotic. Something in me was ready to be reckless in unknown territory.

There's a place where my hand fits, moulded over and under my pubic bone. On the train I had put my back-pack on my lap, hiding the movement of my hand as it went under my long shirt and into my combat trousers. With the flesh of my sexlips spread wide and my clit pushing up between two fingers, the tips of my fingers curled into the sensitive ring of my cunt. This is the gateway to the sex goddess, to her pleasure-trove. Every stroke and rub of my hand lets free a thief who is hunting for pleasure; who slinks through the gateway and then pulls back with his reward. As the thieves come thicker and faster, so my sex awakens and the goddess rises up, chases after them and devours them for her own ultimate pleasure. On the train she had to be surreptitious, absorbing the pleasures without drawing too much attention to herself. Today she was up in a flash and devoured them quickly. Quickly, and rather noisily.

The tap dripped. I sighed; my flesh trembled slightly. After a few minutes I climbed out of the bath. This has always been my favourite place for masturbating and I was amused and yet annoyed with myself; I was supposed to be living hard and alone, traversing India from north to south, proving the strength of my inner character and that I could do without all sorts of luxuries. Including baths, and sex.

'Humph.' The mutter echoed round the gaunt room.

I picked up the worn, ropey towel I had been issued with on entry to the hostel in exchange for my passport. Checking in had been far too reminiscent of the opening scene of a prison documentary, but I'd been willing to sell my passport and my soul by then for the chance of a proper bed and a bath. The bed was thin and hard. The towel was threadbare and rough.

'For fuck's sake,' I muttered, stomping away from the tub. Sometimes a wank was far from enough to quell the need for action; in fact, sometimes it had quite the opposite effect. My sex was now nagging most insistently for something hard inside it.

I tied the towel around my chest and stalked determinedly to the bathroom door, wishing for a keen and able man to appear – as if by magic – and tugged the door open. At that I heard a great cracking sound that suggested the door was about to fall off its hinges. No sign of a man though. I smiled wryly to myself and glanced down the corridor, poised to cover the twenty-odd feet to my room as quickly as possible. I set off, but was brought to a standstill after but two paces by another loud cracking sound. I realised it hadn't been the door at all – the sound had come from the stairwell, or beyond. A sudden tirade of raised voices and running footsteps confirmed that all was not well in the Madhya Pradeshi Travellers' Hostel. It began to dawn on me what the sound was: a gunshot? Was it? Yes, it was a gunshot! Panic set in, in a heartbeat.

The skin on my back prickled with alarm. The footsteps were running in my direction. I glanced around, looking for cover. My options were limited. My room was just at the top of the stairwell. There was no way I could get to it before whoever was pounding up the stairs right now appeared right around that corner. There was a pair of louvered doors to my left, and one was slightly ajar. I had an image of opening it to find a blank wall. Another gunshot and a woman's voice screaming a string of what sounded like Hindi curses suddenly made the louvered door look like the best option.

I grabbed the door, twisted my body inside what appeared to be a gloomy store cupboard, and pulled it closed behind me, very nearly smashing my fingers in the process. Slats of light from the corridor helped my eyes get accustomed to the gloom; a stack of laundry stood slightly to my left. I leaned into it, and huddled for safety. My heart was thudding mightily. I shut my eyes, praying to a god I didn't even believe in. When I heard the door creaking open I peeked and pulled it shut, with a fingernail hooked over a slat. I snatched my finger away as a shadow passed outside the doorway. The figure moved past; I breathed again, giving a sigh of relief. It was then that I was suddenly grabbed from behind.

It happened so quickly I was barely able to gasp a breath before a hand fell over my mouth, and another arm grabbed me and hauled me back against a large body. A large male body. I kicked back and jagged my elbows but the man had a mighty grip, his arms hauling me back against his rib cage, almost completely winding me. I was locked in against him.

My arms went limp; all my self-defence training flashed before my eyes, but I was hardly in a position to kick him in the balls. If he loosened his grip on me I could maybe twist enough to get free and wind him back – but what then? Was what was outside the door worse, or were they in it together with my assailant? In what together? I was very confused and hot, and barely able to breathe. My mouth opened against his hand; I tasted his salt on my tongue, together with a hint of mint, and the warmth of cumin.

'Stay quiet,' he hissed against my ear. 'Your life might depend on it.' What was that supposed to be – a threat, or a warning? I wondered. I rested back against him, though. It seemed the simplest and safest option, if you could call it an option. He gradually loosened his grip on my mouth so I could at least breathe a bit easier. He held onto my body tight, still, moulding against me. I noticed how I fitted almost perfectly against him; he was about two inches taller than I was. I shifted my arm to get more comfortable and he also moved, blowing some of my hair; it flew out from my face. His breath was warm and caressing against the side of my neck. He gave a quiet groan and it was then that I felt it: his cock, stirring against my buttocks.

My blood hit boiling point in a flash. A mixture of

fear, outrage and something I couldn't quite admit to myself at that point raced through me: sheer, rampant lust. I reacted out of instinct, bit against his hand and twisted away to face him, my elbow winding him as he loosened his hold in reaction to the teeth I sank into his palm.

'Wait,' he whispered, his body doubled over, one hand held up as if to signify peace.

He regained his footing and stood up in front of me, his towel shimmying down from his waist to his feet. He had both his hands held up now. It was then that I realised to my surprise that he must be a guest at the hostel, like myself, and he'd obviously taken shelter in the store room, just as I had. He was a well-built bleach-blond hunk with startling green eyes and a devilish goatee beard; a prime piece of best beef, by the looks of him, and with the most impressive erection I had seen since I'd left my cushy London gym for the wilds of Nepal.

I realised I was staring and looked back up at his face. He suddenly broke into a smile, lifted his shoulders in a slight shrug, and eyed me back, up and down. It was then that I realised my towel had also dropped to the floor in the sudden scuffle.

'Oh, shit,' I muttered and bent to rescue the towel. As I did, the man suddenly grabbed my arm and pushed me back into the furthest recess of the cupboards with the bulk of his body, careering us both into a teetering stack of sheets and towels. He put his fingers against my mouth, more gently this time, and nodded towards the corridor. I couldn't hear anything, but then . . . yes. Someone was moving back along the corridor, very quietly, whispering along the walls. What were they searching for, or whom? I clung to the shoulders of my fellow traveller; I suddenly felt like he was my life raft, my saviour. How quickly the tables can turn, I taunted myself, wryly.

His jaw was about level with my forehead. I was pressed wholly against him and leaning back slightly to look up at him. My position pivoted my hips forward as a result of being pressed onto the mound of towels stacked on the ledge behind me. A whispered conversation filtered down the corridor to us. It was calmer than before; a discussion. He held my eyes with his, looking at me intimately and reassuringly as we strained to hear. It wasn't the only thing straining. My nipples rubbed hard against his chest, and his cock had now embedded itself upright against my abdomen. God, that felt so, so good.

'Sorry,' he mouthed, glancing down to where our hips melded together, as if suddenly embarrassed by the waywardness of his manhood. But I was starting to enjoy that particular aspect of the situation far too much. My sex had already begun to cloy; I could smell the scent of my own desire mounting alongside his. The space we were enclosed in was a riot of pheromones. My hands slid down his back to trace the firm outline of his buttocks. He arched one eyebrow at me, amusement tingeing his expression, then he suddenly glanced away as the conversation started up in the corridor again, this time louder.

'I think it's OK, we're safe.' He had leaned down and whispered against my ear. I didn't know what startled me most: that he understood Hindi, or his Australian accent. I was still trying to make sense of the conundrum – which was difficult enough, while also managing my residual fear and an extreme case of arousal in his physical presence – when he broke into another very endearing grin. 'I thought it was regional troubles and

it's a marital breakdown.' He started chuckling to himself, trying unsuccessfully to hold it inside.

'What?' I replied, incredulous. I had also assumed we
were about to be thrust into the civil unrest I had heard
so much about in the past couple of weeks.

He nodded. 'The husband has been here before to
meet with his concubine, and the wife has hunted him
down with a pistol that she stole from her brother-in-
law. She's demanding to know where the other woman
is, and he's more worried about where she got hold of a
pistol, and her eyesight.' He put his hand over his mouth,
quelling another chuckle. 'Apparently he thinks she
wouldn't be able to see straight to shoot and he's pointed
out that she has already shot out two of the lights on
the stairs, so he's worried about how much he will owe
the landlord.'

His whole body was starting to shudder with amusement. So, we were merely bystanders in a crime of
passion. I suddenly realised how ridiculous the situation
was. There I was, relieved. I was relieved to be trapped
in a cupboard in the arms of a naked and very aroused
man – a man that I had never met in my life before –
simply because it was only a half-blind woman shooting
up the place out there. Fine. We were all completely safe,
then! His eyes were warm on me, he was still smiling,
and he smoothed my upper arms with broad warm palm
strokes. I began to chuckle too.

He didn't seem in any rush to move and, instead,
pressed forward again, giving me an inquisitive nudge
of the cock that had been nestled against me for so long.

'I do apologise,' he said, again, with more than a quirk
of amusement in his expression.

'Well, at least one of us was armed,' I replied and
pushed him to arms' length, looking down at the fine

piece of weaponry that rested against my thigh. It wasn't quite the sort of sight I expected to be enjoying in India, but it was a nice surprise. He chuckled, then I heard his intake of breath and saw that he was looking down at my tell-tale nipples, my breasts bouncing free when our bodies moved apart for the first time in some several minutes.

He glanced up at me and his hand closed over one breast; he watched me for my reaction. I pushed up against his hand, showing him my willingness and consent. He began to stir his palm over my nipple.

'I couldn't help it. I was holding a red-hot piece of ass in my arms.'

I smiled at his directness; it wasn't something I was used to, but I quickly decided I could get used to it. He bent to kiss my shoulder, his mouth breathing the promise of intimacy over my skin, across shoulders and neck, until I turned my mouth into his.

His kiss was strong and suggested a deep sensuality, his tongue teasing along the inner side of my lower lip in a way that sent shivers down my back. When I moved in his arms he moved his mouth to my nipple, sucking and teasing it erect again. I could hear the audible purr in my own breathing. Voices flared up in the corridor and he chuckled, his mouth moving from my nipple.

'What now?' I asked, rather annoyed.

He looked up at me; he was truly gorgeous, especially when he was smiling that way. 'It's the landlord, demanding his money.'

I laughed. 'How dare they interrupt!' I grabbed his hand, leading it to the heat between my thighs.

'Indeed,' he replied, slipping one finger inside me to test my wetness. I groaned and then he pushed me up against the shelves again. I balanced my hips on the narrow ledge behind me and clutched at him, one leg climbing against him, inviting him close against me again. He looked down at my open legs and touched his hand against my moistness, stroking my sex, then took his fingers to his mouth and slowly licked the juice off them. I was so surprised at his complete blatantness, and then he shocked me even more.

'Oh, woman, I want to eat you, now,' he said, groaning, and pushed my legs wider apart.

'Oh, yes . . . please,' I mumbled, in a mix of raging lust and confused embarrassment. Was I dreaming this out of sheer hornyness? But, no, he knelt down, right there in front of me, and nestled his face in against my hot cunt. Oh, God! His words and actions flushed yet more heat and moisture inside me. I could hear the need in my own breathing.

He stroked the folds of my sex with his tongue in long firm movements, and then he let his teeth close over the mound of my sex, pulling at my flesh. He slid up and down then paused with my clitoris sucked hard into his mouth, and attacked it with the quick flicking movements of his tongue. In a flash I was gone on it, and arched over his shoulders; my body lifting up away from the intense pleasure laced with the hint of sweet pain.

He pushed his fingers deep inside, opening me to his tongue, and licked at me inside my cunt, his whole face moving against me, his free hand running over my thigh in quick strokes. He was pumping me fast, bringing me to fever pitch. My throat ached, my whole body burned; my orgasm was blistering just beneath the surface. He curled two long, strong fingers inside me, his knuckles nudging at a spot that wired the rest of my body into its intensity. I gripped his shoulders and, as the first bolt of pleasure hit me, I heard myself let out a muted scream. He flexed his fingers out again, and the effect was dynamite. That was it: both my legs were over his shoulders and I was grinding onto his face; grinding every second of exquisite release. I bit my lip to silence myself, and he pulled free and rose up.

'Oh, my, you are noisy. Noisy *and* hot ... my favourite kind.' He gave me a wink and a positively sinful smile, and then glanced at the doors, but all seemed quiet outside. He grabbed my hair around the back of my head with one hand, drew my mouth to his, and lunged into me with his tongue. With his other hand he offered me his erection and I closed my hand over the hot, rock-hard surface. The taste of my own pleasure on his skin stirred me up even more. I couldn't believe this was happening; I was fucking around with a complete stranger in a cupboard. I felt totally wild. As he moved nearer, slowly thrusting his cock into my hand, I pulled away and leaned back against the wall to look down at his equipment. I was captured by its shape, its vitality reaching out through the space between us. It looked so powerful. I felt weak and hot, my body still running rivers of heat in my orgasm.

'I want to see it spurt,' I breathed, as I looked down at the column of energy resting in his hand. He groaned and rested against the wall to steady himself. I let my feet move wider, spreading my hips open, leaning back. My hand went to my wet cunt, my fingers sliding inside, bringing me back to bliss with quick sharp strokes.

'Make yourself come. I want to watch you do it.' I managed to pant the words out. I felt wild. I had never ordered a man to wank in front of me, but I suddenly realised I had always wanted to do just that very thing. He watched my fingers pushing in and around the moist folds of my sex, my clit jutting between the length of two of my fingers, just the way I like it. His eyes were burning me up as he watched me stroking myself and I totally loved it. His hand closed over his erection again and he began to move on it. I moved my free hand over his, sliding up and down his shaft with regular movements, my other hand echoing the rhythm on my sex.

'You are so hard,' I whispered. He leaned into me, his mouth against my head. His cock glistened wet and fierce. He was fit to burst; I could feel his teeth on my hair. He wanted to be inside me; every atom of his body told me that. I wanted him inside too, but all in good time. I let go of his shaft and pushed him gently back.

'I want to see. Let me see it,' I demanded. He moaned quietly and his hand moved faster. He reached down and locked my hand over my splayed sex. I could feel the reluctant control in his touch.

'God, woman, you know how to drive a man insane,' he muttered. I gave a gentle chuckle at the strangeness of his Australian accent and then let my eyes take in the look of the fierce pulsing head of his cock. It was so swollen; the sheen of it glistened in the gloomy heat of the cupboard. His fist rode it faster, his body arched before me to fulfil my request. I glanced up, and he was looking at my face. His eyes were like hot coals, burning with lust as I watched him. His eyebrows were drawn close together, concentration holding them. I could see how much he wanted me. That was quite, quite delicious. My mouth opened, and I enjoyed the feeling of my fingers still moving inside my sex. My eyes were locked to his, but the pressure was building in my clit again.

'I thought you wanted to see it,' he said quietly, his voice dropping to a low growl. His mouth opened and his hand moved faster still, then it slowed to a complete stop. I looked down and saw the upward surge of the flesh in his hand. As it pumped and spurted the jets of come flew across my inner thighs and up across my stomach. I gave a small cry at the sight of it and then he fell against the wall, closing over my body. His cock still moved slightly as it rested against my thigh. My fingers knotted and twisted on my clit, pushing against the folds of my sex. That did it: I spasmed again. I was totally drenched.

'I'm Oliver,' he panted, against my ear. 'How do you do?'

I began to chuckle and let my legs close around his hips.

'I'm Natalie, and I'm very well, thank you, Oliver,' I replied. 'And you?'

'Marvellous . . . but I'll be even better when I have got you on your back . . . on my bed.'

I smiled and purred my consent to him and he lifted me gently from my perch, wrapping my towel around me in the most gentlemanly manner. I loved his directness; I loved it right from the moment I had felt it pressed up against my behind. He asked me if I was ready to make the quick dash to his room. Too right, I was.

We spent a week in that hostel, venturing little further than the market for food and supplies. It's not quite what I had expected from my time sightseeing in the East, but I certainly wasn't about to complain. It was hot; very hot – the weather, and the sex. Particularly the sex. The next time I go travelling I plan to go sightseeing down under in Australia where, I am led to believe, it can sometimes get even hotter.

Spiced Coffee
Fransiska Sherwood

He wasn't coming till three o'clock, but all morning I'd been arranging and rearranging my studio. Not that there's really much to arrange for a few black and white photos. One or two shots – his biceps, his chest, his bum – that's all he wanted.

It's not the sort of thing I normally do. And I told him so when he rang. Fruit and vegetables are more my line, shining with pearls of moisture and oozing juice, for cookery magazines and recipe books. Art you can eat – as pioneered back in the 1980s by that icon of advertising photography, Reinhart Wolf. Not male models. Naked.

I wander into the kitchenette and put the coffee on. It's so hot today, an iced coffee would be more appropriate. Really, I could do with a shot of something alcoholic to calm me down. I wipe back a few tendrils of hair that are sticking to my forehead while the water chugs through the machine. The smell of roasted coffee starts to pervade the studio, filling it with its steamy vapour. I undo a couple of buttons on my floppy black linen dress and fan my cleavage with a printing prospectus. Sometimes I envy girls with pert little breasts.

A knock at the door makes me jump.

Who can that be? Nobody usually calls at this time in the afternoon. Must be the blond guy from parcel deliveries with those stills. I've been expecting him for days.

I slip my glasses into my pocket and open up. Standing before me is a tall boy with cropped black hair and skin the colour of sepia prints.

'Sorry I'm early. I've got to do some deliveries for my uncle later. Is it OK?'

It takes me a few seconds to realise he's my model.

'Sure, sure. Yeah. Come in.'

'Khalid.'

I look into a smile full of teeth, a white crescent in his face. 'Corinna,' I stammer back when I realise that was his name.

Oh, God, I wasn't expecting a prince from distant lands. And he can't be above seventeen.

'How do you want me?'

I swallow, the lump in my throat as tight as the knot in my stomach. Talk about getting straight down to business!

So, how do I want him? My brain goes into overdrive. I can't put him against the dark background. Should I use an extra flash – or will it make shiny patches on him? Am I going to use the large-format Hasselblad – a must for advertising quality? Or my 35mm Leica? I'm sure he's expecting more than a few snapshots. Yes, the Hasselblad – then he can blow the pictures up poster-size and they'll still be so sharp you could cut yourself on his contours. Did I load the film?

I lead him to the couch, desperately trying to regain my composure. 'You can get undressed behind the screen. I thought I'd have you up against the white backdrop.'

He flashes me that fluorescent smile again, and his eyes sparkle with amusement.

God, this is going to be a disaster. I don't know what I'm saying. Don't know what I'm doing. I wish he weren't so good-looking; such a gorgeous fudge-brown colour. It just makes it even more difficult.

Hey, wait a minute. Should I be doing this at all? Don't I need permission from his parents? But if he's doing the deliveries, he must have a driving licence. So he's got to be at least eighteen. Unless he's doing them by bicycle.

There's a queasy feeling in my stomach. And a furrow in my brow that probably ages me by another ten years. Why didn't I say no? I should never have let him persuade me. Just a few artistic poses, nothing dirty, for his portfolio, is what he'd said. I suppose it was the 'artistic' that did it; awakened a lust for something other than aubergines and courgettes. I had visions of doing for the male form what Michael Boys once did for the female form: the objectified body as a work of art, enhanced by the tricks of lighting and steeped in atmosphere. Aesthetic perfection.

I leave him to get undressed and I faff about with some lenses. The Zeiss 120mm, or the 150mm? Or the 180mm, even? I've no idea what I'm playing at. How ever am I going to be able to focus?

He comes out from behind the screen dressed in white underpants that show off his bronzed skin. A little shudder of excitement runs through me and I stare, open-mouthed.

'OK like this? Or should I take them off?' he asks. He lets the elastic waistband snap back against his stomach and I read the name Calvin Klein running through it.

'No, no. They're fine. You're fine as you are.'

Stupid woman, get a grip on yourself!

But a hot wave of anticipation surges through me at the thought of one or two close-ups. That's when I'm going to need the razor-sharp 120mm lens.

Just a few artistic poses? Wow! For all my college antics, and the odd encounter since, I've never seen a body so full of Eastern promise. I'd been conned into thinking he was just a boy. That's the look, isn't it? Today they're all smooth-chested, naughty-boy baby-faced models. But his physique and the bulging package in his Y-fronts tell a different story. So why am I even more nervous about doing this than before?

I try to make conversation, dispel the tension, like you're supposed to when doing portraits. In that respect vegetables are easier. 'You've been putting time in at the gym, haven't you?' I ask.

'No. Humping boxes around.'

I run an appreciative eye over his contours. 'Very nice.' I clear my throat. 'I mean a nice chest ... and biceps, side shot to begin with, I think,' I say, stumbling over the words that were meant to sound so businesslike and professional.

We go over to the chair I've set up against the white backdrop. In the glare of the lights his skin turns golden.

'Just say what you want me to do.'

I nod. I would if I could think straight.

I remove the lens cap, get the camera to my eye, and start walking round him, lining up potential frames. That's the problem with the Hasselblad – you've got to know what you're doing. Take your time. Set everything up properly. It's no good just clicking away madly.

Christ, I can't see a damn thing. What am I playing at? He's not interested in me. He's probably gay. All good-looking male models are, aren't they? I take my glasses out of my pocket and pop them on. Right, concentrate!

Yes, this is going to be a good session – the way his skin reflects the light, its burnished-gold texture, the curves of his muscles, the firmness of his body.

Once my brain has registered the first click, I seem to switch over into professional photographer mode. Suddenly I find myself telling him the poses I want. It now just seems to fall into place. I vary the angles, juggle with lenses. Come in close, take the odd long shot. And he does everything right. Patient and relaxed. But how could anything go wrong? He was made to be captured on film.

His arms ripple with muscle, like a wrestler's or ironsmith's – his biceps encapsulated powerhouses. His torso is sleek and lean and his chest smooth, with nipples that stand out proud: tiny dark-brown peaks in an expanse of burnt sienna. I have to stop myself from reaching out and touching him, testing the tautness of his flesh, running my tongue over the hard points.

'Were there any other shots you wanted?'

I've exploited every inch of his chest and arms, neck and shoulders.

His grin is long and slow.

My heart lurches. Normally the only feasts I get to see are of the culinary kind.

'I'll take some shots of your bottom, then,' I say, and see my face turn pomegranate-coloured in the mirror.

He goes to the couch and slips out of his underpants. I put a new roll of film in the camera. When I next look up he's standing before me, his penis lying softly on a bed of chocolate-brown curls.

I fetch the tripod. No way am I going to be able to keep the camera still now. I adjust the length of the legs, then fit the camera in place. I crouch and undo the buttons to the skirt of my dress, so that I can straddle the cumbersome object as I move round him. The cold metal stings the soft flesh of my inner thigh, sending a frisson right through me.

I home in on his dimpled buttocks. Rounds of solid

muscle. Neat and tight. Cheeks that catch the light like the polished surface of a gong, the skin smooth and of a lighter beige than the rest of him. Towards his anus it becomes coarser and bristled. I zoom in, study the prickly little hairs where he sits. How I'd love to run my finger over them. Feel their delicious tickle.

'I'll have you lying down now. Over there on the couch,' I say, and reap another of his shimmering smiles. Why can't I talk sense? I'm sure Annie Leibovitz doesn't make such a fool of herself in front of her subjects. But then, beardless youths do more for me than bearded ladies.

He picks up his pile of clothes and dumps them on the chair. I drape a white sheet over the garish, zig-zag covers of the couch. Don't want any distractions in the picture. This motif speaks for itself. I bring over the reflectors and lighting, bathing him in a pool of gold as he reclines majestically like some oriental deity. There must be temple sculptures that look just like him hidden deep within the jungle somewhere. Temples dedicated to the goddess of love, with scantily clad male servants to guard her shrine and practise her rites. Visions of frenetic orgies flick through my mind and, absurdly, the goddess is a white, full-bosomed red-head.

'Can you lie on your front?' I ask.

He arranges his generous assets comfortably beneath him.

I hear the coffee machine hissing away in the background. I'm steaming in my clothes. What I need now is a long, cool drink. 'God, it's hot in here,' I say.

'Yeah.' Under the lights his back is moist with sweat.

I bend closer and peer at the wet film. The spicy scent of his skin makes my mouth water and my senses reel.

'Won't be a second.'

His muscles tighten in a spasm of shock when the

first jet of ice-cold water hits him. 'Hey! That's bloody freezing!' he yelps.

'All in the name of art,' I say. I normally use the spray can for drops of water glistening on the skin of tomatoes and peppers, to suggest their freshness. Picked at dawn and still coated with dew. And the beads of water reflect the light well. Stars twinkling on the smooth, shiny surfaces.

I start to take a few shots of the pearls of water on his skin before they disperse and become a gleaming rivulet in a valley of sand dunes.

He rolls onto his back, revealing all that was hidden beneath him. 'Spray the front of me,' he says, inviting wicked thoughts.

A little spasm shoots through me. It's not all I'd like to do to the front of him.

I pick up the spray can and mess about adjusting the nozzle. I'm in dire need of a cold shower. My back's dripping and there's a river flowing between my breasts. Its tickling is excruciating. How I'd love to rid myself of my own clothes; lie next to him, wet and naked.

I shake off the notion and engulf him in a fine mist, like the hazy spray carried from a waterfall. My glasses steam up. I take them off and slip them into my pocket. Then I take photos of his chest with beads of water trickling across it. It is every bit as tempting as my dew-moist, dawn harvest. And my own juices are starting to run.

'Khalid, I've had an idea,' I tell him. I load the camera with a colour film then skip into the kitchen and fetch all the pots of spices I can find: cinnamon, nutmeg, paprika, ginger, turmeric, curry, cayenne pepper. A kaleidoscope of reds, yellows and browns. I'm going to portray him as The Spice God – to show off the beautiful shade of his skin.

I shake little piles from each pot onto the white sheet in front of him. But when I look through the viewfinder, the effect is disappointing. Nobody's going to notice the spices – not with everything else that's on offer!

I scoop them back into their pots, splodges of colour on the white sheet all that's left of my vision.

'How about this?' Khalid tips a little heap of paprika onto his stomach.

'That's going to itch like hell,' I say.

'All in the name of art.' He grins at me. Soon there are several neat little heaps. I photograph them close up, like russet and gold mountains rising from a desert.

He starts to laugh.

'Hold still, you're shaking it everywhere!'

What I manage to salvage, I spoon back into its pot. The rest dusts his skin, merging patches that become trickles of brown and amber as they're mixed with sweat. He begins to trace patterns and spirals with his finger, painting himself in a swirl of desert colours. The pores of his skin, in close-up, form wells of deeper hue. I click away in quick succession.

When I've finished I wipe a wisp of hair out of my face. The loose knot I tie it up in while I work is coming undone. Khalid reaches for the water can and sprays himself clean. His cock gives a little twitch. It's matched by a violent spasm deep within me.

'Coffee?' I take myself off into the kitchen, half choking on the word, my cheeks probably redder than the paprika he smeared over his stomach.

'Only if it's got ice in it,' he calls after me.

I shake my head. And my hair springs out of its tie, tumbling about my shoulders and into my face – a cascade of coppery corkscrew curls.

I pour a coffee and busy myself with stirring it. The

steaming mug-full isn't the only thing that needs cooling down.

'So what sort of things do you deliver, Khalid?' I ask.

'Groceries.'

I'm hoping the inane questions will take my mind off what I can't help thinking about.

'And you model in your spare time?'

'No. Not yet. First I need a portfolio.'

Of course he does. How stupid of me. A professional model wouldn't need to come here to have his photos taken; he'd go to someone with a bit of gumph.

So maybe he is only a kid, just starting out. And they start pretty young, don't they? Fifteen or so.

Oh, God, this has all been a huge mistake. I'll probably be prosecuted.

I notice he's watching me stirring the enamel off the inside of my mug.

But I haven't done anything indecent. So why should I be?

Why is he eyeing me like that? If he wasn't just a boy, I'd think he was imagining what I might look like without my clothes. And what he'd like to do to me given half the chance.

I feel my cheeks colour at the wanton thought. So much for cooling down.

'Why don't you put drops of coffee into my belly-button? Could make some good pictures. I saw an advert once.'

I stare at him. I remember a drop of coffee on skin, but nothing about belly-buttons.

He grins when I come back over to him. Isn't his cock a little thicker than before? I mustn't let this get out of hand. But I do love playing about with food.

I take a teaspoon of coffee and fill his navel with it,

like an inkwell. Then carefully I place drop after drop of the mocha-brown liquid in a line over his stomach, stopping where a fine stripe of hair starts to taper into the fuzz around his shaft. I bring the lighting in close, so that each bead of coffee reflects a patch of gold. Perfect.

'I like women who wear white underwear,' he says, out of the blue. He looks at me sleepily, through half-closed eyelids, a slow smile creeping across his lips. I must have been so intent on getting the right angle for my shots I didn't realise I was showing my knickers.

'It's a black dress,' I say. 'White shows through it.' I guess it's meant as an explanation. Or a warning.

'Aren't you going to drink your coffee?' he asks. 'It's getting cold.' He points to the little well in his belly-button.

A giddy thrill runs through me. I look at his solemn, expectant face. He's not joking.

I kneel and slowly bend my head to his stomach. In one swift draught I sip up the miniature espresso. Then I lick his belly clean. I taste coffee laced with cayenne pepper – an explosive mixture that sends my senses spinning. Or is it the heady frivolity of what I've just done? I eye his penis, so near. And before I know what I'm doing, I'm taking it in my hand and my mouth is closing round its tip.

I begin to suck. And feel how something pulls at my stomach – a wrench deep within me. Khalid lets out a low moan. Mmm, he's enjoying this photo session as much as I am. I fondle the squashy flesh of his balls. He parts his legs. I stroke the bridge of soft skin that leads to his anus. I want to explore every bit of him – inside and out.

'You've been saving the best till last,' he says. 'And I

thought you were gonna say we were finished, and send me home.'

It's what I should have done. But don't I always eat my subjects afterwards?

'Why did you come to me?' I ask when I've taken myself back in check.

'You're the only person I thought might do it. And I knew you were good. I saw an exhibition in the library.'

I smile. I had to remove one or two of the photos. The aubergines were too phallic.

I look at his thickened cock. A noble specimen, and a worthy subject for my camera. But that would really get me into trouble.

'Why not?' he asks, reading my thoughts. 'These are "artistic" photos.'

Little ringlets of hair curl about his penis, framing it in dark brown. Thank God I'm near-sighted. How tragic if all this were out of focus. I tweak a little curl.

'Mmm. Can I spray you?'

'Go ahead. Whatever you want.'

His penis shrivels when the cold water hits it. A pity. I begin to form the moistened hair into coils round my finger, patting them into place. Curl upon curl. Creating the picture I want. And as I fondle them into shape, his cock recovers from its shock and nestles among them in all its glory.

I fit the remote release cord. My fingers are now trembling so much I don't trust myself to press the shutter release without a shake. I adjust the tripod, angle the camera, crouch to take the photos. And as I lean to look through the viewfinder, the bud of my clitoris rubs against the hard metal of one of the tripod's legs. The spasm that rocks through me makes me cry out.

Khalid gives a little chuckle deep in his throat.

As I bend to realign my frame, he leans forward and slips a hand between my legs, gently stroking the black lace of my panties. I open my legs wider, to let him insert a finger inside me, if he wants to. He obliges. And he's no amateur. While I take photographs of his responding cock, he caresses my inner walls, making me shiver with pleasure.

Why didn't he do this sooner? Tiny spasms have been shooting through me since he walked in the door. A torment only exacerbated by crouching with my legs open. And now the desire is growing so strong, I'm having to hold onto the tripod for support. Thank God I'm working with remote release!

He rubs the nub of my clitoris with his thumb. I'm now past caring whether I'm able to contain my moans. He knows what he's doing to me. Knows he's gorgeous. Can tell I want to fuck him. My desire is transparent.

He plucks open the last few buttons of my dress and lets it fall open. He likes what he sees. There's a smile on his lips and his chest heaves with the increase in his breathing.

He rolls onto his side and pulls me closer to him, one hand cradling my hip while the other closes over the lacy cup of my bra. As the palm of his hand searches out my nipple, his nostrils flare and his panting begins to match mine. He does seem to have a thing about black underwear.

'I think you could do with another touch of cold water,' I say.

'It's a touch of something else I'm more interested in,' he replies.

He swings his legs off the sofa and encases me between his thighs. My dress flops into a heap behind me as he sweeps it from my shoulders. His hands stroke over my shoulder blades and meet in the centre of my back. Adept fingers squeeze open the hooks of my bra.

Freed of their confinement, my breasts bounce into his face. Greedily he nuzzles the lace out the way and his mouth seeks the rosy point of my nipple. His lips close round it and his tongue plays with its sensitive tip, tickling deliciously and sending spasms of pleasure pulsating through my sex. He sucks and sucks, drawing more and more of me into him until I can bear it no longer.

I prise his head away, and it homes in on the other side – until that is as sore and swollen as its twin, and my desire is reaching breaking point.

I slip out of my panties and thrust his torso against the backrest of the sofa. He slides further onto the seat, so I can climb onto it and straddle him. I take his cock between my fingers. It's firm and straight, a phallus worthy of any oriental god. He takes my hips in his hands and helps me impale myself on him.

Never have I been so full; never have I stuffed myself so urgently with such a feast. He fills me like he were tailor-made. As I begin to ride him, he kneads my breasts, the rocking and kneading motion growing ever more frenzied.

God, I've been wanting this all day. And was it what he was hoping for, too? Is that why he sought me out? Because of the aubergines? Did he already know what I looked like? That my hair was Celtic gold? That my tits rival anything ever imagined in a bad boy's dreams?

The spasms now shooting through me near turn me inside-out. My climax is quick and urgent. Rippling waves of pleasure that roll over me, again and again. But I'd been holding back for so long, the floodgates just had to break. And they break, releasing a torrent of ecstasy that almost drives me insane and robs me of my consciousness.

As the last violent contractions rock though me, Khalid drags me from him, spraying my stomach with semen. We collapse against each other, smaller spasms still ebbing through me that he can surely feel.

When we've regained our breath and senses we stretch out, side by side, on the sofa.

'Do you mind this mess?' he asks, massaging his semen into my skin.

I shake my head, too content to spoil the moment with words. I don't mind it at all; it leaves the surface feeling silky. I wouldn't even mind if he covered me in honey. Then licked it all off. Not that I haven't produced honey enough of my own, if he wants to taste it.

He reaches over me and picks up the spray can. Gently he rinses away all traces of his come, then pats me dry with a corner of the sheet. I kiss his forehead, his eyelids, his nose, his high, sculpted cheekbones. Then his mouth. He tastes of a spice all his own.

We're lying curled up together, our bodies entwined like coffee with a swirl of cream, when a shadow passes in front of the light.

'Sorry. But I need a signature.'

I look up to see the blond punk from parcel deliveries. I sit up and take the clipboard from him and scrawl a 'C Delaney' on the invoice slip. As I pass it back I notice a definite bump in his brown uniform trousers. He mumbles apologies and backs away. Probably cursing himself that he hasn't got the time to stay a little longer. That he never has the time to stay.

But maybe next time he'll come with a few minutes to spare? I've always wanted to test those spiky points of hair ...

'Fuck! It's nearly four o'clock. My uncle's going to skin

me when I get there.' Khalid starts to pull on his underpants. 'But with a bit of luck, I won't have to do deliveries for much longer. So the photos had better turn out well.'

'And if they don't,' I say, 'I'll do the whole lot again for you. Free of charge. My pleasure.'

Glass House Lisabet Sarai

'What have you got to lose?' he asks with a wicked grin. Lithe and gypsy-dark, he leans toward me, deliberately invading my personal space. My thoughts flash to sensuous, fragile Rebecca, waiting for me in LA, and to Daniel in Boston, his quiet strength and natural dominance. Both my lovers deserve my fidelity.

But I am worn down from three years of this bicoastal ménage, the delicate balancing of demands and desires. Complexities, compromises, guilt, the unvoiced accusations in their eyes when I leave one of them to go to the other: it makes me tired, much as I love them both; makes me vulnerable to someone like Lukaš.

He is young, arrogant, uncomplicated. He prowls this city of cobblestones and castles as if it were his private hunting ground. He does not remember the spring of the tanks; he had not even been born. On mild autumn evenings, he joins the crowd on the bridge singing 'Imagine', but he was in diapers the day John Lennon was shot.

With his leather jacket and narrow hips, sideburns and cigarettes, he could be a modern James Dean. He has that same overwhelming physicality. Still, there is something totally European about him. His interest in me is transparently sexual, but he is unhurried and graceful in pursuit of his prey. As he leads me through the ancient lanes off Old Town Square, shepherds me to museums and concerts, buys me flowers and little souvenir trinkets from Prague's famous glass shops, he touches me, but only occasionally. A brush on the shoulder, a casual pat on the rump: I notice, and he knows that I do. His familiar manner stops just short of being proprietary. I am simultaneously annoyed and aroused by his hands on my body. He is teasing me.

I am old enough that I should be immune. But I'm not. I want him. I remember the way Rebecca shivers as I trace the sweet curve of her breast with my tongue. I see myself kneeling before Daniel, eagerly offering my mouth for his use. The memories make me damp, but they do not distract me from the tantalising presence of Lukaš across the table. I imagine Daniel's silence, Rebecca's hysterics, if I were to surrender to Lukaš. The bright image of my surrender, though, makes those self-reproaching pictures fade away.

Lukaš knows nothing of my domestic arrangements. To him, I am merely available: an attractive, mature, American journalist visiting Prague on a one-week assignment. An opportunity. A challenge. An episode. A diversion. I sigh, and take a sip of my beer.

'I'm not sure that I want to be just a one-night stand, Lukaš.'

'But, *milačku*, what a night it will be!' He grasps my hand. It feels as though he has just grabbed my sex. There is heat, and pressure. He strokes my palm with one finger, watching my face. I swear, I can feel that finger brushing ever so lightly across my clit. He is still grinning.

'Give me the chance, *milačku*,' he says softly, 'and I will make for you memories that you will cherish until the end of your days.'

I cannot help melting into a smile. What American youth would ever say such a thing?

I met him my first night in Prague, in the bar next to my hotel. It was a crowded, smoky cellar of a place with huge beams and rough plaster walls. Blurry with jet lag, I sat nursing a beer, listening to the animated, incomprehensible voices around me. I felt simultaneously lonely and exhilarated.

A pale, slender woman with a mane of dark hair came down the stairs. My heart thudded painfully against my ribs. She reminded me of Rebecca. I remembered our last evening together, before I flew to Boston and on to Europe. Champagne and olives. Candles. Her sensitive artist's hands dancing over my body, coaxing the pleasure from my flesh the same way she coaxes form out of cold clay. Then my pleasuring her, roughly, as she likes it, a dildo in each hole, while she writhed and screamed profanities completely out of keeping with her ethereal, medieval beauty.

Lost in this sensual reverie, I felt his gaze before I saw him. I had the sense that I was not alone, that someone was spying on my lascivious thoughts. I looked up, flustered, and our eyes met.

He lounged against one of the beams, holding a half-empty glass in one hand and a cigarette in the other. He wore all black: tight jeans, turtleneck, that biker's jacket. His hair was a bit too long, a bit unkempt. His eyes bore down on me. There was a trace of the sardonic in his smile.

My reactions were confused. Dangerous, my mind said. Slippery, shifty, not to be trusted. Meanwhile, my body burst into flames in the heat of his gaze, nipples taut, sex wet, a flush of embarrassed arousal climbing up my neck and into my cheeks.

Lukaš sauntered over to my table and sat down on the bench next to me. His denim-covered thigh pressed lightly against mine. I swallowed hard and discreetly tried to shift my position. The contact made me too nervous. He did not react to my retreat. I still felt the ghost of his touch. I found that I missed it.

Politely, in fluent though accented English, he introduced himself. A student, he said, vaguely implying some literary or historical subject. (I never saw him reading, or carrying any books.) Would I like a cigarette? I was American, was I not? How long had I been in Prague?

I answered his questions in monosyllables, undone by the challenge of his nearness. Meanwhile, as he made small talk, he was looking me over thoroughly.

Next to someone so young and vital, I should have felt inadequate, old, used up. Strangely, he had exactly the opposite effect on me. I felt totally desirable. Lust surged in me, heightening my colour, making my eyes sparkle. He saw me as I truly was – gorgeous, sensuous, insatiable. He knew me – knew how hot I could burn in the right hands.

Illusion, whispered my mind. He is a stranger. He doesn't know you. Not the way Daniel knows you, every crevice and hollow, every fantasy and fear. Not the way Rebecca knows you, from the heart of womanhood. You would be awkward and strange together. Afterwards, you would feel empty. Old. Ashamed.

I pushed the thoughts away, but Lukaš sensed me cooling. He was not deterred in the least. 'Allow me to be your guide while you are visiting my city,' he offered. It would be my privilege and pleasure. I was too weak to refuse. He escorted me to the front door of the hotel and shook my hand with mock ceremony. Back in my room, I was simultaneously relieved and frustrated.

I dreamed that night of a shadowy figure in black, leading me through a misty cityscape of towers and spires. Chill moonlight lit the scene, casting stark shadows, but my skin was hot as though I had a fever. I could not see the face of my companion. Nevertheless I recognised his accent and his mocking tones.

'Look up,' he ordered. 'See my people.' Reluctantly, I obeyed. Tall windows pierced the old stone walls. All were barred. Behind the iron bars, naked figures writhed in self-pleasuring. A full-breasted woman squatted in full view, her fist buried to the forearm in her sex. A wiry, ebony-skinned man with a huge red penis stroked himself with one hand. With his other, he wielded a vicious-looking whip, lashing at his own back until it was as crimson with blood as his swollen organ. Their mouths were all open, as though voicing cries of pain or lust. But the scene was eerily silent.

I was overwhelmed simultaneously by disgust and desire. My guide grabbed my wrist. He was not gentle. 'Come,' he commanded, practically dragging me through the street. I wanted to refuse, but I wanted his touch more. My juices smeared my thighs as we hurried along through a maze of deserted lanes lined with stern granite façades and fabulous, time-eaten carvings. I knew that I was lost. Even if I were to break away from his grip, I would never find my way back.

We reached a cul-de-sac where an ancient fountain in the shape of a monstrous face dripped into a moss-grown bowl. He pushed me to my knees on the cobblestones. I could not bear to look at his face. All I could see was black denim, black leather.

'Open,' he said, his voice gruff with need.

I could only obey. My lust left me no choice. I dripped in time with the leering old fountain. As I stretched my jaws to accomodate my escort's hardness, I finally dared to look up.

Mists swirled around the man's features. Everything was dark, shadowy and uncertain. Then the moon stabbed through the clouds. In the sudden, silvery illumination I saw the two windows above us, and recognised the figures of Rebecca and Daniel standing pale, silent, and motionless as I hungrily swallowed Lukaš to his very root.

I woke to a pearly dawn, damp with sweat and arousal, my heart a painful hammer in my chest. Only a dream, I told myself shakily. I have not betrayed them. I will not, no, no matter how charming this young man may be. No matter how horny he makes me. I am older and wiser than that.

For the next few days, as he had promised, Lukaš revealed to me Prague's treasures. He showed me the museums, the cathedrals, the cemeteries. He bought me pale-gold effervescent Pilsner and savory dumplings, watching my mouth as I chewed and swallowed, a half-smile on his own sensual lips. We sat together in a gilded opera house, a Mozart symphony swirling magically around us, and he held my hand. But his blatantly sexual aura was so at odds with this innocent gesture, I had to take my hand away.

He also accompanied me as I worked, while I took photographs, conducted interviews, and pored through dusty archives of old documents. He did not demand my attention. He simply watched me. I would be leafing through a file folder in some dim library and the hairs on the back of my neck would suddenly stand up. He could be across the room from me, but I would still feel his eyes on me, hungry but patient. His intensity was unnerving. My dream would come back to me, hazily. I would push the memory away.

Lukaš occasionally acted as translator when my subject did not speak English. I was suitably grateful for his help. I offered to pay him, but he told me, archly, that my company was more than adequate recompense.

All would be smooth and businesslike: my questions recast in tongue-twisting Czech, the answers relayed to me in clear, slightly old-fashioned English. Then he would look at me in that way of his, and I would totally lose my train of thought. He knew, too. I could tell from that self-satisfied grin. Meanwhile, the subject of my interview would look anxiously from my face to his, confused, perhaps even a bit suspicious.

He was incorrigible, and delightful. I wanted him with a purity of lust that I had not felt in fifteen years.

I was very proud of myself. I had not given in, despite the temptation. I had remained strong, faithful to my partners, as I had promised myself that I would. By tomorrow afternoon, I would be on the plane, headed back towards safety, towards Daniel, towards Rebecca; away from the damnably seductive young Lukaš.

'Let us walk down to the river,' he says, bringing me back to the present. 'It is nearly sunset. And there is something that I would like to show you.'

We make our way westward towards the Vltava in companionable silence. As we stroll along, close but not touching, I am struck by the fact that, after all, I do trust Lukaš. For all his swaggering and sexual innuendo, he has treated me with respect. I know how easily he could have taken advantage of me; he probably knows it, too.

Somehow, though I have told him nothing, I believe that he also senses my conflicts. He knows without being told that I am not free. I am surprised by his perspicacity, unusual in one so young. I am grateful.

Clouds stained by the sunset heap high over the water, which flows grey and smooth like molten lead. Vermilion, ocher, coral, azure: ordinary colour names do not apply to these flowing, burning shapes.

Against this multicoloured background, the spires and towers of Prague Castle on its crag across the river are fairytale silhouettes, the romantic and faraway past made tangible. For a long time I simply stare, as the forms merge and change in the dying light. When I finally remember Lukaš, I see he is grinning again, as if he could take credit for this spectacular display.

'Is this what you wanted to show me? It is wonderful!'

'Not exactly. Look across the street.'

The first thing I see is a massive rococo building of yellow stucco, dripping with ornamentation and topped by an onion dome. Impressive, certainly, but only one of many such edifices that I have admired in recent days. Then I see the building beside it, and stop short.

It is totally fantastic, whimsical and bizarre. It begins as an ordinary, modern office building, with square windows and a flat roof, facing the river across Smetanova Street. But grafted onto this edifice is a second building, all of glass, shaped like an asymmetric egg timer and leaning at a crazy angle against the staid office block. The sunset colours reflect in its multifaceted façade, so that the building seems to shift and move.

I hardly notice that Lukaš has put his arm around my shoulders. 'Do you like it?' he asks, his grin even wider than before. 'We call it "Ginger and Fred".'

I laugh, catching the reference immediately. The glass tower's conical base narrows, like a skirt, up to the 'waist', then fans out again. The whole structure inclines toward the office building, like a dancer leaning on her partner. On the left side, the flared lower edge of the glass completes the illusion, seeming to flow as the dancers swirl away in the opposite direction.

'It is absolutely fabulous. Thank you.'

'You are welcome,' says my smiling young guide with his delightful Czech accent, and then he is kissing me.

He kisses with his whole body. His arms wrap all the way around me. His lean thigh insinuates itself between mine, just as his tongue snakes into my mouth. His hands are on my back, my breasts, my buttocks. I am swallowed up in this hot wet kiss. The jungle has claimed me. I am sinking in quicksand. He tastes of tobacco and beer, completely delicious.

Just when I think I will stop breathing, he releases me. I am shaking. My sex is drenched and throbbing. Unbelievably, I am close to orgasm. From just a kiss. But no one has ever kissed me like that. Not Daniel. Not Rebecca. I am frightened by my reactions.

Lukaš acts casual. 'Do you want to go inside? The view from the top floor is very fine.' He stands close, but does not touch me. I ache for another all-consuming kiss. I fear it.

'Today is Sunday,' I comment, trying to keep my voice steady. 'Won't it be closed?'

'No problem.' He pulls me across the street with him, towards the apparently deserted building. The entrance is hidden under the edge of the 'skirt'. It is clearly locked. To my amazement and horror, Lukaš takes a pouch from his jacket pocket, opens it, selects a thin metal rod, and calmly inserts it into the keyhole.

'What are you doing?' I whisper frantically. 'You can't do that. We'll be arrested.' I remember the Czech police I have seen in the museums and the squares, with their formal uniforms reminiscent of the Soviet era and their prominently displayed firearms. I try to recall travel adviseries about Czech prisons.

'Not unless we are caught,' he says with his signature grin, as the lock succumbs to his probing and the door swings open. 'Come on.'

I want to resist. This is suddenly a different game. This is not the hormone-ridden young student who has been pursuing me for a week. I recognise his pick set: professional tools.

I look around me, slightly desperate. The street is nearly empty. Light is fading from the banked clouds, which are now an ominous grey streaked with rose. The wind whips my dress around me, but the chill creeping down my spine does not come from the weather. 'What do you want from me?' My voice shakes.

The breeze stirs his tangled black curls. He smiles down at me; engaging, dangerous. 'There is going to be a storm,' he says. 'Come inside.'

I should run, but his touch rivets me, his heat melts me. He pulls me into the foyer, and then his lips are on mine again, and I lose all will to fight. His hands slide under my jacket, moulding my breasts through the fabric of my dress. My nipples leap to attention, begging for his touch. He begins undoing my buttons, then stops. I almost cry out in disappointment. 'Upstairs,' he says. 'The view.'

A spiral staircase rises at the center of the transparent hourglass. Before I can object, he lifts me and begins to climb.

I would not have believed that his slender frame had such strength. Four, five, six flights he carries me, and he is not even breathing hard. I love the sensation of his arms around me, but then my stomach sinks as I look down the dark stairwell. I cannot even comprehend the risks I am taking. Where is my usual sensible self? What happened to my strength, my resolve?

Tears prick the corners of my eyes, but I am distracted by wetness gathering in my sex. I bury my face in his jacket, breathing in his odour of sweat and tobacco. I am quivering all over. Fear and excitement are suddenly indistinguishable.

The whole place is dim, illuminated only by the shadowy dusk. Seen from the inside, the building is no less bizarre. There are no walls, only partitions of glass.

Even from the stairs, I can see out to the river and beyond. The fluid shapes and angles of the windows distort the view, making the castle towers shimmer and shift.

We finally reach the top floor. Lukaš opens a (glass) door and invites me into a chamber. It must be an office: there is a desk, a chair, a filing cabinet. But all are made of glass, or some other transparent material. I am thankful that the carpeted floor is not transparent. A wave of vertigo takes me as I imagine walking on glass, looking down eight storeys to the foyer.

He flicks a switch, and the room floods with warm light. 'No!' I cry. 'Someone will see us.'

'So?' he says softly, returning to the unfastening of my clothing. 'I want to see you. At long last. I don't care who else sees.'

He pushes my jacket and dress off my shoulders, rips my bra and lays me bare. 'Are you afraid?' he whispers, nipping at my earlobe with sharp teeth.

Lust and terror war in me. I nod dumbly, remembering his incredible strength, understanding finally that he is not the man I thought he was.

'Good,' he whispers, burying his face in my bosom. 'I like that.'

He sucks my swollen tits like a greedy baby, then bites them, not gently. Images flash through my mind: Daniel tying my wrists, applying the silvery clamps; Rebecca playing with her little nubs while my fingers dance in her crotch. Daniel straddling me, working his prick between my breasts; Rebecca holding her cheeks apart, begging me to enter her. My brain is hazy with present and past lusts.

Lukaš suddenly forces a hand into my panties, roughly squeezing my clit. 'Stop!' he growls. 'Forget them. Forget everyone else. I want you here with me,

one hundred per cent here. Every sense, every thought.
Every dream. Every fear.' There is an evil glint in his eye.
'You cannot run away,' he says. 'I want you here.'

He pulls away from me. Every inch of distance hurts.
'Take off the rest of your clothes,' he says. 'Then go stand
by the window.' Meekly, I obey him. This feels so different from the games I play with Daniel, those carefully
negotiated acts of submission. The glass, cool against my
nipples, makes them tighten further, and I realise: I
really am out of control here. This is not a scene, not a
fantasy. This is me, naked with a stranger, encased in a
pillar of glass.

I am terrified, and flooded with want. I almost scream,
but I know he will not approve. So I wait – exposed, raw,
aching. I am ready for anything, pressed against the
curved glass like an insect trapped in a jar.

It seems that I stand there, alone, for a long time. I
hear small sounds, but I know that I am not permitted
to look. Finally, he is behind me, his hands caressing, his
lips nibbling at my neck. I exult when his engorged
penis brushes the back of my thighs. I can hardly bear
it. He takes his cock in his hand and rubs it slowly, back
and forth against the sensitive skin there. I arch my
back, silently pleading for more. He slides one finger
forward between my legs, thrums it over my clitoris. I
writhe, forgetting everything except his touch.

'You want me, *kočičko*? You want my cock? You want
my mouth? What do you want? Where? Tell me.'

'Yes,' I manage, hoarse, gasping for breath. 'Yes, Lukaš,
yes, I want you. Everything. Everywhere.'

'Are you sure? Anyone can see, you know.' He is
taunting me, making me pay for the days of frustration
I inflicted on him.

I imagine myself, seen from below, spreadeagled,
silhouetted against the glass. I am reckless, desperate,

dying for him. 'Oh, God, yes! I know. I don't care. I can't bear it any longer. Take me. Please! I beg you!'

'Gladly, little bird.' He grabs my butt cheeks and pulls them apart. Still, for a long moment, he does nothing more. I am suspended, obscenely displayed. A fleeting thought: I can still refuse; hold on to my past and my sanity. The thought whirls away as he plunges his cock into my ass.

Thunder cracks, and lightning slashes through the clouds. I am riven like the sky, bursting apart. I do not remember how Daniel buggers me, tentative, considerate, building slowly to climax. I think that I am a virgin, impaled by some anonymous marauder. I think that I will die, as I come again and again, my juices dripping down my thighs, my bowels threatening to betray me. I do not think. When he finally explodes, searing my insides with his hot spunk, I can only twitch and whimper.

Now he is asleep, exhausted on the carpet, while the rain drums against the glass. The city lights are smeared. The river is hidden in fog.

Still, I am not thinking. I do not dare. Mechanically, I gather my clothing and make myself as presentable as I can. I turn off the light as I leave, and stiffly navigate the spiral stairs, every step reminding me of my exquisite violation.

On the sidewalk, I wonder where I should go. The city is foreign and strange. I am fragile and lost, but not, as I had imagined, empty.

There is something in my pocket: the delicate glass unicorn Lukaš gave me. The horn has broken off, but it is still a lovely thing.

I do not know what will happen next. But I sense that something will shatter.

Hot and Hard Sasha White

My favourite way to unwind after a shift behind the bar was a good hard fuck – and I instinctively I knew that *he* could give it to me. Leaning his six feet of solid muscle against the hardwood of the bar he nursed his beer and watched the antics of the inebriated people around him. Everybody in the bar was performing in some way: bronzed beach girls in glittery tops and jewellery danced on tables; gap-year guys twirled devil sticks and attempted juggling with the pool balls; couples put on spectacular displays of affection in darkened corners – yet none of them could hold his interest. I suppose even I was performing but, as bartender, and therefore ringmaster of this circus, I was pretending to enjoy it. What really got to me was that I couldn't seem to hold his interest either.

Watching him from the corner of my eye as I worked, I noticed a few intriguing things. He wasn't performing, for one thing. And he was completely comfortable isolating himself with an invisible wall from everyone else in the room. He wasn't a great-looking guy but that didn't stop the girls from smiling at him and flirting from a distance. Yet not one dared to approach him.

I grinned widely; I never could resist a dare.

'I'm goin' in,' I warned Alex, the other bartender. She knew I was interested in him because she wasn't. It worked out good that way with us; we were rarely attracted to the same guy so we got along great behind the bar together.

'Find anything interesting out there?' I asked as I leaned across the bar, displaying my cleavage nicely.

'Not really,' he answered softly as he turned towards me. Making small talk, I learned his name was Hans and he was a writer travelling around South Africa doing research for his new book. He skirted any questions I asked about the subject of his book so I dropped it. Occasionally I had to tear myself away and pour a few shots and do a little dance with Alex to keep the customers happy. When I did I could feel his eyes stripping my clothes from me as I kept up my performance, but whenever I looked at him he smiled serenely and said something completely innocent.

It was his blasé confidence, I think, that was getting to me. I could feel the sexual heat just radiating off him and heating my blood as it flowed into the pit of my stomach, where it settled heavily. This was a man who could give me a night of energetic entertainment I would never forget. I just knew it.

When I turned to him once again, I caught his eyes on the hard nipples poking rudely through my skimpy tank top. He raised his eyes and, when they connected with mine, I felt the hard punch of lust in my belly. 'Will you wait for me to close up the bar?' I asked bluntly.

'Why?' he returned.

'Because . . . I think we could hang out, and it could be fun.'

'I don't think you know what you want,' he replied, enigmatically.

'Really?' Raising an eyebrow in surprise I confidently continued. 'I'm a big girl, you know. I know what I want, and I usually get it.'

'Do you?' He looked hesitant for a brief second before going on. 'I think you are scared to look too deep into yourself. Scared to admit what it is you really want, even to yourself.'

'And you know what it is I *really* want? After a bit of flirting?' I laughed at him. How could he? All I wanted from him was a good fuck – nothing more, nothing less. What was so hard to believe about that? 'OK, go for it,' I dared him. 'Tell me what you think I want.'

'I know that you are bored. You smile and laugh and flirt with everyone in here, yet none of them interest you in the slightest. Your mind is straining to get free of the tight rein you keep it on, just like your body is aching to be used. You encourage others to let loose and be free, yet you yourself are just pretending to be loose and free-spirited. Why? Because you are too scared to let loose yourself; scared that you may discover something that will change who you think you are. Or who you think you should be.'

I stared at him blankly, caught between shock, anger and laughter.

'Good night, Samantha,' he said with a small smile and turned away before any words could escape my lips.

My God! I thought to myself. What an ego! Don't know myself. Scared to let loose ... I've jumped from airplanes, travelled around the world on my own with only a backpack, learned to surf in an ocean rife with sharks ... scared! What does he know?

Picking up the vodka bottle in response to the request by a pretty Irish girl at the bar, I tossed it in the air, spinning it on the palm of my hand after catching it and poured her a shot. 'This one's on me, sweetie.' I winked at her and turned towards Alex. 'Let's shut it down now.'

She gave me a knowing look before jumping up on the bar and shouting out 'Last call', so that everyone in the small bar could hear her.

I put a little more energy into my performance for the end of the night. Flipping bottles, flirting and telling the raunchy jokes I was known for. Word spread fast it was last call and some ordered drinks while others headed for their nearby cottages. The best thing about this gig was that I didn't have to worry about how my drunken customers were getting home. Since they were guests of The Pirates' Hideaway they all had beds within stumbling distance of the bar.

I shook my head and wondered at myself. I used to live for nights like these. What better way to spend a cold Canadian winter than running a bar on the Wild Coast of South Africa? I was living in paradise. Spending my days on the beach swimming, surfing and playing volleyball with assorted hard-bodies from all over the world while I imagined my friends and family at home scraping the ice off their cars before driving to work every morning. The nights were spent just like this one. Watching people relax and let go, helping them party it up and pick each other up. Partying myself, and having plenty of hot men to choose from.

Yet, I'd turned down a gorgeous young stud from England, and been rejected by a not-so-gorgeous German one. Why? What was wrong with me? I used to jump at the chance for a night of playful sex with a good-looking man. What had drawn me to the one that didn't want me? Deep down I acknowledged what it was – the challenge. I was bored; a nice smile and a hard body weren't enough to get my juices flowing anymore. Hans had known that just from watching me work the bar.

I'd tried flirting with him when he first came in, just as I flirted with everyone that came in to my bar, male and female alike. The way his eyes had roamed my body let me know he appreciated my curves but there was no encouragement in his smile when he thanked me for his beer. More disturbing than his rejection of me was his analysis. Could he have been right?

A soft finger caressing my cheek brought me back to the present with a smile. 'What's wrong, Chica?' Alex asked softly.

'Nothing's wrong,' I replied with a forced smile. 'Just got slam-dunked by the guy. He hurt my ego.'

'I know what will make your "ego" feel better.' She smiled seductively at me, her hand now running up and down my arm, brushing against my breast. 'See the cutie by the door? He is waiting for me. We will make you forget that man. Join us.'

It was something we had enjoyed before when a particular guy interested us both, but I wasn't in the mood for that sort of entertainment anymore. I sent Alex off with her man for the night with a quick kiss and a pat on the ass. 'Have fun!'

Fifteen minutes later I made my way up to the communal self-catering kitchen to nuke my bag of microwave popcorn. My mind went back to what Hans had said. I was bored – he'd been right about that. Was he onto something with the rest of his comments?

As I reached for the doorknob I heard tell-tale groans and whispers from inside the kitchen. Curious to see who it was, I gently turned the handle and peeked in.

My breath caught in my throat. It was him: Hans. I watched his tense face as he worked to prevent himself from coming. I couldn't see over the counter to who it was that was sucking his cock but, from the look on his face, whoever it was knew what they were doing. 'Damn it!' I thought. 'That should be me!'

'Enough,' he commanded. 'Get up.'

I felt my eyes widen as I saw a young blond guy get

up off his knees only to turn around, bend over the counter and eagerly present his bare ass to Hans. It was one of the surfers that lived across the lagoon – a local.

'Spread your cheeks.' Hans reached for a bottle of cooking oil, unscrewed the cap, and generously coated his prominent dick, then his fingers. One hand gripped a shoulder and the other, one finger extended, was shoved, none too gently, into the waiting asshole. The man grunted.

'Keep quiet and place your hands on the counter top. Leave them there,' he said before inserting a second, then a third finger. His hand was thrusting in and out, twisting around, stretching the entrance to accommodate his impressive cock.

Hans pulled out his fingers and took up a solid stance. I watched him grip his hard cock and inch closer to the hole in front of him. My own hand dipped underneath the sarong I wore. I heard another moan, this time louder and clearer, as I watched Hans slowly feed his meat into the well-slicked hole. The moan was cut off when Blondie bit his lip and let his head drop onto the counter top.

My own fingers were now circling my rigid clit as I watched the scene in front of me. Lust kept my feet rooted to the floor, one hand teasing my nipples as the other left my clit to thrust up my wet channel. I desperately wanted to either leave or join in, but my feet wouldn't move in either direction.

My eyes were glued to where Hans's prick thrust fast and hard into the stretched hole. I matched my rhythm with his. The faster his hips thrust, the faster my finger moved. I tried to stifle a gasp of pleasure as I felt my orgasm approaching. Hans must've heard me. His head turned and he stared directly into my eyes.

His piercing gaze showed no surprise at seeing me; only pleasure. His lips slid into a small smile as he increased his speed, eyes dropping to my hand to see if I followed suit. I did. One of his hands released its grip on Blondie's hip only to pull back and slap him smartly on his rounded ass-cheek.

My pulse jumped and my pussy clenched around my finger as if it were *my* ass that had been spanked. My eyes flew back to his as I bit my own lip to remain quiet.

'Now,' he mouthed, only his lips moving, no sound.

And I came. Hard.

When I opened my eyes again he was still watching me. He hadn't come yet and the effort it took showed in his tense muscles. I watched as he reached around to grip Blondie's erection and give it a few tugs.

'Now,' he commanded again, aloud this time.

A loud groan sounded as jizz came shooting out of Blondie's cock. Hans's eyes slid shut and I watched with fascination as his buttocks clenched on his last thrust. He let out a silent breath. He had control in spades. I liked that.

The next morning I awoke drenched in sweat, the temperature already in the nineties. I slipped into my bikini, wrapped a sarong around my hips, then filled my bag with essentials and headed to the beach. I knew my friends would already be lazing about on the soft sand.

When I got there I saw that Alex was the only one lazing; the others were already surfing, or playing in the waves. The warm waters of the Indian Ocean were the most popular way to escape the blistering heat of the South African summer sun. Not ready to join in the play yet, I stripped to my bikini bottoms and dropped down next to Alex. 'Guess what I saw last night!' I blurted out. Reaching for the bottle of lotion she was struggling with, I told her about the night before.

'The thought of two men together has never turned

me on before,' I said as I rubbed the sun lotion into her smooth skin. 'It's never repelled me either; it just wasn't something I thought about.' Yet there was no denying how hot watching Hans fuck that surfer's ass had made me.

'Maybe it's because it's new for you.' The Italian's voice was soft and gentle when she replied. 'New is always exciting. Remember the first time you peeked at your father's magazines? Or touched yourself?'

'It's more than that, Alex. It was so total. I was so wrapped up in them I wasn't even aware of how close I was to coming until he told me to. Then BAM! I came.'

'All right, maybe it wasn't the actual fucking that made you hot. Maybe it was the way he controlled everything. He is obviously a dominant man, and he is only interested in those that will let him be in control. Even I noticed him last night: he has a powerful aura; not your typical backpacker. I believe there is not much in his life he doesn't control.' She slid a sideways glance at me. 'You're the same in that way, only you hide it, and he does not.'

'Yeah, maybe,' I mumbled as I flopped down next to her and let the sun work its magic on the pale skin of my tits. 'You know, Alex, no matter how long I tan topless my tits are never gonna catch up with the rest of me, are they? I'm always going to have these tan lines.'

She smoothed a finger over my bare breast and ran it back and forth over the nipple till it peaked for her. A slow smile spread across her beautiful face. 'No, they will never catch up, but they will always be tempting.'

I looked jealously at her mountainous chest, then down the rest of her body, all evenly tanned to the colour of lightly creamed coffee. 'Whatever,' I muttered to myself before closing my eyes. 'The grass is always greener ...'

My eyes slid shut and I let the heat seep into my bones. Drifting around in my mind was a plan of action. I wanted Hans, and everything I sensed he could offer me. Deep down I knew that she was right about him, and me. Getting tied up and being made to lose control was a fantasy I often used to get myself off. Unfortunately I'd never met a guy man enough to take control away from me in the bedroom. And I wanted someone to take it from me, not wait for me to give it to him. People appreciate the things they earn, or take, more than the things they are given. My control would be a prize, not a gift.

'Did you like it last night?'

Just the sound of his voice put a flutter in my stomach. I thought I was dreaming for a moment, but when I turned my head and opened my eyes I saw Hans sitting on the sand next to me. He wasn't looking at me but at Alex, playing in the waves. I was so deep in thought I never even noticed her get up and leave.

'I think you know the answer to that.' And if he didn't then I'd given him far too much credit.

A slight smile appeared on his full lips as he turned and met my gaze. 'I would like to see that you enjoy tonight as well.'

'Yeah? I thought you were only into men.'

'You don't think that. I am a sexual person; both men and women attract me. Much like yourself.' He flashed that enigmatic smile again.

'I'm working in the bar tonight. Why not now?' I challenged him, trying to gain control of the situation. We both knew I would lose it later – that I wanted to lose it later – but for now I needed to feel that I was in control. He let me.

He gathered up my beach paraphernalia while I tied my bikini top into place and waved to Alex before strolling up the beach towards cottage one. We didn't speak or touch as we walked; but when we entered the cottage I dropped my bag, turned and pressed my body into his. Our lips met and immediately opened into a hungry, eating kiss. My hands gripped his shoulders and slid around to his back. He felt so hard and hot, his muscles playing under my fingertips as they roamed his body, already slick from the heat. Hans gripped my hips and spun us around so my back was against the wall. He pushed his hips against mine and, before I could push back, I felt his fingers grip my hair. He pulled my head back sharply.

'I want you to sit over there and do not move.' Hans directed me to the table and chairs in front of the picture window before going into another room. He emerged from the room a minute later with a black scarf dangling from one hand and a toiletry bag in the other. He strolled over, stepped behind me, and firmly tied the scarf over my eyes. It was folded over so many times that my view was completely blocked. I couldn't even see shadows through the material. All of a sudden another scarf was placed roughly between my lips and stretched tight, gagging me. My breath came faster and I felt a rush of heat flow to my pussy. It had begun.

With no words, only by touch, Hans got me to lean forward and place my hands behind my back, where he tied them together before removing my bikini top. When I was sitting upright again he whispered in my ear. 'You are now my personal playground. And I am going to enjoy this very much.'

With my sight disabled, all my other senses came alive. I could track where Hans was as he walked around my chair by both the sound of his movements and his scent. He smelled of sun, saltwater and a hint of sweat. The fainter sound of people walking past the cottage to the beach could also be heard, and I wondered if any of them looked in through the window. I knew if they did they would see me sitting there, blindfolded and topless. I hoped they would look. I imagined a crowd gathering to watch the show Hans was going to put on. They would soon be reaching to satisfy themselves as I had done last night when watching Hans in another performance.

I felt his presence in front of me a split second before I felt his hands on my knees. Sliding them up under my sarong he told me to lift my hips. With one smooth move he slid my bikini bottoms down my legs and over my feet. Firm pressure from his warm hands pressed my knees wide. My sarong, still tied loosely at the waist, was on the outside of my thighs, leaving my pussy exposed. I heard him shaking what sounded like an aerosol can and wondered what was in store for me.

Then I felt something cold and damp on my bush. He was spreading it all over my lips and inner thighs. A shiver ran up my spine and I felt my tits swell, aching for a hand to touch them, cup them and fondle them. The muscles in my thighs tensed as I tried to spread them further than the arms of the chair would allow. Hans's fingers were just brushing over my cunt, not touching, just teasing. 'You are ripe. Your juices are flowing already and I have yet to touch you. I must clean you up first; shave all these messy curls away, so I can see you better. You must sit still for this. I do not wish to cut your precious skin.'

His words brought another rush of heat to the pit of my stomach. I knew the hairs covering my pussy were neat; I waxed and trimmed them on a regular basis. Those words, coming out of his mouth, made me feel slutty and dirty, the way I always want to behave but rarely do.

He placed a hand on my belly and I felt a blade skim down towards the crack of my pussy. Ommigod, he's using a straight blade! my mind screamed.

'Stay still.' He continued with another firm skim of the blade. The hand left my belly and was placed on my inner thigh, stretching the skin to get to the sensitive area between pussy lips and thigh. 'You are a dirty girl to enjoy this so much.'

I am, I am, I thought to myself.

I was terrified he was going to slip and cut me, but I was so turned on it was all I could do not to squirm around and rub my thighs together for friction. He continued stroking from the blade; the competent way his fingers moved, stretched and played my lips as he shaved my pussy completely bald was torture.

'Keep your legs spread,' he ordered. I heard Hans get up and walk away, the sound of water running from a nearby tap, and him returning. Something wet, warm and rough was pressed between my thighs and shifted around. 'Now I will be able to see all your secrets. I already see your pretty little button. Red and swollen. It is begging for attention.'

I could feel my clit peeping through my now bare lips. A moan escaped me when he gave my pussy one last wipe with the warm cloth, the firm pressure lingering for just a second on my hard little nub, before I heard it hit floor a few feet away.

His fingers then spread my outer lips to reveal all to him. 'Look at you, all pretty pinks and deep reds shiny with wanting. I can smell you. Nothing is more intoxicating than the scent of a woman's lust.'

I listened as he dragged in a deep breath and felt the breeze on my wetness when he released it. 'Your thighs are trembling,' he noted. 'You must remember that you are my playground now. Your pleasure does not matter, only mine. You are not to come until I say it is all right.'

There was no punishment threatened. None was needed. This dominance was what I wanted from him; what had attracted me to him. I felt his hot breath get closer to my pussy, and my insides clenched in excitement when his tongue swept firmly over the length of my crack, stopping just before contact with my clit. My mouth was dry from the gag and my shoulders ached from being pulled back. The discomfort only made the pleasure in other regions of my body more intense.

Hans's tongue was firm and agile as it lapped at my pussy before his mouth moved higher and focused on my neglected button. He swirled around it, then flickered across it a few times before he went for whole mouth suckling.

'Ummm.' A groan reverberated through my chest and escaped when I felt two of his fingers invade my cunt and begin to thrust steadily in and out. The sensations spiraling around my insides increased and my breath rasped loudly in the quiet room. I felt bereft when his fingers slipped out of my grasping hole and slid between the cheeks of my ass. They played around the rim for a second or two before steadily invading the virgin territory of my anus.

Unintentionally I tensed up and Hans sucked harder on my clit in response. His distraction worked and his finger slid into my tunnel with little difficulty. The sensation was a new, but not unpleasant one. The probing of his finger caused shivers and more tremors to run through me. When he began to fuck my ass with that finger the image of him fucking Blondie the night before came up on the blank screen in my mind and I knew I couldn't hold back much longer.

As if sensing this, Hans pulled away from me all at once and left me feeling unbearably empty and aching. A whimper escaped from behind the gag when I heard him get up and felt his body move behind me. I felt the chair turn and knew I was now facing the window. 'People are watching you,' he whispered in my ear. 'They see all of you, spread open and shaven clean. They see the juices glistening on your thighs and your hole gaping hungrily.'

His hands played lightly over my collarbone and inched down to my swollen tits. The tickle of his fingertips playing over my skin was not enough, just a tease. Then suddenly his hand slapped at my tits – first one then the other. 'You are a dirty girl,' he said as he continued spanking them. Inwards, then outwards, but never directly on top. 'I think you enjoy having the people see you like this, eh? You want them to wank over you. Your tits are a nice rosy colour; your nipples are so hard and red, calling out for attention. This is what the young man wants me to do. He is watching us and pinching his own hard nipples with one hand, the other fondling himself through his trunks. The women are more shy; they just watch you and lick their lips, too scared to touch themselves, but wanting to.'

The pain of sharp fingers gripping and twisting my nipples sent shafts of pleasure to my pussy. I could feel it gape open rudely, grasping at air, searching for something to fill the void. The thought of people watching this, watching me, turned up my internal heat, and at the same time filled me with shame. It also filled me with a hunger for more.

One hand still on my aching tit, pinching and pulling the nipple roughly, his other slid down over my belly to spread my outer lips. 'There are no secrets from them, or me, now.' A straight finger was shoved roughly into my sex and pumped in and out, the wetness dripping out in a steady stream, leaving no doubt that I loved every minute of the humiliation. 'You have no shame.'

His hands left me again and I felt tears start to wet the blindfold. My chest was shaking, the harsh rasping of my breath being sucked in and out through the gag very loudly in the quiet room.

'Shift forward,' he said from in front of me. I heard the rasp of a zipper and I knew he was undoing his pants.

When my buttocks were on the edge of the seat he lifted my legs and placed them over his shoulders. The position had me lying on my tied hands with my neck resting uncomfortably on the hard wood of the chair back. I didn't care. I knew he was going to fill my cunt with the seven inches of hard cock I saw in action last night, and that was all I cared about.

He played the head of his cock around my slit, brushing against my swollen clit before edging it into my opening. He stayed there. Just inside my entrance. I tried to lift my hips into him but my position was completely submissive. I had no choice or input into what was happening.

I felt his fingers grip my hair, pulling my head forward, as he thrust his hips sharply, filling me up and stretching my inner walls. Muffled groans and whimpers sounded from behind my gag as he pumped in and out, hitting deep inside me. The sounds were getting louder and more frantic as I felt all my muscles tensing with the effort of holding back my orgasm.

'Now,' he commanded as he ripped the gag away from lips.

My cries filled the air as my pussy clenched and unclenched in ecstasy.

When I came back to my body Hans was still hard

and throbbing inside me. 'My turn,' he whispered in a thick accent, before gripping my hips and roughly plunging in and out again. I imagined the watchers outside hypnotised by the sight of his buttocks steadily hollowing and filling with each of his hard thrusts into me. Thrusts that brought another tingle to life inside me. With a final deep thrust his head fell onto my chest and a small groan escaped his lips, causing a tremor to ripple through my pussy.

We stayed like that for couple of minutes before Hans pulled away, letting my legs fall gently to the floor. I heard him get up, water running again, and once more I felt the damp warmth of a cloth between my thighs.

'I will untie your hands and you may go. If you wish to return before I leave at the end of the week you are welcome.' His hands gently leaned me forward to gain access to my bound wrists. I felt a gentle kiss on the top of my head and listened to him walk away before I took off the blindfold.

Rubbing my hands up and down my arms to encourage the circulation, I looked around the cottage and saw that the bathroom door was closed, but he had left some moisturiser on the tabletop for me. I stood up on shaky legs and walked to the table, where I uncapped the bottle and spread some gently over my newly shaven pussy before replacing my bikini.

I stood there for a moment looking at the empty window. I had wanted that window to be full of strangers, and Hans had known it.

I wonder what else he knows, I thought as I strolled out the door.

Cycles Jean Roberta

'Are you using both machines?' The voice managed to combine a certain well-bred politeness with a hint of desperation. I was in the laundry room, bending over the dryer, so I couldn't see him at all. I was sure he was getting a clear view of me.

I straightened up fast. 'Yes,' I said, willing myself not to feel embarrassed – I didn't want to tell my fellow tenant that every machine in the entire apartment complex was filled with my clothes. That's how I do it when I have a lot of laundry. I figure this is actually more considerate than using the machines in my own building for long periods.

'Will you be finished soon?' he persisted. He was trying to control a grin, but his dark piercing eyes were disconcerting. They were set in a face with prominent cheekbones, a chiselled nose and full, sensuous lips. He seemed to be in his thirties. He was of average height, but his slim body and graceful stance suggested an unusual occupation: dance, theatre, fitness or martial arts.

'Do you need to wash something right away?' I heard myself asking. Why offer this man favours? howled the voice of my self-respect.

'Well, yes.' He flashed me a smile, intended to be charming. 'I need to wash this.' He shook out a silk turquoise evening gown with a 1920s-style dropped waist and a handkerchief hem. 'It's washable,' he explained, as though we were friends, 'though I'm not sure I can get the stain out of the skirt.' I didn't want to know the origin of the stain.

He obviously wanted a reaction from me, and I wanted to maintain my cool at all costs. I ignored his need for advice on removing stains; I was hardly an expert on the subject. 'You can put it in before I do my next load,' I told him.

My reckless phrase brought the tickled grin back to his face. 'Thank you,' he intoned deeply, like a lion purring. He seemed to be suggesting thanks for something I hadn't offered. 'I'm Serge, by the way, in 3-D.'

I resisted the urge to make a smart crack about his apartment number. 'I'm Sherry,' I answered, not wanting him to know more about me than that.

Luckily, I had to turn away from him to pull my laundry out of the washer and stuff it into the dryer. I felt his eyes on my behind as though they were hands.

'Sherry.' He tasted my name on his tongue. 'Foyer, I think it is, though you use the pen name Palabra, at least for some of your writing. Do you want to keep that identity separate from your role as a librarian?' His words jolted up through my guts like an electric shock.

I faced him, showing my anger. 'How –' I began, but he interrupted me.

'Do you feel threatened?' he asked gently. His eyes looked unbearably sympathetic. 'I didn't mean to invade your privacy. I came across some of that information by accident. But after all, you can't expect your life to be a secret once you've been published. As a certain critic once said, anyone who has published a book is standing around in public with their pants down, waiting to see what will happen.'

This felt like the last slap, in some sense, especially from a man who had a taste for women's clothing, who probably looked more convincing in it than I did, and who clearly enjoyed goading me – though he probably had no interest in getting my pants off for any reason I wanted to think about. But I was thinking about it. Damn my hyperactive imagination.

'Well, I'm not standing around,' I retorted, wanting to get away. 'I have other things to do.'

'Sherry,' he tempted, 'won't you come to my place for a drink, just until our clothes are ready to come out?' It was my turn to grin at an unintended double-entendre. 'I've been horribly rude, and I'd like to make it up to you. It's my Good Neighbour policy.'

My curiosity wouldn't let me resist the bait. 'OK,' I accepted. 'Just for a minute.'

His apartment was tastefully furnished, mostly in pale woods, cream-coloured fabrics and reflective surfaces that appealed to vanity and gave an illusion of space. I liked the way my short reddish-gold (or sherry-coloured) hair framed my lightly freckled face and grey-green eyes in his hallway mirror, as though he had invited me in because my colour scheme complemented his. I also liked the way my faded T-shirt and paint-splattered jeans clashed with his decor, like graffiti on the walls of a trendy boutique.

'What would you like?' Serge asked suggestively. 'Beer, domestic or imported; wine, scotch?' I was glad he had the good sense not to offer me a glass of sherry.

I asked for a beer from the local brewery. 'I don't need a glass,' I added. Seated on his sofa, I waited to be served. When he placed the bottle on a coaster on the coffee table in front of me, I jumped up to admire the view from his picture window. He was making me nervous.

'Are you running away from me, Sherry?' he needled. He approached me so quietly from behind that his hands on my shoulders were a surprise. I could smell his cologne, and the clean smell of his skin underneath.

Nothing about him was careless or masculine in the style of the football-playing men of my youth. I felt like an animal, maybe a raccoon, that he had discovered washing something in the local stream and had lured to his home with food, to see if the creature could be domesticated.

From my shoulders, his hands moved up to the edge of my neck, where he began massaging tension out of my muscles. I couldn't stand it. 'Don't you prefer men?' I demanded.

He laughed as though I had told him a witty joke. 'Sometimes,' he admitted. 'It depends who it is. I don't understand why so many people think plumbing is everything, do you? Human beings have so much else to offer. And besides, I spend most of my time working with women's bodies, deciding what would cover them best.' His hands suddenly tightened on my upper back. 'Oh, is that why you thought I was a queen? Because I'm a designer and dressmaker?'

I felt myself turning hot. I didn't want to admit that I had thought he was washing one of his own favourite dresses.

He guessed. 'Oh, you thought I was going to wear the silk!' He chuckled. 'It doesn't fit me, honey. I made it for someone else. I can show you the clothes I wear, and the ones I make for other people, so you can see the difference. When I design for my customers, I'm guided by their taste, not mine.'

Don't tell me what I should wear, I thought, especially on my weekends at home. 'OK,' I said aloud, as though taking up a dare. 'Show me your work, and show me through your place.' I was terrified that if he didn't stop touching me soon, I wouldn't be able to resist any other offers he might make.

'Fair enough,' he agreed, tugging me gently by the

arm. 'I've read your work, but you haven't seen mine. Or you didn't know it.'

He pulled me into a bedroom that was as seductive as I expected; the *pièce de résistance* was a canopied bed piled high with pillows and matching duvet. I couldn't help admiring the round, muscular cheeks in my host's tight pants as he strode to the closet, where he rummaged briskly through the contents until he found what he was looking for. When he turned around with a red beaded gown in his arms, he looked uncannily like a grieving madonna holding the bloodstained body of her son. He laid it carefully on the bed so that I could see it whole. 'I made this,' he explained simply, 'for him.'

Serge glanced at a framed photo on the wall near the carved oak bureau. It showed him with a shorter, younger man who had curly black hair and a devilish grin. Both men were wearing jeans and shirts in macho shades of putty and navy blue, but with a certain ironic self-consciousness. Despite their arch expressions, they both looked so innocent that at first I could hardly recognise the man in the picture as the one standing beside me.

'He used to perform,' Serge explained. He was obviously struggling to control his voice, and this effort made him uncharacteristically terse – more like me. 'The gown –' he paused and sighed '– goes with a fake ruby necklace and earrings. They went to his sister after he died.' Serge's eyes shone with the dark brightness of a very deep well.

I felt feverishly hot, then icy cold. I was appalled to the bone by this man's unwanted revelations: first the low comedy of a transvestite relationship, and then the shock, grief and survivor guilt of losing a fairly young lover, probably to a sexually transmitted disease that had stolen him away like a successful rival. I wanted to scream: what do you want me to say? Why did you burden me with this?

'Dick,' he told me, as though I had asked. 'That was his name. Actually Diego. Five years ago.'

I couldn't look at Serge. 'I'm sorry,' I murmured, falling back on a conventional phrase. I wasn't willing to hug him, and his strong, silent expectation of physical comfort made me furious. I didn't want to admit to myself why hugging him would feel dangerous.

I began backing out of the bedroom, his cave of memory. 'I'm sorry,' I repeated, 'but you don't know me very well, and I don't think it was appropriate for you to tell me this.' If I sound like a cold bitch, I thought, so be it. 'You invited me in for a drink. That was all. I think I should go check on my wash now.'

Serge opened his arms towards me as though expecting me to walk into them. 'I feel as if I know you, Sherry,' he defended himself, 'because I've read some of your stories. *Survival* moved me. You know something about grief too. Your life isn't a secret, you know. I think we both have things to offer each other.' He waited for me to answer, but none of the words in my head seemed suitable, and I knew from hard experience that words, once thrown into the air, can never be taken back. 'Your laundry can wait,' he urged gently.

'No it can't,' I insisted. 'Every machine in this complex is full of my clothes, and they must all be ready by now. If I don't take them out soon, the Tenants' Committee will have an emergency meeting and put *me* through the spin cycle.'

The change in his expression was like a sudden burst of sunlight. Opening his mouth as though to taste something delicious, he let out a guffaw that sounded much too hearty to go with his usual style. 'Sherry, you are too much!' he howled, slapping one of my shoulders before

I could stop him. 'OK, then, let's go.' I hadn't invited him to come along.

He followed behind me like a shadow, and his unseen presence at my back somehow felt threatening and comforting at the same time. I speeded up, and we both scampered briskly down the steps to the basement laundry room. We probably looked like a comic dance team to the other tenants who passed by at a distance. No one else seemed interested in us.

I rushed to the washing machine, planning to pull out my clothes as quickly as possible. As soon as I bent over, though, Serge did something so crude that I felt lightheaded: he pressed his crotch against my denim-covered bottom as he wrapped his arms around my waist. 'Sherry,' he chuckled calmly, leaning toward my ears, 'you know I want you.'

Lust flooded through me like another surge of alcohol in my veins. My feelings weren't any subtler than his, but they were certainly complicated. The hardness of his cock through his pants spoke directly to the wetness in mine; what had he said about the irrelevance of sexual plumbing? He was male and I wanted him, or did I want him because he was male? But I also wanted him because he was feminine, with everything that involved: charm, sensitivity, an eye for detail, a good smell, a certain body language. My heart ached for those qualities when I couldn't find them in another person. And yet I knew he was tempted to fuck me like an animal in this gathering-place; a modern city version of a streambank.

'Serge . . .' I began. I had no idea what I was going to say, but I wasn't willing to surrender without conditions.

He pulled me up and turned me around as though he were leading me in a dance. With an urgency that was almost scary, he pulled me close and nuzzled my hair.

'Just for now, honey,' he assured me. 'One minute at a time. That's all I'm asking.' He kissed my throat in such a way that I could feel it in the soles of my feet. I moaned, and that was my answer.

'Serge –' I said again. I twisted halfway out of his arms, making him laugh; he knew now that I wasn't rejecting him.

'Let's get your clothes,' he agreed. Like a helpful brother, he waited for me to reach into the washing machine and bring out armfuls of damp cloth. After taking them from me, he loaded them into the dryer. Our task was done with impressive speed.

As soon as I turned away from him, he slapped my behind with so much relish that I knew he had wanted to do this from the moment he first saw me bent over the washing machine. The slap seemed to be a comment on my torn and stained jeans as well as on the cheeks they covered. Instead of making me angry, the slap made me feel weak in the knees as echoes of the warm sting flooded through my guts and teased my pussy. For a moment, I couldn't move. 'No, you won't get it again,' he chuckled with a hand on my waist, 'unless you hurry up.'

At that moment, I decided to suspend caution, good sense, and possibly even my self-respect. I had been hungry for human touch for a year, since the abrupt departure of my last lover. I had been in shock for at least three months after the door had slammed, and after that I had plunged into solitary activities, especially my writing, like a diver searching for treasure at the bottom of the ocean. No one could come between me and my Muse, I thought, since she seemed more reliable than any fickle human companion.

Now I was faced with my hunger, and I had to admit that I was ready for what Serge was offering. Of course, it would mess up my sense of identity and the image my friends seemed to have of me. That was actually part of the lure, like the call of my imagination: what hidden part of me would Serge summon forth, and vice versa? I was willing to find out.

We raced from building to building, and in each one we pulled wet clothes from a washing machine and stuffed them into a dryer, or pulled warm clothes from a dryer and folded them. Almost my entire wardrobe was in the machines because I hadn't done any laundry while working on the last chapter of my novel. I had an image of all my clothes catching fire in the dryers, leaving me with nothing but what I was wearing. I wondered if Serge would design me a new wardrobe in that case, and if he would find it amusing to keep me in his apartment, naked (or clad in the lingerie of his choice) until he was finished.

He kept a hand on the back of my waist as we walked to the stairs leading to his apartment and, as we climbed them, his hand slid down to one of my cheeks where he could feel my muscles moving. I couldn't help wondering if he had usually done this with his male lovers, yet he seemed to appreciate my ass for its own qualities, and I was sure it didn't feel like a man's behind. I also suspected that he would enjoy discovering the rest of me in due course.

Somehow his apartment looked different when I entered it the second time, probably because I was entering with different expectations. Every piece of furniture now seemed to offer a different sexual experience: the carpet invited me to lie down on it and pull him down with me; the cream-coloured sofa seemed to need some human fluids to spice up its blandness, and the matching chair looked like a suitable place for its owner to sit with an alert cock, waiting for me to ease myself onto it. But the bedroom was obviously where we were headed, and I was glad. I promised the living-room I would get to know it better before long.

Of course, Serge wanted to undress me first. He gently pulled the ends of my T-shirt out of my jeans, and I pulled it over my head and threw it aside as though I would never need it again. He smiled. He was looking at my old grey bra, and a blush spread over my face. He unhooked my bra at the back with one smooth move, and it fell off my breasts like flotsam falling off a Venus rising from the waves. I thought I heard him sigh 'ahh' as my nipples tightened and hardened under his gaze.

I was tingling from head to foot as he helped me pull my jeans and panties down my legs. Why hadn't I known how horny I was? After I had kicked the last of my clothing aside, he held me for a moment, pressing my skin against the wholesome texture of his cotton shirt and pants: his version of casual wear. When he pressed his lips to mine and slid his tongue between them, he seemed to be making a silent promise: don't worry, I'll feed you.

I helped him take his clothes off, and I was too impatient to be careful. He seemed to be laughing silently. Sliding his pants down over the bulge at his crotch, I was flattered to feel its hardness. As soon as his cock was released from his jockey shorts (so white they hurt my eyes), it pointed towards me, begging for attention.

To my surprise, Serge slid away from me, then threw himself on his back onto his luxurious bed, spreading his arms wide. It was a melodramatic gesture that served a practical purpose: with one hand, he reached a packet on a bedside table, brought it to his mouth and released a lime-green condom. 'Come on,' he invited me, grinning with his eyes. I dove on top of him, kissing him teasingly and then sliding my breasts over his surprisingly muscular chest.

'Wait,' he told me, reaching under me to roll the latex sheath over his straining shaft. 'Won't you sit on it?' he asked, as sweet as a girl but with a certain ironic undercurrent. 'Baby?'

'Gladly,' I chuckled, 'but not yet.' I slid down his body until I could take his cock into my mouth, and I discovered a vein that bulged even through the sheath. I teased it with my tongue, and probed the underside of the head. I hadn't done this in so long that I felt slightly amazed, as well as reassured, that even the cocks of unusual men behave predictably. Serge stroked my hair in appreciation.

My pussy felt like something beyond my control, as if it was likely to start drooling onto his clean sheets at any moment. My clit felt almost unbearably sensitive, and I could feel a certain maddening itch that longed to be scratched, deep inside me. Somehow my hunger felt dominant and submissive at the same time: I felt as if I could tear walls down, or tie Serge to his own bed, if that's what it took to get what I needed. I also felt as if I would offer him anything in exchange for relief. The dimensions of 'anything' could be explored later.

Serge's cock looked thicker than the last one I had seen, and it bent slightly at an angle. I found it endearing. As I knelt over the impatient animal, its owner smiled serenely at me as though he could wait forever. I grasped the shaft to guide it into me as I slowly slid down on it, feeling it twitch as I watched Serge's expression. He casually reached down with both arms. Just as I began to move, one of his fingers, slippery with lubrication, slipped into my anus. As I descended on the thick, delicious organ that filled my pussy, the modest finger gaining territory alongside it. Serge's other hand held one of my hips as I rode him.

Our dance felt perverse in the best sense. I didn't feel like half of a conventional couple; I felt like a moon goddess playing with her brother, the sun, to make stars. I squeezed him to give him pleasure, and I was surprised at how much I got in return. The friction of his shaft seemed to be striking sparks in my clit, and I knew I was going to come before he did. 'Ohhh,' I sighed, wanting to warn him but unable to put words together.

The man responded with another unexpected move: he pulled his finger out of my ass so he could bring both his warm hands to my bouncing breasts. As he rubbed, kneaded and squeezed them, a pang from each nipple rushed into my guts, filling them with the sweetest sadness. My eyes stung with tears. With a mighty effort, I blinked them back. 'Come on,' he encouraged, almost under his breath. 'You can let go, honey.' I wasn't sure exactly which kind of release he was urging on me, but I was determined not to cry.

For a long, unbearable moment, all my feelings seemed to be centred in my bursting clit. Like a daredevil in a barrel, poised at the top of Niagara Falls, I wondered if I would go over the edge. Then it was happening – my cunt squeezed and squeezed as though it wanted to milk all the juice out of the strange manfruit inside it. I felt as if I could never get enough air into my lungs. Sweat popped up on my skin as more water welled up in my eyes; no part of me was dry.

Serge stayed hard and stayed calm. After my frenzy had subsided somewhat, he resumed pumping to a steady, persistent beat. Wanting to please him, I bent down to kiss his warm mouth, and gently scratched the fine dark hair on his firm chest. Holding both my hips, he settled me on his cock with increasing roughness as his need grew. I squeezed him deliberately and with all the art I could summon. Before long, he rose up off the bed to plunge into me as deeply as he could, groaning as a stored load of fluid shot into the snug green bag. I almost wished I could feel his sperm bombarding my womb, its intended goal. 'Baby,' he sighed, stroking my sweaty back.

'Honey,' I sighed back. I couldn't help remembering the last person I had addressed this way. I told myself that the differences between my present and my previous lover were irrelevant; a sweet body, animated by a need to connect, was a gift from the Goddess, who surely created balls and chest hair as well as breasts and clits.

Serge's spent organ began sliding out of me. Reluctantly, I rose up to give it breathing-space, then gently rolled the condom off as he watched me with interest. 'The wastebasket is near the bureau,' he advised. I sat up, slid my legs off the end of Serge's luxurious bed, and walked two steps to the wicker object that waited to receive the product of his hunger for me. I was tempted to save it as a souvenir. I wondered whether Serge would be disgusted by my lack of disgust; I was not willing to find out yet.

My lips felt as dry as if I had been crawling through a desert for days. I licked them as Serge watched me. 'Lip balm is on the bureau, Sherry,' he said in a voice that suggested a desire to smear various exotic substances on me. I went looking for the magic ointment which could make my lips as kissable as I wanted them to be.

The confusion of small bottles, jars, tubes, business cards and envelopes on the bureau posed a delicate moral issue: did I have the right to rummage through his belongings for the thing he had offered me? An hour ago, the answer to this question would have been clear.

Now I wondered if he assumed I was on intimate terms with the minutiae of his life. Glancing quickly over the picturesque mess, I noticed a square envelope decorated with butterflies. It obviously contained a matching greeting card, probably given to him by some affected man or woman. In a moment, I recognised the return address; it hit me in the stomach like a blow from a lead pipe. Numbly, I kept looking until I found a small jar of lip balm and returned with it to the bed.

'What's wrong, baby?' he demanded. He took the jar of lip balm from my fingers, opened it and carefully smeared some on my lips. I took a deep breath as he wrapped an arm around my waist. With the same hand that had touched my lips like a butterfly's wing, he slapped my ass. 'What is it?' he insisted.

'How do you know Blaine Wishfort?' I blurted. 'Why did she send you a card?'

The man looked me in the eyes. 'I knew her as Janice,' he told me. 'She said Blaine was her middle name. I saw her a few times, Sherry. She told me about you.'

I couldn't stand it. 'Oh, I bet she did,' I answered furiously.

'Sherry,' he interrupted. 'She didn't blame you for anything. She told me she left you. I think she felt quite guilty about it. I didn't have what she wanted either, and it didn't take her long to figure that out.'

'I don't see why she wasn't happy with you,' I told him bitterly. 'She wanted a man.'

'You think so?' he challenged. 'No, baby. She was looking for status, power, an image she could attach herself to. She thought I had all that, or I was likely to get it. She didn't want me. After I got to know her a little, I realised she wasn't who I thought she was at first.' Serge held me, trying to ease the pain I couldn't hide. 'The worst thing either of us could wish on her is that she'll get what she's looking for. She probably will. I wish her luck.'

I wiped my eyes with one hand. To my chagrin, Serge dabbed at them with a corner of the sheet. 'So it didn't take you long?' I demanded sarcastically. 'You or her? So I'm the only fool who thought it could work?'

'Why torture yourself, woman?' he asked, rocking me gently. 'You thought you saw what you wanted. We all do that. A long time or a short time, what difference does it make?'

I wasn't willing to let it go. 'She used to clean my apartment while I was writing. And she'd make me coffee and bake cookies. She said she loved everything I wrote. She would take my manuscripts to the post office to send off. I should have known. It was too good to trust.'

Serge brushed my hair away from my face, exposing what I didn't want him to see. I jerked back. 'Mm,' he murmured consolingly. 'Sherry, she told me how much she admired you.'

This comment almost made me puke. 'She believed in me, she said. Believed in what? If she really thought I was ever going to become rich and famous, she was a worse fool than I was for believing –' I couldn't say it.

Serge knew. 'She told me she wanted to move in with you; keep house for you.'

Now my humiliation was complete. 'As if any sane person really wants to be a wife nowadays. Did she offer to do that for you?'

Serge chuckled. 'Baby, we would have killed each other. She wanted to redecorate this place. I had to set her straight.' I couldn't help laughing, even though it hurt my heart.

The pain of loss still flowed nauseatingly through my guts as Serge slid me beneath him and lay on top of me, resting on his elbows. He slid down and licked my nipples like a cat. 'Such beautiful breasts, honey,' he said. 'Do you ever show cleavage?'

I guffawed. 'Where, Serge, at the library? At –' I censored my thought in time. 'No.'

'I know you go to the gay bar,' he remarked casually, tweaking my nipples to make them rock-hard. 'I've seen real women with cleavage in there. It's not a crime. You've got it, you might as well flaunt it.' I was growing too hungry again to argue.

One of Serge's hands snaked down to my pubic hair. Two comic fingers strutted through it, marching down to find my clit and distract me from the past while tickling my resistance away. Before that could happen, I wanted him to know what I was thinking.

'Listen,' I told him, grabbing the mischievous hand. 'I won't wear a dead man's evening gown. I won't. But I might wear something else. I'm sorry I was so abrupt when you told me about Dick. I am sorry you lost him. It must have been terrible. Was he sick for a long time?' I've never been known for my tact or my timing.

Serge sighed and lay his head on my upper chest for a moment before answering. 'It was a car accident, honey,' he informed me quietly. 'Totally unexpected. I was driving.'

'Jesus,' I reacted without thinking. 'I'm sure it wasn't your fault.'

'It wasn't,' he sighed, 'according to the insurance company. I know that in my head.' I kissed his forehead, his nose, his cheeks, wanting to kiss away the mess of tangled emotions, knowing I couldn't do it.

'It's OK,' he lied. His mouth searched for mine and found it. The warm, soft pressure of his lips on mine sent a message directly to my now-neglected clit. I wiggled slightly beneath his half-awakened cock. He paused for breath. 'I got a lot of emotional support at the time,' he assured me. 'Thank the Goddess for my women friends.' This reference to the deity of my faith sounded very strange coming from him, but then I thought, why not?

I laughed, reaching down to find his sensitive joystick, like a live toy that was permanently attached to his flesh and his feelings. I didn't envy him for having it, but I loved what it could do for me. 'Well, thank the horned god of all horny animals for this,' I told him. 'And the rest of you,' I added generously.

Serge was determined to find my clit before I could encourage his wilful cock to plunge into me again. 'So crude,' he clucked. 'So natural and unpolished. What can I do with you?'

His question didn't seem to need an answer. He stroked and teased my clit into a swollen state of excitement. 'Is this unfair?' he demanded suddenly, knowing I couldn't think clearly.

'Yes!' I laughed breathlessly. I knew that his fingers were now coated with my fluid. 'But maybe I'm using you too,' I shot back while I still could.

'I can live with that, honey,' he said, rising up gracefully to reach for another lime-green coat for his demanding cock. I felt as if I could melt when he guided it into my hungry, shameless cunt. As I pulled him into me with all my will, the smell of his cologne came to my nose in gusts, mixed with the rich smell of our bodies.

I felt as if my life had entered a cycle that was spinning me out of control. I didn't know where I would be when it ended, but for now, I was loving the ride.

Love the One You're With
Lois Phoenix

The first Tuesday of the month and Lauren toyed with her visitation order as she sipped her first coffee of the day. She thought of her man, incarcerated fifty miles away and wondered if he had woken with a hard-on knowing she was coming to see him. Who was she kidding? Marv always woke with a hard-on. And so did she these days. Her clit had been neglected so long it was on permanent alert.

She had been living alone in their trailer for the last six months, working nights, waiting tables in the local diner. She seemed to spend as much time ducking away from straying, sweaty hands as she did taking orders. And though she managed to fend them off with a quick quip or a friendly slap, her smile was becoming thinner and thinner. She slept in late and woke each morning feeling swollen and juicy, aroused by dreams of conjugal visits and unable to dull the ache between her thighs despite her own well-practised fingering.

Dan, Marv's best friend, often called by first thing, freshly showered and ready for his day shift. He towered in the doorway, politely waiting to be invited in, and never failed to offer his services for any repairs or jobs she needed doing around the trailer. She knew what services he was really offering, and they weren't much in the way of being a best friend. Dan was a nice guy, and he was certainly all man, but he knew deep down that she wasn't the philandering kind. They batted a little conversation back and forth over the breakfast table and he was nothing if not courteous. Lauren watched his huge calloused hands toying with his coffee cup and would have loved to have lain face down on the dinette table with her hot, hard nipples pressed to the chipped Formica, legs spread wide, and order, 'Do me, Dan. Don't speak, just stick your long, hard cock into my pussy, and do me.'

She wondered if he would rise to the occasion or whether he would bail out at the last minute. Whatever, she had promised Marv she would be faithful, so when Dan came knocking she made sure that she had on her baggiest T-shirt and no make-up. Nothing about her implied that she was enticing him in any way. But she knew that he often came to the restaurant for a drink and sat at the far end of the bar to watch her in her waitress uniform. She wasn't sure if it was like having a bodyguard or a stalker. Lauren knew that in Dan's mind the line between being a good friend to Marv while he was in the can and the urge to fuck his best friend's girl was getting blurred. She reckoned that even Dan didn't know which he was following more ardently: his loyalties or his cock.

This morning, he caught her daydreaming. She hadn't had time to duck into the shower and, as she passed his coffee across the small table, she knew he caught a whiff of pussy on her fingers where she had been playing with herself. His nostrils flared and he shivered like a wet dog. He watched her over the rim of his mug as she cooked them both eggs, and she hated him. Violently hated him for coming around every day dressed in his tight vest; for squeezing his huge frame behind her kitchen table and reminding her of what she couldn't have. She hated him for flaunting his biceps, tanned and solid; she hated him for his thick thighs; she hated him for the tufts of underarm hair, damp from his shower; and she hated him for his flat stomach, hiding taut beneath his vest, with its line of soft hair from belly-button to zipper. This morning she caught herself imagining the fat head of his cock poking out over the waistband of his jeans, and what it would be like to dip her tongue into the glistening hole. She looked up to catch him watching her again, his Adam's apple bobbing mockingly as he chewed his breakfast.

The eggs were dry and tasteless in her mouth and she was glad when they had finally finished eating. She leaned across the table and gently wiped away a crumb from his lip, making sure she left traces of her honey smell on his mouth to haunt him all day. Dan left soon after, giving up on their stilted conversation. Lauren smiled grimly and threw their dishes into the sink. 'Serve you right, you bastard,' she muttered, knowing that seeing Marv today but not being able to touch him was going to add fuel to an already highly explosive fire.

Three hours later she was parked up in the desert dust and sweating behind the wheel of her trusty Chevy, anxiously watching the daunting prison fence for signs of life. Her visitation order was safely tucked away in the glove box and she had an hour to kill. She couldn't afford the gas to keep the motor running for the air conditioning and her perspiration was sticking her to the seat. She slipped out and stretched.

Looking up she saw an eagle circling high in the azure sky. Her stomach dipped and her heart beat furiously at the thought of walking into the visitors' hall. She knew that the men all checked out each other's visitors for hot pussy and the thought of all that pent-up testosterone sent her pulse racing; especially the one in her groin.

She wanted to look her best. Her sandals were all dusty in the dirt and she bent to brush them off. Her toenails had taken ages to get right and she didn't want them to look grubby as if she were slummy trailer trash who didn't take good care of her appearance. She adjusted a shiny strap, nervous and fidgety now, and grew slowly aware that the low whistling she could hear wasn't the eagles overhead but was coming from behind her. She straightened and turned slowly, her face burning with the realisation that she had given the prison guard a fantastic view of her butt in a skimpy thong and her short skirt dancing in the warm breeze. He was grinning through the metal fence at her, sweating in his uniform, and panting nearly as much as the German Shepherd he held straining on its leash.

Her head thumped with embarrassment and she pretended to ignore him, bending to fiddle with the other shoe, this time with her ass turned away from him. It must have made his day when the slow thud and shuffle behind her had to be ordered to keep moving and fourteen men, chained together at the ankle and all dressed in prison regulation boilersuits, all rubbernecked the sight of her ass-cheeks exposed to the warm desert air. She hid behind the truck, mortification making breathing difficult. Eyes squeezed shut, she clamped her thighs together and crouched behind the truck, her breasts rising and falling rapidly as she struggled to compose herself.

She thought her heart had stopped altogether when she opened them again and saw, behind the prison fence, maybe twenty men or so, hands clasping the metal links and watching her as if she were an exhibit in the zoo. She shrank in embarrassment, her mouth dry, her mind racing. She took deep breaths and calmed herself down, telling herself that all she had to do was climb into the truck and drive around to the visitors' entrance.

Then it struck her: these men weren't expecting visitors. They were out in the yard while the other inmates eagerly awaited loved ones. Marv was sitting there waiting right now, in his boilersuit, hoping for a quick feel under the bolted-down table, feeling all sorry for himself when he shouldn't have gone out thieving in the first place; when she had begged him not to, in fact. She didn't want much; just for him to find a decent job – like Dan had. The thought sent a frisson of anger running straight through her.

One of the men – a tall Hispanic with a thick moustache – rattled the fence and called out something that she didn't understand. The other men laughed. They made her think of a group of young boys, prodding a snake with a stick, not sure if it would spit or not. She straightened and they quietened, watching her. One of them lifted a hand to wipe his mouth and she saw his erection, huge in the front of his boilersuit.

She licked her dry lips. *She* wasn't in the zoo; they were. She had been humiliated enough by her old man in the slammer. Working crappy hours. Having to sleep in a cold lumpy bed every night. Almost every man on the park thinking she was game for a quick feel. Anger pulsed in her crotch. These men weren't going to humiliate her. She was a free citizen. And she was bored with waiting for her man to be one too. She stretched slowly and pushed her breasts out so that they strained against the thin fabric of her blouse. She stood on tiptoe, flexing her thigh and calf muscles and letting her skirt dance around the tops of her legs.

That certainly provoked a reaction. They shook the metal fence, calling out to her and whistling. She smiled slyly at the guard who was trying to calm his agitated dog, but who couldn't quite bring himself to move the prisoners away from the fence. She walked around to the cab of the Chevy for her purse and heard the men calling out in hoarse deep voices for her to stay. She smiled to herself; she was going to stay all right, and when they were all lying on their bunks after lock-up they were all going to think of her, the free citizen, when they jerked off. Then maybe Marv would get to hear of the hot chick in the blue skirt and the white blouse and he'd be sorry that he hadn't listened to her when she'd asked him to stay home that night.

She got her purse and carried it around to the trunk where she found her key and opened it up, making sure she bent right over so that her skirt blew up. She smiled to herself at the hushed excited tones of the men behind her. She wiggled her butt and heard the fence shake. So they liked her fat ass, did they? She looked over her shoulder at them and smoothed her hands down over her bare cheeks. The men fell silent and she imagined how they must be feeling with such a display going on. Her thong was damp between her legs and she reached behind her to pull it up against her poor tortured clit, kept waiting for so many months, and snapped it playfully so that the elastic flicked against her skin.

Lauren was loving this now, the fire well and truly burning between her legs, and she turned back to face her crowd of admiring felons. One man poked his long, pink tongue though the fence and waggled it suggestively at her. You wish, she thought to herself, and undid a top button to reveal a couple of inches of jacked-up cleavage. The men whistled appreciatively. Then she sat on the edge of the trunk and slowly crossed her legs, giving the men a whisper of quim, her skirt blowing around her thighs. She reached in her purse and pulled

out a compact and a lipstick and sat preening herself for
a moment, checking her reflection and painting her lips.
When she had finished she shut the compact with a
snap and blew them a kiss. One man was pressing
himself hard against the fence and mumbling incoher-
ently with lust, oblivious to the dog snapping at his
heels.

She adjusted her bra, checking her straps for non-
existent kinks and giving her breasts a good squeeze to
make sure that they were settled properly in the cups.
She had to check those sandals again but, instead of
bending over, she lifted her foot up onto the edge of the
truck to fiddle with the strap. She heard a collective gasp
as the men fought to catch a glimpse of her pussy. She
wriggled against the lace of her thong as it dug in her
cleft; the scent of her own arousal rose up to her. She
swapped feet, the lace chaffing her aroused clit, and her
own needs suddenly became more important than tor-
turing the men trapped behind the fence in front of her.
Her finger strayed of its own accord under the lace but
she caught herself in time; she had done enough self-
pleasuring. It was time for the real thing.

She watched the men, squirming and calling through
the fence, some clasping their erections through the
well-washed fabric of their suits, and she knew that she
had given them something to think about in the long
nights ahead. She had one last parting gift for them.
Reaching under her skirt, she hooked her thumbs into
the elastic of her panties and pulled them down slowly.
The men fell quiet once more. She crouched facing them,
her thong around her ankles and her thighs spread, and
hoisted her skirt around her waist. Then, with a shudder
of satisfaction, she pissed long and hard into the sand in
front of her as the silent men looked on in awe. With a
little shiver she emptied her bladder and rose, pulling

her panties up as she did so and smoothing her skirt down neatly. She took her purse and locked the trunk and, with a wave, she climbed behind the wheel, leaving the men staring at a wet patch in the sand.

Her quim throbbed all the way home and she had to concentrate hard on her driving to take her mind off the ache between her legs. Her visitation order remained folded in the glove box. Well, it was tough; Marv should have listened.

She didn't wash before she went to work; if the men wanted to slip their hands up under her skirt then it served them right. The thought of them running their hands up her damp thighs actually excited her tonight. She undid an extra button on her blouse and hoisted her skirt up just a little bit. As usual, Dan perched at the end of the bar when he finished his shift and watched her over his beer. She smiled at him and relished the heavy throb of anticipation in her crotch.

Dan was knocking her up before she was properly awake and she answered the door dressed in an old shirt that allowed him to catch a glimpse of her bush as she leant on the door jamb. He turned scarlet with embarrassment and she gestured to him to come in with a tilt of her head. He stepped nervously into the trailer, his boots sounding heavy on the thin carpet, and shut the door carefully behind him. He sensed a change but was unsure what it was.

'How's Marv?' He looked about him as if expecting his old pal to appear.

Lauren filled the kettle noisily at the tap. 'Angry, I should imagine. I've dumped him.'

Dan slipped his hands into the back pockets of his jeans. 'Excuse me?'

'I've thought about it long and hard and Marv and I are over. So your obligations to me are finished. You don't need to look out for me anymore.' She plugged the kettle in, feigning nonchalance, but her heart was thundering in her throat and her crotch.

Dan looked down on her, scowling. 'I can't believe that.'

She shrugged. 'Whatever. It's over. For good.' Her flashing eyes defied him to argue further.

His eyes flicked down the front of her crumpled shirt and back up.

'So,' she drew a deep shuddering breath. 'Don't you think it's time you fucked me?'

Shock replaced the scowl. 'Exc–'

She pressed a finger to his lips to silence him. 'Get that vest off, Dan, and fuck me, good and hard.'

She didn't have to ask twice. He reached over his left shoulder and dragged the vest off his back, throwing it into a corner. She pressed herself back against the sink, her quim melting with lust as she took in his work-honed muscles and flat belly.

He took a step towards her. 'I've wanted to fuck you for the longest time.' He closed the gap between them and ran a huge hand up between her smooth thighs.

'I know.' The words snagged in her throat as he pushed a finger deep inside her.

She let her head fall back as his finger worked higher. Her thighs automatically opened wider around his warm hand and she angled herself so that her clit was rubbing against the ball of his hand. God, how she needed this.

He kissed all along her neck and murmured in her ear, 'The smell of your cunt has driven me almost insane.' He withdrew his finger and tore her shirt open. The ripping material stung her skin but was nothing compared to the heavy ache in her groin. She resisted the urge to grab his hand and guide it back in.

His mouth opened over hers, his tongue pushing

inside her mouth, and she reached out for him, pulling him close. His hands were all over her hot skin, pinching her nipples, delving into the cleft of her buttocks, rubbing her sopping wetness and opening her up. He pushed against her and the dishes on the sink clanked and rattled.

Her hands were greedy for him, too, feeling the hard contours and planes of his body that her eyes had coveted so badly. She reached down for his zipper and frantically released his cock, feeling it slip warm and velvet over her palm. She trembled at the sweet promise of it. 'Do me,' she groaned into his mouth. 'Just do me.'

He buried his mouth in her neck. 'Where? Tell me where.'

She pushed him away and his eyes were all over her, his cock throbbing in front of him, quivering and splendid. She looked like a slut, her chin and breasts red from his bristle, the shirt half torn from her back, her pussy wet between her thighs. She bent over the small kitchen table, her legs spread and her pussy offered up to him. 'Here,' she whispered, 'and everywhere.'

She watched over her shoulder as he pushed his jeans a little further down his hairy thighs. He grabbed her waist and held her still as he pushed his cock sharply into her from behind. She groaned and pushed herself back against him, her bare feet treading on his own heavily booted ones.

'Hold still,' he barked gruffly, 'while I do you good and hard.' He punctuated each word with a thrust and her sounds were lost as her mouth opened in an 'O' of pleasure. His cock was deep inside, up where the pleasure was almost pain. He held it there for a long moment, sensing her exquisite hurt, savouring it after the long months of denial. She shook beneath him and he was skewering her again with long, deep strokes. She pressed her torso down onto the table top and she held onto it for support, moaning with pleasure at the feel of the cold plastic against her hard nipples. His heavy balls slapped against her clit as he ground himself into her hot pussy. Above her he sucked the finger he had dipped into her earlier and, still grasping her waist with his other hand, he screwed it slowly into her puckered asshole until she groaned and bucked beneath him, as her climax swept her out.

And he did her. Good and hard and everywhere.

It was the first time he had ever called into work sick. They curled up in bed for the best part of the morning; sweat sticking them together, dozing then becoming aroused again. And later she did him.

Dan, who had offered his services every morning for the last six months, was finally taken up on the offer. After all, she was a free citizen, and how did the old song go? Love the one you're with.

Visit the Black Lace website at
www.blacklace-books.co.uk

FIND OUT THE LATEST INFORMATION AND TAKE
ADVANTAGE OF OUR FANTASTIC **FREE BOOK OFFER!**
ALSO VISIT THE SITE FOR . . .

- All Black Lace titles currently available
  and how to order online

- Great new offers

- Writers' guidelines

- Author interviews

- An erotica newsletter

- Features

- Cool links

BLACK LACE – THE LEADING IMPRINT
OF WOMEN'S SEXY FICTION

TAKING YOUR EROTIC READING
PLEASURE TO NEW HORIZONS

LOOK OUT FOR THE ALL-NEW BLACK LACE BOOKS – AVAILABLE NOW!

All books priced £6.99 in the UK. Please note publication dates apply to the UK only. For other territories, please contact your retailer.

BEDDING THE BURGLAR
Gabrielle Marcola
ISBN O 352 33911 X

Maggie Quinton is a savvy, sexy architect involved in a building project on a remote island off the Florida panhandle. One day, a gorgeous hunk breaks into the house she's staying in and ties her up. The buff burglar is in search of an item he claims the apartment's owner stole from him. And he keeps coming back. Flustered and aroused, Maggie calls her jet-setting sister in for moral support, but flirty, dark-haired Diane is much more interested in the island's ruggedly handsome police chief, 'Griff' Grifford. And then there's his deputy, Cosgrove, with his bulging biceps and creative uses for handcuffs. **A sexually charged tale of bad boys and fast women set in the teeming backwaters of 'gator country!**

MIXED DOUBLES
Zoe le Verdier
ISBN O 352 33312 X

When Natalie Crawford is offered the job as manager of a tennis club in a wealthy English suburb, she jumps at the chance. There's an extra perk, too: Paul, the club's coach, is handsome and charming, and she wastes no time in making him her lover. Then she hires Chris, a coach from a rival club, whose confidence and sexual prowess swiftly put Paul in the shade. When Chris embroils Natalie into kinky sex games, will she be able to keep control of her business aims, or will her lust for the arrogant sportsman get out of control? **The gloves – and knickers – are off in this story of unsporting behaviour on court!**

Coming in December 2004

CREAM OF THE CROP
Savannah Smythe
ISBN O 352 33920 9

Aspiring artist Carla Vicenzi has caught the eye of Alex Crewe, a serial seducer who owns an exclusive retreat where artists hone their craft. Alex wants a high-profile exhibition, but corporate shark Crewe embodies all the values Carla despises. As she tries to resist his advances, he woos her the old-fashioned way, unaware that she can be dirtier than him. Eventually they are drawn together by forces neither of them can resist, and their resulting affair is explosive, pushing each of them to their sexual limit. Meanwhile Carla's dishy but dumb boyfriend is lured into depravity by Ruth, Alex's slinky PA. Amid the scheming and double-crossing, Carla still manages to find time to seduce a few of New York's fittest firemen! **A story of lust and honour, revenge and greed, set against Manhattan's glittering skyline.**

EDEN'S FLESH
Robyn Russell
ISBN O 352 33923 3

Eden Sinclair is director of the exclusive Galerie Raton in Atlanta's
prestigious mid-town district. As summer temperatures soar she finds it
increasingly difficult to adhere to her self-imposed celibacy, and spends a
lot of time fantasising about the attractive young artists who pass
through the gallery. Among them is Michael MacKenzie, the flame-
haired sculptor whose sexy masculinity sets her pulse racing. Almost
delirious with unrequited passion, Eden sets out to seduce him – despite
her professional promise never to become involved with her clients.
Things become even more charged when she finds out gallery owner
Alexander is having an affair with her best friend. In downtown Atlanta
it's going to be a summer of saucy surprises and steamy encounters.

Also available

THE BLACK LACE SEXY QUIZ BOOK
Maddie Saxon
ISBN 0 352 33884 9

- What sexual personality type are you?
- Have you ever faked it because that was easier than explaining what you wanted?
- What kind of fantasy figures turn you on – and does your partner know?
- What sexual signals are you giving out right now?

Today's image-conscious dating scene is a tough call. Our sexual expectations are cranked up to the max, and the sexes seem to have become highly critical of each other in terms of appearance and performance in the bedroom. But, even though guys have ditched their nasty Y-fronts and girls are more babe-licious than ever, a huge number of us are still being let down sexually. Sex therapist Maddie Saxon thinks this is because we are finding it harder to relax and let our true sexual selves shine through.

The Black Lace Sexy Quiz Book will help you negotiate the minefield of modern relationships. Through a series of fun, revealing quizzes, you will be able to rate your sexual needs honestly and get what you really want from your partner. The quizzes will get you thinking about and discussing your desires in ways you haven't previously considered. Unlock the mysteries of your sexual psyche in this fun, revealing quiz book designed with today's sex-savvy girl in mind.

Black Lace Booklist

Information is correct at time of printing. To avoid disappointment check availability before ordering. Go to www.blacklace-books.co.uk. All books are priced £6.99 unless another price is given.

BLACK LACE BOOKS WITH A CONTEMPORARY SETTING

☐ SHAMELESS Stella Black	ISBN 0 352 33485 1	£5.99
☐ INTENSE BLUE Lyn Wood	ISBN 0 352 33496 7	£5.99
☐ A SPORTING CHANCE Susie Raymond	ISBN 0 352 33501 7	£5.99
☐ TAKING LIBERTIES Susie Raymond	ISBN 0 352 33357 X	£5.99
☐ ON THE EDGE Laura Hamilton	ISBN 0 352 33534 3	£5.99
☐ LURED BY LUST Tania Picarda	ISBN 0 352 33533 5	£5.99
☐ THE NINETY DAYS OF GENEVIEVE Lucinda Carrington	ISBN 0 352 33070 8	£5.99
☐ DREAMING SPIRES Juliet Hastings	ISBN 0 352 33584 X	
☐ THE TRANSFORMATION Natasha Rostova	ISBN 0 352 33311 1	
☐ SIN.NET Helena Ravenscroft	ISBN 0 352 33598 X	
☐ TWO WEEKS IN TANGIER Annabel Lee	ISBN 0 352 33599 8	
☐ PLAYING HARD Tina Troy	ISBN 0 352 33617 X	
☐ SYMPHONY X Jasmine Stone	ISBN 0 352 33629 3	
☐ SUMMER FEVER Anna Ricci	ISBN 0 352 33625 0	
☐ CONTINUUM Portia Da Costa	ISBN 0 352 33120 8	
☐ FULL STEAM AHEAD Tabitha Flyte	ISBN 0 352 33637 4	
☐ A SECRET PLACE Ella Broussard	ISBN 0 352 33307 3	
☐ GAME FOR ANYTHING Lyn Wood	ISBN 0 352 33639 0	
☐ CHEAP TRICK Astrid Fox	ISBN 0 352 33640 4	
☐ THE GIFT OF SHAME Sara Hope-Walker	ISBN 0 352 29935 1	
☐ COMING UP ROSES Crystalle Valentino	ISBN 0 352 33658 7	
☐ GOING TOO FAR Laura Hamilton	ISBN 0 352 33657 9	
☐ THE STALLION Georgina Brown	ISBN 0 352 33005 8	
☐ DOWN UNDER Juliet Hastings	ISBN 0 352 33663 3	
☐ ODALISQUE Fleur Reynolds	ISBN 0 352 32887 8	
☐ SWEET THING Alison Tyler	ISBN 0.352 33682 X	
☐ TIGER LILY Kimberly Dean	ISBN 0 352 33685 4	

Her face changed, from her usual happy, confident smile to dismay and misery, an awful sight that immediately brought a lump my throat. She bit her lip, obviously close to tears, then spoke.

'I'm sorry, Hazel. What are you going to do?'

'Tell me why, first.'

'I don't know, I ... I suppose I was just lazy, and there was too much to do, and I knew I'd make a mess of it, and ... and I couldn't bear to disappoint you!'

'But you're a bright girl; you'd have done well anyway. You essays are exceptional.'

She shook her head.

'Phil did them for me too. Sorry.'

She'd hung her head, unable to meet my eyes. I wanted to cuddle her, to tell her it was all right, but it wasn't.

'Your essays don't count towards your final mark, but the assignment does, and ... and I don't know what to do, Tiggy. You've put me in an impossible situation.'

'I know. Sorry.'

'What were you doing at Brancaster anyway, just messing about with Saul?'

'Yes, but not at Brancaster. That day, when you came up, we'd been to Norwich.'

'Tiggy!'

I didn't know what else to say, my exasperation boiling up inside me, until it occurred to me that it might be even worse.

'Have you shown any of your work to Dennis Woolmer?'

'No, nothing. You're the only person who's seen it. Couldn't we ... couldn't we just burn it, and start again?'

'Start again? It has to be in next week, Tiggy. No,

hang on, maybe you're right. If we destroy it you won't get any credit, and you can do something else instead, quickly, something simple, and ... and I'll say you couldn't cope with your original choice, which is what Dennis half expects anyway. Yes, that's it, but I hope you realise what I'm doing for you, Tiggy.'

She burst into tears.

That evening and the next three were spent desperately putting together Tiggy's replacement assignment, on species diversity in urban parks, which was the only thing simple enough I'd been able to think of on the spur of the moment. It was hardly original, and I had most of the data in my head anyway, which I gave her without feeling I was compromising myself much more than I already had. By Thursday night it was done, brief, crude, but viable, and she accepted that in the circumstances she could hardly expect high marks.

We had slept together, but we hadn't had sex. It just hadn't felt right, but with the assignment ready to hand in I finally allowed myself to relax a little. Phil Paddon, I could be absolutely sure, was not going to say anything, and with Tiggy's original work safely consigned to the flames it looked as if we were safe. She had burned her diary at the same time, a single blue corner among the ashes the sole remaining evidence of its existence. I didn't ask, but from some of the things she'd said I knew it was because she'd felt there to be a major change in her life. In her head at least, she was no longer a virgin.

As if peace of mind was something to which I simply was not entitled, Friday raised a new difficulty. Miles called to remind me he was coming up at the weekend, which we'd already agreed, so I could hardly turn him down. What I wasn't sure of was Tiggy's reaction, because for all her remarks about jealousy I'd seen the hurt in her eyes when I'd first been with him. It needed to be sorted out, and tactfully.

That night I finally let my feelings out, by giving Tiggy a blistering spanking with my hairbrush, not that I wanted to at first, but after she'd dropped about the hundredth hint I could no longer resist. The consequences were inevitable, a night of passionate, uninhibited sex at least as rude as our first together, and which went on until the early hours of the morning.

It was nearly ten o'clock when I woke to the sound of the doorbell being rung incessantly. For a moment I though it was part of my dream, in which Robert, Dennis Woolmer and for some reason Mary Whitehouse had all turned up in the car park at Brancaster to find me fellating Miles Shelldrake while Tiggy spanked me with a copy of Phil Paddon's thesis. Reality wasn't quite as bad, but it might have been better, Sarah's voice calling up to me, full of impatience.

'Hazel? Hazel! It's time to go.'

I shook myself, wondering what she was talking about but far more worried about getting the fast asleep, stark naked Tiggy out of my bed. Sarah called again as I clamped a hand over Tiggy's mouth and tugged at her shoulder, my rising panic blowing the sleep from my head faster than any coffee. Her eyes came open in surprise, but as Sarah's increasingly irate voice rose up one more time she realised, tumbling herself out of bed and skipping through to her own room as I quickly put on my robe. Sarah was about to throw some gravel at my window when I stuck my head out.

'What's the matter?'

'What are you doing, Hazel? Aren't you ready?'

'Ready? For what?'

'To go to the solicitors about the hunt case, of course. Don't tell me you've forgotten? You're bringing the original tape.'

'Um ... no, of course not. Sorry, I had a bad night, overslept. I'll get it. Two seconds.'

She gave an impatient sigh as I ducked back inside. I had to go, because the last thing I wanted to do was make any obvious changes to my behaviour, but I was cursing bitterly as I splashed water onto my face and hurried on the first clothes I could lay my hands on. My hairbrush at least was easy to find, still on the floor where I'd left it, but not the tape. It wasn't in the machine, but I eventually managed to find it on my chest of drawers and hurried downstairs. Sarah was less than sympathetic.

'Really, Hazel, this is important.'

'Sorry. Look, we'd better drive.'

She turned her eyes up to the sky, as if my actions were going to be a major factor in rising pollution levels. I ignored her, in no mood to discuss anything, and stayed silent as we drove into town, Sarah's voice as she described the situation with the case a mere background drone.

I was not happy at all, sleepy, hungry and without even a coffee. Worse, my dream had left me feeling insecure, no doubt a reflection of my current worries, and I was wondering if I'd made the right choice after all. Miles was coming up in the afternoon, and he was sure to mention the job again. Had I been fully honest and resigned I would have had little option but to accept, and simply do my best not to be a complete puppet.

Instead I'd covered up for Tiggy, and now there was no going back. It was done, and would always be there to haunt me, as would my relationship with her, however it turned out. There was Miles too, a lesser problem, but still a problem, both because of the need for secrecy and having to balance my two relationships. That at least had its good sides, but otherwise I could look forward to a future of constant worry.

I forced myself to think of something more cheerful, the small but not insignificant possibility that at some time in the future the situation with Miles and Tiggy might become more exciting still. Perhaps a little absinthe, and maybe, just maybe, she might be persuaded to join in, even if just to watch as he tied me and spanked me, because to have it done in front of her would be so good.

'Hazel, are you listening at all? Turn left!'

'Sorry, Sarah, I was miles away.'

'So I notice.'

I managed to park and we walked across to the solicitors' office. Robert, Eve, Paul and several others were already there, all looking at me as I was one of the hunters, but I couldn't be bothered to defend myself. In the office of the man who'd agreed to represent us I quickly linked the camera to his computer and called up the right program as he addressed me.

'And this is the original tape, not a copy?'

Robert answered for me.

'The original, exactly as I took it.'

I was ready, and clicked on the play icon before retreating to the only remaining chair, behind Eve. For a moment the video window was blank, then a green blur before the picture swam into focus – bushes, the Breckland and Fen Hunt in full cry, heading right towards the camera, and another image altogether, quite different and horribly familiar. It was accompanied by my own voice.

'You're going to spank me. You're going to turn me

over your knee and take down my knickers and spank me.'

'What am I going to spank, Hazel?'

'My bottom.'

'Say it, properly.'

'Yes, Miles. You're going to turn me over your knee and take down my knickers and spank my bottom.'

'That's better. One more time for Daddy.'

'Oh God ... You ... you're going to turn me over your knee and take down my knickers and spank my bottom. Yes. Yes, please do it, Miles. Do it now, you bastard. Spank me. Spank me really hard, really, really hard!'

LOOK OUT FOR THE ALL-NEW BLACK LACE BOOKS – AVAILABLE NOW!

All books priced £7.99 in the UK. Please note publication dates apply to the UK only. For other territories, please contact your retailer.

THE STRANGER
Portia Da Costa
ISBN O 352 33211 5

When a mysterious young man stumbles into the life of the recently widowed Claudia, he reignites her sleeping sexuality. But is the handsome and angelic Paul really a combination of innocent and voluptuary, amnesiac and genius? Claudia's friends become involved in trying to decide whether or not he is to be trusted. As an erotic obsession flowers between Paul and Claudia, and all taboos are obliterated, his true identity no longer seems to matter.

Coming in February

BARBARIAN PRIZE
Deanna Ashford
ISBN O 352 34017 7

After a failed uprising in Brittania, Sirona, a princess of the Iceni, and her lover, Taranis, are taken to Pompeii. Taranis is sold as a slave to a rich Roman lady and Sirona is taken to the home of a lecherous senator, but he is only charged with her care until his stepson, General Lucius Flavius, returns home. Flavius takes her to his villa outside the city where she succumbs to his charms. Sirona must escape from the clutches of the followers of the erotic cult of the Dionysis, while Taranis must fight for his life as a gladiator in the arena. Meanwhile, beneath Mount Vesuvius, there are forces gathering that even the power of the Romans cannot control.

MAN HUNT
Cathleen Ross
ISBN O 352 33583 1

Fearless and charismatic Angie Masters is on a man hunt. While training at a prestigious hotel training academy, the attractive and dominant director of the institute, James Steele, catches her eye. Steele has a predatory sexuality and a penchant for erotic punishment. By seducing a fellow student, Angie is able to torment Steele. But she has a rival – the luscious Italian Isabella who is prepared to do anything to please him. A battle of sexual wills ensues, featuring catfights, orgies and triumph for either Angie or Isabella. Who will be the victor?

Coming in March

CAT SCRATCH FEVER
Sophie Mouette
ISBN 0 352 34021 5

Creditors breathing down her neck. Crazy board members. A make-or-break benefit that's far behind schedule. Felicia DuBois, development coordinator at the Southern California Cat Sanctuary, has problems—including a bad case of the empty-bed blues. Then sexy Gabe Sullivan walks into the Sanctuary and sets her body tingling. Felicia's tempted to dive into bed with him . . . except it could mean she'd be sleeping with the enemy. Gabe's from the Zoological Association, a watchdog organization that could decide to close the cash-strapped cat facility. Soon Gabe and Felicia are acting like cats in heat, but someone's sabotaging the benefit. Could it be Gabe? Or maybe it's the bad-boy volunteer, the delicious caterer, or the board member with a penchant for leather? Throw in a handsome veterinarian and a pixieish female animal handler who likes handling Felicia, and everyone ought to be purring. But if Felicia can't find the saboteur, the Sanctuary's future will be as endangered as the felines it houses.

RUDE AWAKENING
Pamela Kyle
ISBN 0 352 33036 8

Alison is a control freak. There's nothing she enjoys more than swanning around her palatial home giving orders to her wealthy but masochistic husband and delighting in his humiliation. Her daily routine consists of shopping, dressing up and pursuing dark pleasures, along with her best friend, Belinda; that is until they are kidnapped and held to ransom. In the ensuing weeks both women are required to come to terms with their most secret selves. Stripped of their privileges and deprived of the luxury they are used to, they deal with their captivity in surprising and creative ways. For Alison, it is the catalyst to a whole new way of life.

Black Lace Booklist

Information is correct at time of printing. To avoid disappointment check availability before ordering. Go to www.blacklace-books.co.uk. All books are priced £6.99 unless another price is given.

BLACK LACE BOOKS WITH A CONTEMPORARY SETTING

☐ SHAMELESS Stella Black	ISBN 0 352 33485 1	£5.99
☐ INTENSE BLUE Lyn Wood	ISBN 0 352 33496 7	£5.99
☐ ON THE EDGE Laura Hamilton	ISBN 0 352 33534 3	£5.99
☐ LURED BY LUST Tania Picarda	ISBN 0 352 33533 5	£5.99
☐ THE NINETY DAYS OF GENEVIEVE	ISBN 0 352 33070 8	£5.99
Lucinda Carrington		
☐ DREAMING SPIRES Juliet Hastings	ISBN 0 352 33584 X	
☐ THE TRANSFORMATION Natasha Rostova	ISBN 0 352 33311 1	
☐ SIN.NET Helena Ravenscroft	ISBN 0 352 33598 X	
☐ TWO WEEKS IN TANGIER Annabel Lee	ISBN 0 352 33599 8	
☐ PLAYING HARD Tina Troy	ISBN 0 352 33617 X	
☐ SYMPHONY X Jasmine Stone	ISBN 0 352 33629 3	
☐ SUMMER FEVER Anna Ricci	ISBN 0 352 33625 0	
☐ A SECRET PLACE Ella Broussard	ISBN 0 352 33307 3	
☐ THE GIFT OF SHAME Sara Hope-Walker	ISBN 0 352 29935 1	
☐ GOING TOO FAR Laura Hamilton	ISBN 0 352 33657 9	
☐ THE STALLION Georgina Brown	ISBN 0 352 33005 8	
☐ SWEET THING Alison Tyler	ISBN 0 352 33682 X	
☐ TIGER LILY Kimberly Dean	ISBN 0 352 33685 4	
☐ RELEASE ME Suki Cunningham	ISBN 0 352 33671 4	
☐ KING'S PAWN Ruth Fox	ISBN 0 352 33684 6	
☐ SLAVE TO SUCCESS Kimberley Raines	ISBN 0 352 33687 0	
☐ SHADOWPLAY Portia Da Costa	ISBN 0 352 33313 8	
☐ I KNOW YOU, JOANNA Ruth Fox	ISBN 0 352 33727 3	
☐ THE HOUSE IN NEW ORLEANS Fleur Reynolds	ISBN 0 352 29951 3	
☐ DRAWN TOGETHER Robyn Russell	ISBN 0 352 33269 7	
☐ VIRTUOSO Katrina Vincenzi-Thyre	ISBN 0 352 29907 6	
☐ FIGHTING OVER YOU Laura Hamilton	ISBN 0 352 33795 8	

BLACK LACE BOOKS WITH AN HISTORICAL SETTING

To find out the latest information about Black Lace titles, check out the website: www.blacklace-books.co.uk or send for a booklist with complete synopses by writing to:

> Black Lace Booklist, Virgin Books Ltd
> Thames Wharf Studios
> Rainville Road
> London W6 9HA

Please include an SAE of decent size. Please note only British stamps are valid.

Our privacy policy
We will not disclose information you supply us to any other parties. We will not disclose any information which identifies you personally to any person without your express consent.

From time to time we may send out information about Black Lace books and special offers. Please tick here if you do not wish to receive Black Lace information.   ☐

BLACK LACE BOOKS WITH AN HISTORICAL SETTING

BLACK LACE ANTHOLOGIES

BLACK LACE NON-FICTION

To find out the latest information about Black Lace titles, check out the website: www.blacklace-books.co.uk or send for a booklist with complete synopses by writing to:

Black Lace Booklist, Virgin Books Ltd
Thames Wharf Studios
Rainville Road
London W6 9HA

Please include an SAE of decent size. Please note only British stamps are valid.

Our privacy policy
We will not disclose information you supply us to any other parties. We will not disclose any information which identifies you personally to any person without your express consent.

From time to time we may send out information about Black Lace books and special offers. Please tick here if you do <u>not</u> wish to receive Black Lace information.   ❏